Selected Stories

Éilís Ní Dhuibhne

SELECTED STORIES

DALKEY ARCHIVE PRESS

Library of Congress Cataloging-in-Publication Data
Names: Ní Dhuibhne, Éilís, 1954- author.
Title: Selected stories / Éilís Ní Dhuibhne.
Description: First Dalkey Archive edition. | Victoria, TX : Dalkey Archive
Press, 2017.
Identifiers: LCCN 2017023153 | ISBN 9781943150311 (pbk. : alk. paper)
Classification: LCC PR6064.I127 A6 2017 | DDC 823/.914--dc23
LC record available at https://lccn.loc.gov/2017023153

Selected Stories has received financial assistance from the Irish Arts
Council.

www.dalkeyarchive.com
Victoria, TX / McLean, IL / Dublin

Dalkey Archive Press publications are, in part, made possible through the
support of the University of Houston-Victoria and its programs in creative
writing, publishing, and translation.

Printed on permanent/durable acid-free paper

Contents

Blood and Water   3

The Flowering   16

Night of the Fox   31

Summer Pudding   44

The Woman With the Fish   60

The Pale Gold of Alaska   75

The Day Elvis Presley Died   112

The Banana Boat   156

Illumination   178

Literary Lunch   199

City of Literature   212

The Coast of Wales   222

Blood and Water

I HAVE AN AUNT who is not the full shilling. 'The Mad Aunt' was how my sister and I referred to her when we were children, but that was just a euphemism, designed to shelter us from the truth which we couldn't stomach: she was mentally retarded. Very mildly so: perhaps she was just a slow learner. She survived very successfully as a lone farm woman, letting land, keeping a cow and a few hens and ducks, listening to the local gossip from the neighbours who were kind enough to drop in regularly in the evenings. Quite a few of them were: her house was a popular place for callers, and perhaps that was part of the secret of her survival. She did not participate in the neighbours' conversation to any extent, however. She was articulate only on a very concrete level, and all abstract topics were beyond her.

Had she been born in the fifties or sixties, my aunt would have been scientifically labelled, given special treatment at a special school, taught special skills and eventually employed in a special workshop to carry out a special job, certainly a much duller job than the one she pursued in reality. Luckily for her she was born in 1925 and had been reared as a normal child. Her family had failed to recognise that she was different from others and had not sought medical attention for her. She had merely been considered 'delicate'. The term 'mentally retarded' would have been meaningless in those days, anyway, in the part of Donegal where she and my mother originated, where Irish was the common, if not the only, language. As she grew up, it must have been silently conceded that she was a little odd. But people seemed to have no difficulty in suppressing this fact, and they judged my aunt by the standards which they applied to humanity at large; sometimes lenient and sometimes not.

She lived in a farmhouse in Ballytra on Inishowen, and once a year we visited her. Our annual holiday was spent under her roof. And had it not been for the lodging she provided, we could not have afforded to get away at all. But we did not consider this aspect of the affair.

On the first Saturday of August we always set out, laden with clothes in cardboard boxes and groceries from the cheap city shops, from the street markets: enough to see us through the fortnight. The journey north lasted nearly twelve hours in our ancient battered cars: a Morris Fight, dark green with fragrant leather seats, and a Ford Anglia are two of the models I remember from a long series of fourth-hand crocks. Sometimes they broke down en route and caused us long delays in nauseating garages, where I stood around with my father, while the mechanic tinkered, or went, with my sister and mother, for walks down country lanes, or along the wide melancholy street of small market towns.

Apart from such occasional hitches, however, the trips were delightful odysseys through various flavours of Ireland; the dusty rich flatlands outside Dublin, the drumlins of Monaghan with their hint of secrets and better things to come, the luxuriant slopes, rushing rivers and expensive villas of Tyrone, and finally, the intimate reward: the furze and heather, the dogroses, the fuchsia, of Donegal.

Donegal was different in those days. Different from what it is now, different then from the eastern urban parts of Ireland. It was rural in a thorough, elemental way. People were old-fashioned in their dress and manners, even in their physiques: weather-beaten faces were highlighted by black or gray suits, shiny with age; broad hips stretched the cotton of navy-blue, flower-sprigged overalls, a kind of uniform for country women which their city sisters had long eschewed, if they ever had it.

Residences were thatched cottages 'the Irish peasant house' . . .
or spare gray farmhouses. There was only a single bungalow in
the parish where my aunt lived, an area which is now littered
with them.

All these things accentuated the rusticity of the place, its
strangeness, its uniqueness.

My aunt's house was of the slated, two-storey variety, and
it stood, surrounded by a seemingly arbitrary selection of
outhouses, in a large yard called 'the street'. Usually we turned
into this street at about nine o'clock at night, having been on the
road all day. My aunt would be waiting for us, leaning over the
half-door. Even though she was deaf, she would have heard the
car while it was still a few hundred yards away, chugging along
the dirt lane: it was always that kind of car. She would stand
up as soon as we appeared, and twist her hands shyly, until we
emerged from the car. Then she would walk slowly over to us,
and shake hands carefully with each of us in turn, starting with
my mother. Care, formality: these were characteristics which
were most obvious in her. Slowness.

Greetings over, we would troop into the house, under a low
portal apparently designed for a smaller race of people. Then we
would sit in front of the hot fire, and my mother would talk,
in a loud cheery voice, telling my aunt the news from Dublin
and asking for local gossip. My aunt would sometimes try to
reply, more often not. After five minutes or so of this, she would
indicate, a bit resentfully, that she had expected us earlier, that
she had been listening for the car for over two days. And my
mother, still, at this early stage of the holiday, in a diplomatic
mood, would explain patiently, slowly, loudly, that no, we had
been due today. We always came on the first Saturday, didn't
we? John only got off on the Friday, sure. But somehow my
mother would never have written to my aunt to let her know
when we were coming. It was not owing to the fact that the
latter was illiterate that she didn't write. Any neighbour would

have read a letter for her. It was, rather, the result of a strange convention which my parents, especially my mother, always adhered to: they never wrote to anyone, about anything, except one subject. Death.

While this courteous ritual of fireside conversation was being enacted by my parents (although in fact my father never bothered to take part), my sister and I would sit silently on our hardbacked chairs, fidgeting and looking at the familiar objects in the room: the Sacred Heart, the Little Flower, the calendar from Bells of Buncrana depicting a blond laughing child, the red arc for layers' mash. We answered promptly, monosyllabically, the few questions my aunt put to us, all concerning school. Subdued by the immense boredoms of the day, we tolerated further boredom.

After a long time, my mother would get up, stretch, and prepare a meal of rashers and sausages, from Russells of Camden Street. To this my aunt would add a few provisions she had laid in for us: eggs, butter she had churned herself, and soda bread which she baked in a pot oven, in enormous golden balls. I always refused to eat this bread, because I found the taste repellent and because I didn't think my aunt washed her hands properly. My sister, however, ate no other kind of bread while we were on holiday at that house, and I used to tease her about it, trying to force her to see my point of view. She never did.

After tea, although by that time it was usually late, we would run outside and play. We would visit each of the outhouses in turn, hoping to see an owl in the barn, and then we'd run across the road to a stream which flowed behind the back garden. There was a stone bridge over the stream and on our first night we invariably played the same game: we threw sticks into the stream at one side of the bridge, and then ran as fast as we could to the other side in order to catch them as they sailed out. This activity, undertaken at night in the shadow of the black hills, had a magical effect: it plummeted me headlong into the atmosphere of the holidays. At that stream, on that first night, I would suddenly discover within myself a feeling of happiness and freedom that I was normally unaware I possessed. It seemed to emerge from some hidden part of me, like the sticks emerging from underneath the bridge, and it counteracted the faint claustrophobia, the nervousness, which I always had initially in my aunt's house. Refreshed and elated, we would go to bed in unlit upstairs rooms. These bedrooms were paneled in wood which had been white once, but had faded to the colour of butter, and they had windows less than two feet square which had to be propped up with a stick if you wanted them to remain open: the windows were so small, my mother liked to tell us, because they had been made at a time when there was a tax on glass. I wondered about this: the doors were tiny, too.

When I woke up in the morning, I would lie and count the boards on the ceiling, and then the knots on the boards, until eventually a clattering of footsteps on the uncarpeted stairs and a banging about of pots and pans would announce that my mother was up and that breakfast would soon be available. I would run downstairs to the scullery, which served as a bathroom, and wash. The basin stood on a deal table, the water was in a white enamel bucket on the dresser. A piece of soap was stuck to a saucer on the window-sill, in front of the basin: through the window, you could see a bit of an elm tree, and a purple hill, as you washed.

In a way it was pleasant, but on the whole it worried me, washing in that place. It was so public. There was a constant danger that someone would rush in, and find you there, half undressed, scrubbing your armpits. I liked my ablutions to be private and unobserved.

The scullery worried me for another reason. On its wall, just beside the dresser, was a big splodge of a dirty yellow substance, unlike anything I had ever encountered. I took it to be some sort of fungus. God knows why, since the house was unusually clean.

This thing so repelled me that I never even dared to ask what it was, and simply did my very best to avoid looking at it while I was in its vicinity, washing or bringing back the bucket of water from the well, or doing anything else. Years later, when I was taking a course in ethnology at the university, I realised that the stuff was nothing other than butter, daubed on the wall after every churning, for luck. But to me it symbolised something quite other than good fortune, something unthinkably horrible.

After dressing, breakfast. Rashers and sausages again, fried over the fire by my mother, who did all the cooking while we were on holiday. For that fortnight my aunt, usually a skillful fryer of rashers, baker of bread, abdicated domestic responsibility to her, and adopted the role of child in her own house, like a displaced rural mother-in-law. She spent her time fiddling around in the henhouse, feeding the cat, or more often she simply sat, like a man, and stared out of the window while my mother worked. After about three days of this, my mother would grow resentful, would begin to mutter, gently but persistently, 'it's no holiday!' And my sister and I, even though we understood the reasons for our aunt's behaviour, as, indeed, did our mother, would nod in agreement. Because we had to share in the housework. We set the table, we did the washing up in an enamel basin, and I had personal responsibility for going to the well to draw water. For this, my sister envied me. She imagined it to be a privileged task, much more fun than sweeping or making beds. And of course it was more exotic than these chores, for the first day or so, which was why I insisted on doing it. But soon enough the novelty palled, and it was really hard work, and boring. Water is heavy, and we seemed to require a great deal of it.

Unlike our mother, we spent much time away from the kitchen, my sister and I. Most of every morning we passed on the beach. There was an old boathouse there, its roof almost caved in, in which no boat had been kept for many many years. It had a stale smell, faintly disgusting, as if animals, or worse, had used it as a lavatory at some stage in the past. Even though the odour dismayed us, and even though the beach was always quite deserted, we liked to undress in private, both of us together, and therefore going to great lengths with towels to conceal our bodies from one another, until such a time as we should emerge from the yawning door of the building, and run down the golden quartz slip into the sea. Lough Swilly. Also known as 'The Lake of Shadows', my sister often informed me, this being the type of fact of which she was very fond. One of the only two fjords in Ireland, she might also add. That meant nothing to me, its being a fjord, and as for shadows, I was quite unaware of them. What I remember most about that water is its crystal clarity. It was greenish, to look at it from a slight distance. Or, if you looked at it from my aunt's house, on a fine day, it was a brilliant turquoise colour, it looked like a great jewel, set in the hills. But when you were in that water, bathing, it was as clear as glass: I would swim along with my face just below the lapping surface, and I would open my eyes and look right down to the sandy floor, at the occasional starfish, the tiny crabs that scuttled there, at the shoals of minnows that scudded from place to place, guided by some mysterious mob instinct. I always stayed in for ages, even on the coldest days, even when rain was falling in soft curtains around the rocks. It had a definite benign quality, that water. And I always emerged from it cleansed in both body and soul. When I remember it now, I can understand why rivers are sometimes believed to be holy. Lough Swilly was, for me, a blessed water.

The afternoons we spent *en famille*, going on trips in the car to view distant wonders, Portsalon or the Downings. And the evenings we would spend 'raking', dropping in on our innumerable friends and drinking tea and playing with them.

This pattern continued for the entire holiday, with two exceptions: on one Sunday we would go on a pilgrimage to Doon Well, and on one weekday we would go to Derry, thirty miles away, to shop.

Doon Well was my aunt's treat. It was the one occasion, apart from Mass, on which she accompanied us on a drive, even though we all realised that she would have liked to be with us every day. But the only outing she insisted upon was Doon Well. She would begin to hint about it gently soon after we arrived. 'The Gallaghers were at Doon Well on Sunday,' she might say. 'Not a great crowd at it!' Then on Sunday she would not change her clothes after Mass, but would don a special elegant apron, and perform the morning tasks in a particular and ladylike way: tiptoe into the byre, flutter at the hens.

At two we would set out, and she would sit with me and my sister in the back of the car. My sense of mortification, at being seen in public with my aunt, was mixed with another shame, that of ostentatious religious practices. I couldn't bear processions, missions, concelebrated masses: display. At heart, I was Protestant, and indeed it would have suited me, in more ways than one, to belong to that faith. But I didn't. So I was going to Doon Well, with my aunt and my unctuous parents, and my embarrassed sister.

You could spot the well from quite a distance: it was dressed. In rags. A large assembly of sticks, to which brightly coloured scraps of cloth were tied, advertised its presence and lent it a somewhat flippant, pagan air. But it was not flippant, it was all too serious. As soon as we left the safety of the car, we had to remove our shoes. The pain! Not only of going barefoot on the stony ground, but of having to witness feet, adult feet, our parents' and our aunt's, so shamelessly revealed to the world. Like all adults then, their feet were horrible: big and yellow, horny with corns and ingrown toenails, twisted and tortured by years of ill-fitting boots, no boots at all. To crown it, both my mother and aunt had varicose veins, purple knots bulging hideously through the yellow skin. As humiliated as anyone could be, and as we were meant to be, no doubt, we had to circle the well some specified number of times, probably three, and we had to say the Rosary, out loud, in the open air. And then my mother had a long litany to Colmcille, to which we had to listen and respond, in about a thousand agonies of shame, 'Pray for us!' The only tolerable part of the expedition occurred immediately after this, when we bought souvenirs at a stall, with a gay striped awning more appropriate to Bray or Bundoran than to this grim place. There we stood and scrutinized the wares on display: beads, statuettes, medals, snowstorms. Reverting to our consumerist role, we . . . do I mean I? I assume my sister felt the same about it all . . . felt almost content, for a few minutes, and we always selected the same souvenirs, namely snowstorms. I have one still: it has a painted blue backdrop, now peeling a little, and figures of elves and mushrooms under the glass, and, painted in black letters on its wooden base, 'I have prayed for you at Doon Well.' I bought that as a present for my best friend, Ann Byrne, but when I returned to Dublin I hadn't the courage to give it to her so it stayed in my bedroom for years, until I moved to Germany to study, and then I brought it with me. As a souvenir, not of Doon Well, I think, but of something.

We went to Derry without my aunt. We shopped and ate sausages and beans for lunch, in Woolworths. I enjoyed the trip to Derry. It was the highlight of the holiday, for me.

At the end of the fortnight, we would shake hands with my aunt in the street, and say goodbye. On these occasions her face would grow long and sad, she would always, at the moment when we climbed into the car, actually cry quietly to herself. My mother would say: 'Sure we won't feel it now till it's Christmas! And then the summer will be here in no time at all!' And this would make everything much more poignant for my aunt, for me, for everyone. I would squirm on the seat, and, although I often wanted to cry myself, not because I was leaving my aunt but because I didn't want to give up the countryside, and the

stream, and the clean clear water, I wouldn't think of my own
unhappiness, but instead divert all my energy into despising
my aunt for breaking yet another taboo: grown-ups do not cry.

My sister was tolerant. She'd laugh kindly as we turned out
of the street onto the lane. 'Poor old Annie!' she'd say. But I
couldn't laugh, I couldn't forgive her at all, for crying, for being
herself, for not being the full shilling.

There was one simple reason for my hatred, so simple that
I understood it myself, even when I was eight or nine years
old. I resembled my aunt physically. 'You're the image of your
Aunt Annie!', people, relations, would beam at me as soon as I
met them, in the valley. Now I know, looking at photos of her,
looking in the glass, that this was not such a very bad thing. She
had a reasonable enough face, as faces go. But I could not see
this when I was à child, much less when a teenager. All I knew
then was that she looked wrong. For one thing, she had straight
unpermed hair, cut short across the nape of the neck, unlike
the hair of any woman I knew then (but quite like mine as it
is today). For another, she had thick unplucked eyebrows, and
no lipstick or powder, even on Sunday, even for Doon Well.
Although at that time it was unacceptable to be unmade up, it
was outrageous to wear straight hair and laced shoes. Even in a
place which was decidedly old-fashioned, she looked uniquely
outmoded. She looked, to my city-conditioned eyes, like a freak.
So when people would say to me, 'God, aren't you the image of
your auntie!' I would cringe and wrinkle up in horror. Unable
to change my own face, and unable to see that it resembled hers
in the slightest . . . and how does a face that is ten resemble one
that is fifty? . . . I grew to hate my physique. And I transferred
that hatred, easily and inevitably, to my aunt.

When I was eleven, and almost finished with family holidays,
I visited Ballytra alone, not to stay with my aunt, but to attend
an Irish college which had just been established in that district. I

did not stay with any of my many relatives, on purpose: I wanted to steer clear of all unnecessary contact with my past, and lived with a family I had never seen before.

Even though I loved the rigorous jolly ambiance of the college, it posed problems for me. On the one hand, I was the child of one of the natives of the parish, I was almost a native myself. On the other hand, I was what was known there as a 'scholar', one of the kids from Dublin or Derry who descended on Ballytra like a shower of fireworks in July, who acted as if they owned the place, who more or less shunned the native population.

If I'd wanted to, it would have been very difficult for me to steer a median course between my part as a 'scholar' and my other role, as a cousin of the little native 'culchies' who, if they had been my playmates in former years, were now too shabby, too rustic, too outlandish, to tempt me at all. In the event, I made no effort to play to both factions: I managed by ignoring my relations entirely, and throwing myself into the more appealing life of the 'scholar'. My relations, I might add, seemed not to notice this, or care, if they did, and no doubt they were as bound by their own snobberies and conventions as I was by mine.

When the weather was suitable, that is, when it did not rain heavily, afternoons were spent on the beach, the same beach upon which my sister and I had always played. Those who wanted to swim walked there, from the school, in a long straggling crocodile. I loved to swim and never missed an opportunity to go to the shore.

The snag about this was that it meant passing by my aunt's house, which was on the road down to the lough: we had to pass through her street to get there. For the first week, she didn't bother me, probably assuming that I would drop in soon. But, even though my mother had warned me to pay an early visit and had given me a headscarf to give her, I procrastinated. So after a week had gone by she began to lie in wait for me: she began to sit on her stone seat, in front of the door, and to look at me dolefully as I passed. And I would give a little casual nod, such as I did to everyone I met, and pass on.

One afternoon, the teacher who supervised the group was walking beside me and some of my friends, much to my pride and discomfiture. When we came to the street, she called, softly, as I passed, 'Mary, Mary'. I nodded and continued on my way. The teacher gave me a funny look and said: 'Is she talking to you, Mary? Does she want to talk to you?' 'I don't know her,' I said, melting in shame. 'Who is she?' 'Annie, that's Annie Bonner.' He didn't let on to know anything more about it, but I bet he did: everyone who had spent more than a day in Ballytra knew everything there was to know about it, everyone, that is, who wasn't as egocentric as the 'scholars'.

My aunt is still alive, but I haven't seen her in many years. I never go to Inishowen now. I don't like it since it became modern and littered with bungalows. Instead I go to Barcelona with my husband, who is a native Catalonian. He teaches Spanish here, part-time, at the university, and runs a school for Spanish students in Ireland during the summers. I help him in the tedious search for digs for all of them, and really we don't have much time to holiday at all.

My aunt is not altogether well. She had a heart attack just before Christmas and had to have a major operation at the Donegal Regional. I meant to pay her a visit, but never got around to it. Then, just before she was discharged, I learned that she was going home for Christmas. Home? To her own empty house, on the lane down to the lough? I was, to my surprise, horrified. God knows why, I've seen people in direr straits. But something gave. I phoned my mother and wondered angrily why she wouldn't have her, just for a few weeks. But my mother is getting on, she has gout, she can hardly walk herself. So I said,

'All right, she can come here!' But Julio was unenthusiastic. Christmas is the only time of the year he manages to relax: in January, the bookings start, the planning, the endless meetings and telephone calls. Besides, he was expecting a guest from home: his sister, Montserrat, who is tiny and dark and lively as a sparrow. The children adore her. In the end, my sister, unmarried and a lecturer in Latin at Trinity, went to stay for a few weeks in Ballytra until my aunt was better. She has very flexible holidays, my sister, and no real ties.

I was relieved, after all, not to have Aunt Annie in my home. What would my prim suburban neighbours have thought? How would Julio, who has rather aristocratic blood, have coped? I am still ashamed, you see, of my aunt. I am still ashamed of myself. Perhaps, I suspect, I do resemble her, and not just facially. Perhaps there is some mental likeness too. Are my wide education, my brilliant husband, my posh accent, just attempts at camouflage? Am I really all that bright? Sometimes, as I sit and read in my glass-fronted bungalow, looking out over the clear sheet of the Irish Sea, and try to learn something, the grammar of some foreign language, the names of Hittite gods, something like that, I find the facts running away from me, like sticks escaping downstream on the current. And more often than that, much more often, I feel in my mind a splodge of something that won't allow any knowledge to sink in. A block of some terrible substance, soft and thick and opaque. Like butter.

The Flowering

LENNIE HAS A DREAM, a commonplace, even a vulgar dream, and one which she knows is unlikely to be realised. She wants to discover her roots. Not just names and dates from parish registers or census returns. Those she can find easily enough, insofar as they exist at all. What she desires is a real, a true discovery. An unearthing of homes, a peeling off of clothes and trappings, a revelation of minds, an excavation of hearts.

Why she wants this she does not know, or knows only very vaguely. It is partly a general curiosity about the past of her family, and more particularly a thirst for self-knowledge. Why does she look this way? Like some things and not others? Why does she do some things and not others? If she knew which traits she has inherited from whom, which are independent qualities, surely she would be a better judge of what she is herself, or of what she can become?

When she begins to ask these questions she becomes excited, initially, then dizzy. The litany of queries is self-propagating. It enjoys a frenzied beanstalk growth but reaches no satisfactory conclusions. And the more it expands the more convinced is Lennie that the answers are important. The promise, or rather the hope, of solutions, glows like a lantern in the bottlegreen, the black cave of her mind, where Plato's shadows sometimes hover but more often do not make an appearance at all. Drunk on questions, she begins to believe that there is one answer, a true all-encompassing resolution which will flood that dim region with brilliant light for once and for all, illuminating all personal conundrums.

Of course when Lennie sobers up she knows that such an

answer is impossible. The only thing she has learnt about the truth—she believes in its existence; that is her one act of faith— is that it is many-faceted. This is as true of the past as it is of the present and the future. Knowledge of ancestors would not tell her all she needed to know, in order to see herself, or anything, clearly. But it would provide a clue or two.

Clues. There are a few. Place in particular looks promising. The same location for hundreds of years, if popular belief holds any veracity—the documents suggest that it does. Wavesend. Low hills swoop, black and purple and bright moss green, into darker green fields. Yellow ragweed and cow parsley decorate them. Royal red fuchsia, pink dog-roses, meadowsweet and foxgloves flounce in the ditches that line the muddy lane leading down to the shore. Leonine haunches of sand roll into the golden water of the lough. Golden lough, turquoise lough, indigo lough, jade lough. Black lough, lake of shadows. The shadows are the clouds, always scudding across the high opalescent sky. The terns, the oystercatchers, the gulls swoop into those and their own shadows after shadows of herrings, shoals of shadowy mackerel. Shadows on the other side of the shadowy looking-glass of the water.

The house of stone, two storeys high, with undersized door and narrow windows squinting in the gray walls. Crosseyed, shortsighted house, peering at the byre across the 'street'. A cobbled path brings people limping there to milk the cows or if they are women, and usually they are, since cows are women's work, go to the toilet. The milk bounces into wooden buckets, the other flows through a neat square hole into the green stinking pond. The midden. A ridiculous word which always made Lennie laugh. Piddle, middle, midden. Riddle.

Inside, dark is relieved by bright painted furniture. The blue dresser displaying floral tea-bowls, willow patterned platters, huge jugs with red roses floating in pinky-blue clouds on their bellies—the jugs came free, full of raspberry jam; that's why there are so many of them. A special clock, known as an American clock, with a brass pendulum and a sunray crown. Red bins for corn and layer's mash.

The stuff of folk museums. Lennie gets it from textbooks (*Irish Folk Ways*) and from exhibition catalogues, as well as from her own memory. The exhibited model and the actual house overlap so much that it is difficult to distinguish one from the other now. In her own lifetime—she is in her thirties, neither young nor old—real life has entered the museum and turned into history. A real language has crept into the sound archives of linguistic departments and folklore institutions, and it has faded away from people's tongues. In one or two generations. In her generation. It has been a time of endings. Of deaths, great and small. But this she finds interesting rather than painful. She was, after all, an observer of life in Wavesend, someone who had already moved on to other ways of living and speaking before she came to know it and its ways, before she grew to realise their importance. She was never really part of the Wavesend way of life and so she was not founded or offended by its embalming and burial while some of its organs still lived on, weakly flapping like the limbs of an executed man. Saddened, she was, but not bewildered.

Other clues to her past are folk-museum stuff, school history stuff, too. The Famine. Seaweed and barnacles and herrings for dinner. A bowl of yellow meal given to a tinker caused her immediate death. Ate the meal and dropped dead on the hot kitchen floor, Glory be to God; she hadn't eaten in a month, the stomach couldn't take it. Lennie's ancestors had yellow meal, and seaweed, and barnacles, so they survived, or some of them survived. What does that tell her about them? The litany goes on. Oh Mother most Astute! Oh Mother Most Hungry! Oh Mother Most Merciful! Oh Mother Most Cruel! Give us our gruel! The Lennies turned, became Protestant, and later turned back again. Some of them went to America and later came back again. A U-turn, it's called. What that tells U is that U are a survivor. Is it?

Wolfe Tone passed by the house on his way to France. Drugged. Red Hugh passed by the house on his way to Dublin. Drunk. Lennie's great-great-great-grandmother saw the ship and waved. Hiya Wolfie! We're on your side! (Forget chronology. It doesn't reflect significance, usually.)

The Great War. Artillery practice on the shores of the Lough. The sound of cannon reverberates across the night-still waters. Boom. Men stir in their heavy sleep. Boom. An infant shrieks. In the fragile shelter of daylight soldiers visited the house to buy milk and eggs. So, were they friendly? Did they chat? Did someone fall in love with one of them? They gave Lennie's father a ride in a car. His first car ride. That's the sum total of it. It must have been exciting, Daddy! It was. It was.

A personal experience tale: when daddy was seven he fell off a bike, a man's big bike that he had been riding with his legs under instead of over the crossbar. Ten months in a Derry hospital followed the experience. The wound on his leg would not heal. Home, with the abscess, to live or die. Philoctetes. Folk belief: the miracle cure. A holy stone from the holy well, the well of St. Patrick, was taken by his grandmother. You shouldn't take stones from shrines or ancient sites of worship, from open-air museums, but people did not know that then. She took it home without a by your leave and placed it on the wounded spot, and the next day she returned it to its ancient site. The wound healed. He always limped but he was healed, by whatever was in that stone.

And what was it like, in hospital for ten months all alone? Not a single visit for the little nine-year-old boy. Not a single visit. He forgets. He doesn't remember it at all. Perhaps he cannot afford to remember.

It's enough to drive you crazy. Archaeology, history, folklore. Linguistics, genealogy. They tell you about society, not about individuals. It takes literature to do that. And since the Lennies couldn't write until Lennie's grandparents went to school, and not very much after that, there isn't any literature. Not now anyway. The oral tradition. What oral tradition? It went away, with their language, when the schools started. Slowly they are becoming articulate in the new language. Slowly they are finding a new tradition. If there is such a thing as a new language or a new tradition. Do you have to invent them? Like you have to invent history? Invent, discover, revive? You too can transform yourself. Must transform yourself. Utterly.

But look, there she is, hunkered over the black stool in the bottle-green dimness of that cavernous byre, her long hair cloaking her visage and her long, adroit hands squeezing the hot teats. There she is! Sally Rua. Lennie's great-aunt. A tall girl, with adder-green eyes and a mole on her chin and two moles on the sole of her right foot. Gentle on the whole, sometimes acerbic and brusque. People who dislike her—women, mostly, because she is the sort of reserved woman many men unaccountably gravitate towards—say she is a snake. When her hair is wound up behind her long white neck, the simile is accurate enough, although boys who love her compare her, more conventionally, to a swan.

She lived in that house in Wavesend, slept in the bedroom with the window that has to be propped open with a stick and the green wardrobe with cream borders that her own father made for her. In the mornings she went to school in the low white cottage beside the church. The rest of the day she was engaged in all the busy activities of the home. Baking and boiling, feeding and milking. Teasing and carding and spinning and weaving and knitting and sewing and washing and ironing. And making sups of tea for the endless stream of callers. Rakers, they called them, those who shortened the day and the night and stole the working time. A hundred thousand welcomes to you. Just wait till I finish this skein.

When Sally Rua was thirteen a lady from Monaghan, a Miss Burns, came to Wavesend to open a lacemaking school there. The Congested Districts Board had sent her, and her brief was to teach twelve likely girls a craft which would help them supplement their family income. The craft was crochet. The people of Wavesend, and Miss Burns too, called it 'flowering'. Twelve girls, including Sally Rua, assembled in a room in the real teacher's house, which had been kindly lent to Miss Burns. There she began to teach them the rudiments of her craft.

Miss Burns was thirty-six, pretty and mellow, not acid and volatile like Miss Gallagher, the real teacher who was lending them her room. She wore snow-white, high-necked blouses with a dark-blue or a dark-green skirt, and her hair was fair. What, in those pre-peroxide days, was called fair. Leafy brown, fastened to the nape of her neck in a loose bun. Her face was imperfect. There were hairs on her upper lip, quite a little moustache, and Sally Rua thought that this softened her, made her gentler and more pleasant than she might otherwise have been; more cheerful, more enthusiastic about her work of teaching country girls to crochet.

The atmosphere in the chilly room where they worked around a big table was light-hearted. An atmosphere of well-aired orderliness, appropriate to the task in hand. It had less to do with the embroidery or even with Miss Burns, Sally Rua thought, than with the fact that boys were absent. This resulted in a loss of excitement, of the difficult but not unappealing tension which tautened the air in the ordinary classroom, so that no matter what anyone was doing they were vigilant, aware that extraordinary things were going on all the time under the apparently predictable surface of lessons and timetables. Here in the single-sex embroidery class there was none of that; only peace and concentration.

The first thing they learned to crochet was a rose. Sally Rua had sewed the clinching stitch and severed her thread by the end of the first day, although most of the other girls spent a week completing the project. By then, Sally Rua could do daisies, grapes, and shamrocks, and had produced a border of the latter for a linen handkerchief. She worked on her embroidery at home as well as at the school, gaining extra light at night by placing a glass jug of water beside the candle, a trick Miss Burns taught them on the first day. (She had also told them that a good place to store the embroidery, to keep it clean, was under the pillow, unless they happened to have a box or a tin. Nobody had. 'You've already learnt all I'm supposed to teach you!' said Miss Burns at the end of the week, smiling kindly but with some nervousness at Sally Rua. She had encountered star pupils before and was not afraid of them, but there was always the problem of what to teach next, and the suspicion that they already knew more than the teacher. 'You could stop coming here, if you liked. You can already earn money.'

Sally Rua did not want to stop coming. Her primary education was over now—the flowering was by way of finishing school. The prospect of spending her mornings sitting outside the house at home, working alone in the early light, and being called upon to do a thousand and one chores, was not immediately appealing. She'd be doing it soon enough anyhow.

'Maybe you can show me how to do that?' She pointed at a large piece of work lying on the table. It was a half-finished picture of a swan on a lake. Miss Burns had drawn the picture on a piece of paper and pinned some net to it. Now she was outlining the shape of the swan with switches.

'That?' Miss Burns was confused. 'You won't be able to do that. I mean, you won't be able to get rid of it. The Board wants handkerchiefs, not this type of thing.'

'What is it called?'

It was Carrickmacross lace: appliqué. Miss Burns, who came from Carrickmacross, or near it, was doing a piece for her sister who was getting married in a few months' time. The 'picture' was to form the centrepiece of a white tablecloth for the sister's new dining-room.

Sally Rua offered to finish it for her, if she showed her what to do, and after some deliberation Miss Burns agreed to this, although it was not strictly ethical. However, Sally Rua continued to do her roses and daisies, and was earning twice as much money as any of the other girls already, so the aims of the Congested District Board were not being thwarted completely. And Miss Burns was finding the swan tedious.

It was slow work. Sally Rua spent over a week completing the stitching, which looked anaemic and almost invisible against the background of its own colour. Then the paper behind was cut away. And the scene came miraculously to life, etched into the transparent net with a strong white line.

'It's like a picture drawn on ice,' said Sally Rua. In the centre of the hills behind Wavesend, which were called, romantically but graphically, the Hills of the Swan, was a lake, the habitat of several of those birds. Every winter it froze over: the climate was colder in those days than it is now in Donegal. The children of Wavesend climbed the hills in order to slide, and Sally Rua had often done that herself, and had seen crude pictures drawn on the glossy surface with the blades of skates. Once, she had seen something else: a swan, or rather the skeleton of a swan, frozen to the ice, picked lean by stronger, luckier birds.

Miss Burns gave Sally Rua cloth and net to do a second piece of appliqué. She allowed her to make her own pattern, and suggested a few herself: doves, stags, flowers. Sally Rua drew some foxgloves and fuchsias, in a surround of roses, and this was approved of. It was a complicated pattern to work but she managed to do it. Miss Burns said she would send the piece to a shop in Dublin that sold such embroidery, and gave Sally Rua more material. This time, she did a hare leaping over a low stone wall. There were clouds in the background and a gibbous moon.

'It's beautiful,' said Miss Burns. 'But I'm not sure . . . it's very unusual.'

'I've often seen that,' said Sally Rua, who had never seen a stag or a dove and had already done the flowers. 'It's not unusual.'

'Well,' said Miss Burns, 'we'll see.'

The shop in Dublin wrote back three weeks later, Miss Burns's last week, and said that they liked the appliqué and were going to send it to New York, where it would be on exhibition at the Irish Stand at a great fair, the World's Fair. They enclosed a guinea for Sally Rua, from which Miss Burns deducted 9p. for the material she had supplied.

'You should buy some more net and cambric with some of that money,' Miss Burns advised. 'The address of the shop in Dublin is Brown Thomas and Company, Grafton Street. Do another piece of that Carrickmacross and send it to them. You are doing it better than they can do it in the convents.' And she added, because she was a kind and an honest woman: 'You can flower better than me now, too, you know. You should be the teacher, not I.'

Sally Rua, who had known she was better than Miss Burns on her first day's flowering, took her teacher's advice. She walked seven miles to Rathmullan, the nearest town to Wavesend, and bought some yards of net and cambric. She created appliquéd pictures of seagulls swimming on the waves of the lough, of an oystercatcher flying through the great arch at Portsalon, and of the tub-shaped coracles from which her father and brothers fished. Each of these pictures was despatched to Brown Thomas's, and for each of them she was paid ten and sixpence, half of what had been paid for the first, and, it seemed to her, inferior piece. She heard no more about that or about how it had been received at the World's Fair.

The time required to do the appliqué work was extensive, and in fact it did not pay as well as the ordinary flowering.

Sally Rua continued to do a lot of that, although she did not particularly enjoy it. However, she could turn out a few dozen roses or daisies a week, and that was what the merchant who called to the school in Wavesend every Friday afternoon wanted. For every flower, she received 4p. The money formed a useful contribution to the family economy, and so the aim of the Congested District Board was fulfilled, and Sally Rua's life settled into a pattern which she found rewarding: flowering and housework by day, appliquéing (and some other forms of entertainment) by night. She was happier than she had ever been before.

It did not last. By September, Miss Burns had left Wavesend and the lacemaking school had stopped. In March of the following year, six pictures later, Sally Rua's father and two brothers were drowned while fishing on the lough during a storm. When the wake and funeral were over and the first grieving past, the actual implications of the disaster were outlined to Sally Rua by her mother. She could no longer afford to live on the farm at Wavesend unless her daughters went out and earned a living (the only son, Denis, was married). The flowering would not be enough. Sally Rua would have to get a real job, one that would support her fully and leave some money over for her mother.

She went to work as a maid in a house in Rathmullan, the house of the doctor, Doctor Lynch. She was the lucky one; Mary Kate and Janey, her sisters, had to go to the Lagan to work as hired girls for farmers. Sally Rua's polish, and her reputation as a skilled needleworker, ensured that she had the better fate.

The house in Rathmullan was a square stone block on a low slope overlooking the roofs of the town. It was called 'The Rookery', because it was close to a wood where thousands of crows nested. Sally Rua's room was in the attic, of course, at the back of the house, above the farmyard and with a view of the trees and the crows which she would have been happier without. It was a small, cold room, but she had little time to spend in it. Her days were long hectic rounds of domestic and farm routines. The Lynches kept other staff, but not enough, and there was always something to be done.

At first, Sally Rua was not unhappy. Mrs Lynch was a reasonable woman who wanted her servants to be contented, if for no other reason than she would get more out of them in that way. She spoke Irish to them, since she knew they preferred it, and to her children, because really she felt more at home in that language herself, even though the doctor, from Letterkenny, wished English to be the language of his household. That did not matter: he was not often at home, and never in the kitchen where Sally Rua spent most of the time when she was not in the byre or the dairy. When she described her life in Rathmullan to her mother, whom she visited once a month, she painted a picture of a calm, contented existence.

This description began to change after about three months. Sally Rua, speaking in a voice which had become low and monotone and should itself have been a warning to her mother, said she was anxious. Her mother, legs parted to catch the heat of the flares, looked at her—anxiously—shook her head and did not pursue the matter. Sally Rua, lying that night on her high bed in Rathmullan, watching the shadows of the giant oak trees gloom across the floor, wept. She told herself she was stupid. She told herself she was sad. She told herself she was miserable, lonely.

What she was missing was the house at Wavesend, her sisters, her friends. Her mother. Homesick she was. She had been homesick from day one. But there was more to it than that. What really made her cry with misery and frustration was the way she was missing her work. Her real work. The flowering.

She had hoped, at first, that there would be some need for that here. That Mrs Lynch would ask her to make some antimacassars for her big armchairs and sofa, which could badly do with them, or runners for the dressing tables and sideboard. After about six weeks she realised that such requests would not be forthcoming. There was plenty of needlework to be done in the Lynch household, all right, but it took the form of mending sheets and underwear and nightgowns, rather than of anything elaborate. Sally Rua was expected to spend every night working at the linen closet and wardrobe of Mrs Lynch and her daughters. She had been employed chiefly for her skills in this line; the other work she spent twelve hours a day doing was simply thrown in as a little extra.

There was, of course, no possibility of doing embroidery in her own room during her spare time, simply because she had no spare time. Every minute in the Lynch household that was not spent sleeping or eating had to be devoted to Lynch work. The only free time she had was one Sunday a month, the Sunday she spent visiting her mother. She did a bit of flowering while she was at home, occasionally. But a few hours a month were insufficient. There was never time to get even one flower finished, never mind a whole picture.

Sally Rua became more and more miserable. She also became more and more cross. She snapped at the other maids and at the lads in the yard, and even at Emma and Louise, the daughters of the house. Gradually her personality was transformed and she became renowned for her bad temper as she had once been renowned for her skill at the flowering. She became so crotchety that sometimes on her day off she did not go to Wavesend at all, but wandered around Rathmullan, staring at the ruined abbey, at the boats moving across the shadowy lough to Buncrana, and at the Seagulls wheeling over it. She stared at the crows who built their nests in the high, scrawny oaks that surrounded the Lynch house.

Once, on a winter's evening, when the moon was a full white circle behind the skeletal trees, she saw a hare on the fence that divided the garden from the bog. Its coat of fur was brown and gold and yellow and purple, streaked with odd white patches. It had a small white bun of a tail. Never had she seen a hare at such close quarters. She was so near that she could see its tawny eyes gazing at her, and its split trembling lip. For minutes she stared, and all the time the hare stayed as still as the fence it sat on. Then something happened. A twig fell, a scrap of cloud shadowed the moon. And at that same moment, the hare and Sally moved. She bent, picked up a stone, and flung it hard at the hare's white tail. Before she had stooped to the ground, before she had touched the stone, the hare was gone, bounding over the moonlit turf at a hundred miles an hour.

A few days later, Sally screamed at Mrs Lynch. Mrs Lynch had simply asked her to make a white dress for Louise's Confirmation, and had suggested that she do a little embroidery on the cuffs and collar. It was the first time such a request had been made. Daisies, she suggested, might be appropriate. Sally Rua had taken the material, a couple of yards of white silk, and thrown it into the fire. She watched it going up in flames without a word or a cry, and then, as Mrs Lynch, having got over her shock, began to remonstrate, she picked up all the cushions and tablecloths and textiles that were lying about the room (the drawing-room) and pitched them on the fire as well. At this point she began to scream. This helped Mrs Lynch to regain her presence of mind, and she ran for help to the kitchen. John, the hired man, and Bridget the cook (all cooks are called Bridget) caught Sally Rua and pinned her down to the sofa, while someone was sent for the doctor. There was a certain gratification in imprisoning Sally Rua in this way; it was a slight revenge for all the abuse she had heaped on them over the past months.

There was no lunatic asylum in Letterkenny then, as there is now. But there was a poorhouse, with a wing for those of unsound mind, and that is where Sally Rua went. Later it became a lunatic asylum and she experienced that, too, for two decades before her death. She reached the age of seventy-six, and was completely mad for most of her life.

Sally Rua. She went mad because she could not do the work she loved, because she could not do her flowering. That can happen. You can love some kind of work so much that you go crazy if you simply cannot manage to do it at all. Outer or inner constraints could be the cause. Sally Rua had only outer ones. She was so good at flowering, she was such a genius at it, that she never had any inner problems. That was the good news, as far as she was concerned.

Sally Rua. Lennie's ancestor. Of course, none of that is true. It is a yarn, spun out of thin air. Not quite out of thin air: Lennie read about a woman who had gone mad because she could not afford to keep up the flowering which she loved, and had to go into service in a town house in the north of Ireland. The bare bones of a story. How much of that, even, is true? She might have gone mad anyway. She might have been congenitally conditioned to craziness. Or the madness might have had some other cause, quite unconnected with embroidery. The son of the house might have raped her. Or the father. Or the grandfather or the hired man. People go mad for lots of reasons, but not often for the reason that they haven't got the time to do embroidery.

Still and all. The woman who wrote the history of embroidery, an excellent, an impassioned book, the name of which would be cited if this were a work of scholarship and not a story, believed that that was the cause of the tragedy. And Lennie believes it. Because she wants to. She also wants to adopt that woman, that woman who was not, in history, called Sally Rua, but some other, less interesting name (Sally Rua really was the name of Lennie's great-grandmother, but what she knows about her is very slight), as her ancestor. Because she does not see much difference between history and fiction, between painting and embroidery, between either of them and literature.

Or scholarship. Or building houses. The energies inspiring all of these endeavours cannot be so separate, after all. The essential skills of learning to manipulate the raw material, to transform it into something orderly and expressive, to make it, if not better or more beautiful, different from what it was originally and more itself, apply equally to all of these exercises. Exercises that Lennie likes to perform. Painting and writing, embroidering and scholarship. If she likes these things, someone back there in Wavesend must have liked them too. And if someone back there in Wavesend did not, if there was no Sally Rua, at all, at all, where does that leave Lennie?

Night of the Fox

'WHAT I LIKE ABOUT it is seeing the light in the window when we arrive and then going into the kitchen and it's bright and hot and Nana's there and Granda's there and we get our tea.'

We're going to the country.

It's a long weekend. It's a long way to the country. We've made good headway, however, in spite of some hiccups (roadworks in Dorset Street: 'Dorset Street's not real!' somebody had told me earlier in the week, but I forgot that in the rush of getting away). In any case, we are out of town by six o'clock, out on the road to Wavesend, the North Road. Soon its clipped hedges and depressingly straight line have given way to a narrower winding way overhung with elms. The ditches are creamy with meadowsweet. Hawthorn blossoms drip like lazy snow on to the bonnet of the car.

'When will we get there? How many hours? Five hours? A hundred hours?'

We play 'What am I?' with the boys. Simon, who is almost seven, plays seriously: he is not too old for this kind of thing, or too young. He works indoors. He makes something, something you can eat. He enjoys his job. He is a baker. Timmy's mind is not the kind that focuses easily on games, on any kind of game, or on anything else for that matter. He works outdoors. He grows something. His job is fun. It turns out he's a robber.

'He's chea-ea-tin'.'

'I am not. I'm not cheatin', sure I'm not Mammy!'

Eric turns up the cassette player and shouts at them over the roar of somebody's concerto. The car swerves slightly and I frown. The thing is not to let them get at you. If you let them

31

get at you you could crash the car. You would certainly get a headache.

Sooner than is wise we have to stop for food: Simon is so hungry, he can't last till we're even close to a halfway stage. I turn down an avenue to a place we've often used before for travellers' snacks: it is called 'The Traveller's Rest', like many pubs and cafés along the way. (One of our games, on one of our journeys, was counting them. After five we lost interest.) But unlike most of those establishments it is an old, comfortable hotel, set amidst rolling golf greens and overlooking a lake which might be artificial, might have been constructed a hundred years ago just to provide this elegant place with a view, but looks natural enough to fool us. We park in what I think is the usual place but something has happened: the hotel has disappeared. At least the house we know is no longer there. Instead there are some new buildings, faked to look old. They are half finished; piles of cement and machinery are lying about. We can't see anyone and we can't find anything that looks like an entrance.

'Maybe it's further up. Maybe we've parked in the wrong place!' I suggest. I am always ready to doubt any judgment, to believe myself wrong. Sometimes I am justified in this attitude, sometimes not. And now I realise as I walk that some of the features are familiar. Where the new terrace is, there used to be an old terrace, with a fancy balustrade and pink and white geraniums in stone pots. The new terrace has nothing, as yet, relieving its bareness. Indeed, like all the building, it has the dead wettish look of fresh concrete and its sour smell. Unwelcoming. Eventually we try a door that looks forbidding: I think it might be the way into a golf club, some private exclusive place that we, in our work—and school-weary clothes, with our tired unglamorous faces, have no right to enter.

As we approach the door we meet a stylishly-dressed woman who stares past us: she has the unfriendly eyes of a fashion model or some pampered, oft-stared-at personage. I expect to be repulsed. But once inside the door I have the feeling of being in a familiar place that has somehow changed beyond recognition. It is like a room I have visited in a previous existence, or have become familiar with from the pages of a book. Gradually, however, we realise that enormous alterations have been carried out on the hotel both inside and out, but that the basic ground plan, although enlarged, is the same as before. Thus the lobby is three times as big and ten times as elegant as it formerly was, but it is more or less in the same place as the old, comfortable lobby we used to drink coffee in.

Similarly, the bar is in the same quarters as the old bar: in fact, the bar itself, the wooden counter with a huge mirror behind, is exactly the same; it was good enough to endure the transition, apparently. Only the furniture and the interior decoration has been altered here, altered beyond recognition. Antique, or antique-look, sofas and easy chairs, no two doing anything as vulgar as matching, but all blending harmoniously together. Deep custom designed carpets. The toilets are the most splendid of all, and we all comment on them.

'Of course you pay for all the elegance!'

'How much did it cost, Dad?'

Simon wants to know the cost of everything. It has become an obsession with him, one with which I have difficulty being patient. For once Eric gives him a civil answer.

'Ten pounds.'

'Ten pounds! Ten pounds! For two cups of coffee and two sandwiches and two glasses of coke! Ten pounds! They weren't even big sandwiches, were they, Mum?'

'Not really,' I have to agree. They were small sandwiches. The coffee was not especially good, either; it was probably instant but it was so bad you couldn't tell whether it was or not. Normally I would forgive the faults and the expense in a place as luxurious and splendid as this has become. I like luxury and precious trappings, easy panache. Not this time.

The refurbishing of 'The Traveller's Rest' has left me thoroughly disorientated. It was permeated with a sense of *dejà vu*, elusive feelings I couldn't get a grip on. It wasn't real.

We are going to visit my parents in their summer cottage on the northern coast. They bought this cottage five years ago, five years after my father retired. It was something they'd been planning to do for years, to return to the country, to live in the place, or near the place, where they had been born. But when the time came at long last they found they couldn't stick Wavesend all the year round. It is no longer the place it was when they were young, a place where families lived and worked and which was, purely incidentally, also a very picturesque, beautiful place. Now it is more of a quiet holiday resort and most of its houses are summer cottages. It's hard to live year round in a place like that. So they spend six months there and six months in the city in their old house on Exeter Place. Usually in Exeter Place they are ill, coughing and having headaches and flutterings of the heart. They are up and down to the doctor. On more than one occasion one of them has been in hospital, but so far they've always come out, recovered. Usually in Wavesend they are well. Fat and sunburned, they spend their days planting vegetables and cutting the lawn and going for walks on the beach and drinks in the local pub. It is a good life but not, my mother says, in winter. In winter you have to be in town.

We visit them two or three times each summer, usually during July and August when the children have their summer holidays. Now it is June and we are going because a cousin of ours from Wavesend, Manus, is ill. He is one of the permanent Wavesend people, and he has been a good friend to my mother and father during their retirement: he is the sort of man who will come and fix a burst pipe or mend the motor mower whenever necessary. In fact he comes to the house and cuts the grass for my parents when they are away in Dublin and his wife, Marie, lights a fire in the kitchen to keep the place aired. A few months ago he started forgetting things. The vet made an appointment to come and check his small dairy herd and it went clear out of his head. He promised Marie he would get her a packet of bayleaves when he was in town at a mart (he is a farmer) and came home without them. He forgot to pay the ESB bill and they were cut off suddenly to the great risk of their milk, settling in electrical cooling vats in the dairy. Other incidents like that occurred. Minor but accumulating. Then about three weeks ago he got a bad headache. A tumour was diagnosed. By now he is in a state of semiconsciousness. The tumour is inoperable. He has been given a few months.

The children, our children, do not, of course, know any of this. They know that Manus is sick but it means nothing to them. They hardly remember who Manus is, although I explain. Manus, the man who gives us the asparagus and the milk. Manus has been in the habit of bringing us gifts of unusual vegetables, artichokes, asparagus, eggplants, which he grows organically as a hobby. They are fresh and delicious, but Simon and Timmy have never eaten any of them. They don't eat any kind of vegetable except potato. Neither do they like the milk which Manus carries up to the house every evening. They turn up their noses when they see it frothing and foaming in the white enamel bucket. When they go to bed my mother pours it into bottles and puts them in the fridge. Next day she pretends she's bought them from the shop.

It is midnight by the time we reach Wavesend. When I turn down the lane that leads to my parents' house I see the lights on in their windows. And I see also two smaller yellow lights in their garden hedge. Lights that move, brilliant yellow, yellower than any light I know, against the black hedge. I see these lights, but nobody else does; the boys are half asleep, Eric is talking about Beethoven and Mozart. Simon is like Beethoven, he says. Timmy is like Mozart. I have no knowledge of music and no memory for it. Eric used to play games with me: Guess what

this is? Who wrote it? What instruments are being used? He's
given up on that. It's too late: when I was Simon's age I'd never
heard the names Beethoven and Mozart, let alone any of their
music. But I agree with him about the contrasting characters. I
have picked up the basic biographical clichés.

'Look!'

Eric looks and does not see. Timmy sits up and leans against
his window. Simon grumbles.

'Do you see?'

It is a fox, a small, perfect fox, imprisoned momentarily in
the beam of the headlights. His brush stands firmly up, his little
sharp face is cocked, looking at us with eyes that are not yellow
anymore, but glittering ebony like ponds in moonlight.

'Look! Look, Simon, look!'

Already he has disappeared into the darkness. Nobody has
seen him apart from me: the boys never do see wild animals;
you have to be older than them, I think, or at least quieter, in
order to catch sight of a fox or a hare or even a rabbit, which
I see dozens of times as I drive along through the countryside.
Both boys are sceptical and do not really believe that I have
seen a fox. I can understand their scepticism, and their faint
resentment. I wish Simon, at least, had caught a glimpse of it
because he likes animals so much. In books, that is.

'He's not so well,' my father says in his shy diffident voice. His
bushy old eyebrows meet in a puzzled frown as if he does not
understand why this should be. Manus is less than half his age,
one of the young men he depended upon.

'Ah well, you never know how things will go. He may
improve.' Eric does not know Manus and the subject of illness
is distasteful to him. He has been seriously ill himself in the
not too distant past, not with Manus's illness but with another
serious disease. He does not want the topic broached. Neither
do I. 'I am always optimistic, you know!'

'Yes,' my father laughs his little apologetic but rather gleeful laugh. 'I heard Gorbachev saying something today, yez didn't hear it, did yez? It was very good like . . . what was it, something like "I see the glass half full and the people see it half empty." I thought it was good.'

Eric and I exchange a look.

'Yes,' says Eric, 'oh yes, I always see the glass half full, while Lennie here sees it half empty. If not completely empty. She is a pessimist, are you not?'

'I suppose so.' I am embarrassed when Eric teases me in the presence of my parents. I wish he wouldn't do it. They like it a bit, but no more than me do not know how they are supposed to respond. My father, luckily, can always pretend not to hear anything he doesn't grasp fully since he is partially deaf.

My mother is running in and out of the scullery setting the table and making tea. As usual, we will have cheese and cold ham and bread and tea.

'We had dinner in a hotel on the way. It cost a hundred pounds,' Simon informs her in his loud voice. He is wide awake by now.

I try to correct this. Mother is capable of believing it, of believing that we would buy a dinner costing a hundred pounds on our way to the country and bring her as a gift a bunch of flowers purchased at a garage on the roadside and costing two pounds fifty: the only thing they had, the only thing I had time to get, Eric had got them, actually, along with another item I'd urgently required: a packet of sanitary towels. He'd said: 'I am not going to ask for them!' but I knew he would. He is like Mozart. When he came out, with the bunch of oldish carnations and the see-through plastic bag, he said, 'I had to say the words sanitary towels three times. The fellow in there had never heard of them.'

'Did you have to tell him about the facts of life as well?'

'He's at your window now; why don't you tell him yourself?'

The boy's face at the window, waiting to serve the petrol, was not red or ostensibly embarrassed, but bland, expressionless. So I knew he was either embarrassed or scornful, waiting for us to move on so that he could laugh at us with some companion. I quickly gave my order and money and got away.

My mother, in strong contrast to my father, is loquacious. She loves to talk, to transform the ordinary events of her life into stories. The gory details of illness, any illness, always provide her with excellent copy, and she tells us a great deal about Manus. More than we want to know. 'Poor Manus, there's nothing they can do for him in Luke's. The thing is growing so fast, it's really just taking over the whole brain now.' She uses her hand to demonstrate how it's growing. Her hand has grown puffy lately, and the sun has highlighted its veil of coffee-coloured spots. I glance at my own hand, large but as yet thin. The right hand is a comforting pasty white but the left is freckling, sure enough. I touch the black mole on the left side of my face, where a gland has begun to stiffen. The left is my dangerous side; I have always feared it. That is where the end will come first. Feeling the tinge of nausea which that touch and thought always stimulate, I quickly return my attention to my mother's tale. Her hand is still boldly illustrating the air above the table while her voice continues to provide supporting text. To hear her speak you would swear she had been inside Manus's head with the surgeons, peering at it with a magnifying glass, probing with the scalpel. I see a stalk of meadowsweet putting out more and more white fronds, each one foaming with a myriad tiny blossoms. 'In the end it'll start to bleed and then . . . '

She shakes her head fatalistically.

'We'll miss the milk,' she says.

'And the asparagus,' I acquiesce, observing Eric's expression of disgust. He hates the mercenary side of humanity, a side with which I am very familiar. My mother will, given half a chance, elaborate on Manus's financial affairs and the problems his widow may have to face. She will hint at the plight of the children: to do more than hint would be to go too far, at this stage, but we all get the message. And his imminent death is transformed from a personal tragedy to something akin to a devaluation of the pound or some kind of purely economic crisis. Manus, like a lot of married men, is more than just a human being. He is a breadwinner. Other humans depend on him for their sustenance: his loss will be greater than that of a man or woman with a smaller responsibility. Will it also, in some way, be less? I have my suspicions but I do not want to consider their implications right now, so I shy away from them.

We are going to see Manus on Saturday afternoon, but the morning is ours, for pleasure. First we go to the beach so that Simon and Timmy can play. It is Whit Saturday. My father tells us that when he was a child they were never allowed to go to the shore on Whit Sunday, because if you got a cut on that day it would never heal.

'Don't pay any attention to him!' my mother laughs. 'It's not Sunday anyway, is it? Go on down to the beach and let the boys enjoy themselves.'

The beach, according to my mother, is the most magnificent beach in Ireland. It's the longest and the finest, and moreover it's got some special award from the EC for being the most unpolluted. Possibly it is the best and biggest beach in Europe, possibly, for all I know, in the world. We trudge down to it, across the sandy field that separates it from the house. Lapwings take fright as we pass and wheel around our heads, frantically twittering 'Peewee, peewee!' They sound like a computer game, observes Simon, and Eric and I smile, thinking that Simon is very clever, 'Peewee, peewee!' We arrive at the beach.

Two miles of white sand, reddish when it's rained as it has earlier this morning. A wide bay, shirred by shadows, into which the hills fall gracefully like smooth-haunched bathers. Behind the beach are dunes, giving way to a saucer-shaped valley. The lip

of hills that shelters it is low but variegated, mysterious to look
at. The most distant hills are black, those slightly nearer green.
The closest of all are olive green, moss green, brown and silver. I
look at the hills and the grayish white sky while I kick ball with
Simon, help Timmy build a sand castle. Why don't they build
themselves? I ask Eric. But he doesn't hear; he is walking along
by the edge of the waves plugged into his Walkman, listening
to his eternal music and staring at the terns which dive into
the sea at regular intervals with a shocking white splash. What
does he hear when he listens? I would like to know but I never
will. When I first knew him he didn't seem to care about music.
Gradually it has become an obsession. I think this dates from
the time of his illness, the time he had his heart operation. Four
years ago, at the time of Timmy's birth. I was in Holles Street,
having Timmy, while he was in another hospital, being cut to
bits. We try to forget that time and to forget that Eric is always
in danger, and mainly we succeed. As time passes we assume
that danger lessens, although probably the opposite is the case.
The operation has left its mark on Eric, however, in more ways
than one. He knows something that I don't know, I suspect, and
it is not something he can teach me. The names of concertos,
the lives of the composers, he tries with those. But he can't give
me the music.

I think of a piece of coral. There is no coral, naturally, on
this northern strand. The rocks, however, which border it at
one end are black and soft, lacy with clefts and multi-shaped
fissures. You could guess that the Giant's Causeway is not too
far away. In one part of the bay great arches have formed where
the sea has bitten through the basalt. You can sit and watch
oystercatchers and gulls flying under the arches as you listen to
the waves crashing on the rocks. In spite of their grey and black
colours, their texture reminds me of coral reefs in the south
seas. Stones of pink and stones of white, growing and growing
and growing.

After lunch we drive to the hospital. I am driving: I do not want to concede this power to my father or mother, who have offered to play chauffeur. I am afraid to let them drive me anywhere, afraid of where they will take me and how long I will have to stay. If I drive I will have the ultimate say in what we decide to do. My mother knows this and that is why she is looking disgruntled, climbing awkwardly into the back seat. My father sits beside me in the front. My mother, possibly to atone for feeling annoyed, is doling out peppermint sweets and the air is full of their aroma.

The meadowsweet froths out of the ditches like bubbles on the top of a bucket of new milk. Behind it the rhododendron bushes have gone out of control so that they are not bushes but trees, not shrubbery but forests, dangling their enormous flowers. Mostly purple, some the more brilliant exotic pink.

Eric is asleep. I can hear him snoring, a thin snore like a whistle.

The hospital is on the outskirts of the town and has substantial grounds. The children are not allowed in to visit, we are told in the lobby. Eric is quick to offer his services as minder. 'Sure Lennie can come down and let you up in a few minutes,' my mother, always ready to organise, says. 'I doubt if we'll have to stay long.'

I feel sick, hearing these words. They get me in the gut, not with sadness, but with something closer to either fear or nausea. What is it I am so afraid of?

We walk falteringly up the stairs (falteringly because my mother and father are old and each has one good hip and one bad, the good one made of plastic. They do not negotiate stairs easily, particularly stairs that are strange to them). The hospital is like all others I have been in, rather more spacious and comfortable than some. There are wide corridors with no beds in them, and equipment seems to be stored in its proper place, out of sight. The cutbacks you hear so much about don't

seem to have taken effect here, not visibly anyway. A few nurses
scuttle along. We find the ward Manus is in: Saint Joseph's. It is
a big room containing about twenty beds. 'He's down near the
far corner,' my mother whispers. Her voice is reverent; it is the
voice she uses in church. 'You won't know him. Don't expect to
know him, he looks so different. He's in that second last bed, I
think, do you see there, near that table with the flowers on it?'

The flowers are sweet peas, I can see that much from here,
but my mother cannot since she is not wearing her glasses.
Neither can she see that the bed she has indicated is empty. I do
not point this out to her, but walk slowly, measuring my step to
hers and my father's, until they can see it for themselves.

'Hm, that's odd now,' my mother looks around. Her face
wears a rather sharp and business-like look, an expression it gets
when she is dealing with people whom she considers inferior to
herself. A lot of people fall into this category, including me and
my father.

A nurse comes and tells us. He's been moved. He's in
intensive care. We can't visit him.

My mother is not going to give up so easily.

'My daughter has come all the way from Dublin especially
to see him. Especially. It may be her last chance.'

'You can look in at him, I suppose,' the nurse concedes.
She is quite young but authoritative. She looks at me with an
expression that is both sympathetic and scornful. My mother,
I realise, must seem slightly eccentric to some younger people.
The strong will, the independence, the pushiness which were
powerful when she was younger herself have hardened into
oddness, to be humoured if it's easier, not to be feared.

We follow the nurse to a lift and along a wider, much quieter
corridor.

'There,' she says, and leaves us.

My mother peers through the window. My father, obedient
as always, looks: his eyesight is not the best, he probably can't

see anyway. I stand as far away as I can and fix my gaze on the curtains. They are a dusty pink, smoky pink I think it is called, and are made of imitation linen. I look closely at the little uneven cropped lines, the broken weave.

'Poor Manus,' my mother says, shrugging her shoulders. Shrugging him off, 'Doesn't he look dreadful?'

We nod.

The nurse comes and beckons us away. My mother, on the way out, questions her about Manus. But of course she gives us no solid information.

We all leave the hospital together and walk along the paved pathway to the carpark. The sky is still overcast but the sun is occasionally making an effort to break through. Now it pierces a bank of gray cloud and the slabs at our feet grow lighter, almost yellow, for a minute. Our shadows appear before us, faint diffident shadows. They move along slowly ahead like silent guides, each shadow blending into the next so that you cannot tell where one person's ends and the other's begins.

Summer Pudding

WE CAMPED AT CAER Gybi for three days waiting for Father Toban. Two tinkers we'd met in Llanfair told us he was on his way there from Bangor. But although we'd kept an eye out for him on the road we had not seen him, and we had not heard tell of him either. When we asked about him. people laughed, or gave a useless answer or no answer.

We camped on a patch of ground above the beach, close to the harbour, where we could see the packet sailing in and out. The weather was dry and calm, and the tides were quiet for April. We'd missed three sailings in the three days.

'We should go,' I said, 'without him. We can say our own prayers.'

Naoise did not believe this and neither did I. The truth was, I did not want to say prayers at all any more. But he did. He would not go. He had it in his head that Father Toban would come and that was that. I was getting to know him, and already I knew that he was stubborn as an ass, He had told me that anyway, proudly, and warning at the same time. I was proud, too, when he told me, and I knew that his stubbornness was good for me, a gift for me. Now I could see it could have another side.

There is sharp marram grass on the ground and it is not comfortable to lie on, or to love on. It is dry, however. The dunes are alive with rabbits and we have had a good stew every day—I have onions that I lifted from an old one in the town. I go in during the day for a few hours and sell tin cans. The Welsh here are not as bad as in other parts, being used to us, I suppose, by now. They should be.

Father Toban. Who is he? I have heard him talked about ever since I came but I haven't seen him and everything I have heard about him has a hollow ring to it. Maybe he is an old *piseog*, like the banshee.

'Do you believe in the banshee, Naoise?' I asked him.

He did.

'She must have been busy during the last couple of years. Or does she have helpers?'

'Go away out of that,' he said. He didn't like it.

I didn't tell him that I thought Father Toban was like the banshee. Somebody only your friend's friend has ever laid eyes on.

In July I came over with my sister Mary and a band of people from Kildare. Dunnes and Connors mostly, who had been on the road for years and already knew the tinsmith's trade, as we, of course, did not. Our father was a farmer outside Kilkenny and had just died a few months before we came over. Our mother had died the year before that and all our brothers. We ledged their clothes in a pawnshop in Naas, where we were not known. We had been told we should burn them because of the fever but we needed money and the clothes were good—trousers with no patches, two good frieze coats, a pair of leather shoes and two pairs of wooden brogues. I washed them in the river and dried them two days in the sun and I do not think there could have been any fever left on them. With the money we got for them and for some pots and pans and the blankets from our beds, and the one week's wages our father had got on the Relief, we had enough money for the two tickets. The tinkers we met at the docks and took up with there.

Mary did not like them. 'They are wild animals,' she said. Not 'they are like wild animals', which is what I thought at first. Long scrawny things, with loose arms and legs—loose tongues, loose other things as well. They have bushes of frizzy red hair or fair hair, never combed, sticking up on top of their heads or just tumbling down any old way around their shoulders. The strangest thing is their eyes. The men have mad eyes, that don't seem to blink, like the eyes of cats or foxes. Maybe it is from the *poitín*, which they drink whenever they can—they carry a still with them, on a handcart, so they can make more whenever they camp anywhere for any length of time. The women throw their bodies along the road rather than carry them like Mary does and, I suppose, me as well, as if we were jugs of milk that might spill if we didn't take care. They spread their legs when they sit by the fire and suck in the heat of the flames. Right in. No underpants. They laughed at the way we looked and at our dresses.

'What have you your hair pulled out of the roots like that for?' they said, pulling it down. 'Who do you think you are anyway?'

We have flat black hair, which falls lank down the sides of our faces when the bands are off. Our dresses are plain gray calico.

'You are a sight,' they said, 'for sore eyes.'

They did not ask where we had come from or why we had joined them. They could guess. The surprising thing was that they let us stay with them, and they gave us some of their food.

'I want to leave them as soon as we land,' Mary said. 'I can't stand them.'

We were eating half a loaf of bread we'd got from them. We had not had bread in months.

'How can we do that? We don't know our way around. We don't know the language.'

'Do you think that lot of eejits know any language apart from their own Paddy bad language?'

They did, some of them, speak Welsh and English, because they had been over before. More importantly, they could get food wherever they went. They could snare rabbits and hares, grouse and pheasants, they could make whiskey and tin cans. And they could beg and sell, they could steal and frighten people into giving them things. They could erect a tent that kept out the rain. We couldn't do even one of these things.

We soon learned.

'Into the town and come home with your dinner,' Molly Dunne, the one who talked to us most, said. She had gray hair, curled like carrageen moss, down to her waist nearly, and a huge beak of a nose.

'Will we sell something?'

'What have you to sell?'

'Well . . . '

'You can sell yourselves if you like but I don't think you'll get much of a price with the cut of you. Do what you see the rest of them doing.'

We went off down the road from the camp with nine or ten of them, women and a few men. The women all had their striped cotton dresses on and big blue cloaks flying around them, and their red hair flying, and the men had white shirts and black coats and carried thick sticks on their shoulders. They moved in a strung-out group along the thin road from the sea to the marketplace, and we were among them. I thought they must look like the wind, blowing into the place. People scattered before them as if they were—the wind, or a band of bad mischievous fairies. The little Welsh women in their black clothes, with their little white lace bonnets close to their faces, fled.

Not all of them saw us, or got away in time. The tinkers cornered any who stayed on the street.

'Ma'am, will you buy a pot from me? A good little pot?'

The Welsh women looked terrified and said in their singsong voices, 'Dim Sasenig,' although the tinkers were speaking Irish. The men stood close by, staring at the frightened women with their cat eyes, rubbing their sticks thoughtfully. All the women bought a pot or a pan or a mug and then ran into some shop. I heard the word '*Gwydellion*' for the first time. '*Gwydellion Gwydellion Gwydellion.*' It was a whisper, a whimper and a curse. Also a warning and a plea for help. I knew what it meant without asking.

I stole a loaf, not from a stall or a shop, but from a woman's basket. She put her basket down on the gray slabs while she tested some apples on a stall. In the basket were eggs, butter and something I did not recognise, a thick wedge of red stuff, like butter, as well as the loaf of bread. I pretended to be looking at the apples and pears which were heaped on the stall. The woman behind the stall looked suspiciously at me and muttered '*Gwyndellion*' under her breath but not aloud. She wasn't sure, maybe. I did not look quite like the other Gwyndellion, with my black hair, which I had tied back again behind my neck, and my plain dress.

It was easy to snatch the bread and then I ran away like the hammers of hell.

'Good girl yourself,' Molly Dunne said. 'I didn't think you had it in you.'

Neither did I. I was as proud as punch, and Mary was downhearted and disapproving as you would expect her to be, a girl who had spent a year studying with the nuns who might have been some sort of a kitchen nun herself, if things had gone different.

When we camped near a town we were often attacked. People came and tried to set fire to our tents. Often fights broke out because the tinkers were quick to defend themselves. The Welsh men were smaller than ours but they were strong; they had plenty to eat and did not drink whiskey, only their own sweet ale. Once, one of our lads was killed in one of these battles. What Molly said was, 'Just as well it was not the other way round, or we'd all be on the way to Van Diemen's Land, if not worse.'

That was the first time I heard about Father Toban. It was actually the first time I heard about religion from the band, but now it turned out that they wanted Father Toban to bury the dead boy, one of the Connors. They wanted him to get a Christian burial and Father Toban was their only chance of that. 'He is the only Catholic priest in all Wales,' they said.

'Where is his church?' This was Mary. She'd want to know so she could visit it and get Mass. That she had not got Mass in weeks and weeks was a great heart's scald to her.

'Oh, be quiet, you fool! Do you think he'd have a church in this place?'

'I see a lot of churches.'

'Not one Catholic church.'

'What is their religion, then?'

'They are Protestant, and worse than that.'

'What is worse?'

'They are heathens like the blacks of Africa or the wild men of America.'

'They look like Protestants to me,' I said. And they did. I had never in Ireland seen anyone that looked half as Protestant as the Welsh women, not even in Dublin or Kingstown.

'They are Centers. The Centers is what they call themselves, they are worse than the Protestants.'

We did not find Father Toban and Tadg was buried in a bog on the slopes of the mountain called Wydfa, where we camped after the fight that killed him. It was a remote place, not too close to any town, and there we felt safe. Some villages, Llanberis and Beddgelert, were about an hour or two's walk away, and during the day we could visit them, sell tin cans or steal. I never begged. I couldn't, although Mary became quite good at that. I stole all before me, preferring that, even though I knew what would happen if I got caught. I stole from farms as well as from towns—eggs and milk, bread sitting out to cool on windowsills. I took the red stuff called, I knew now, cheese.

Once, I lifted a lamb from under the nose of a boy on the side of Wydfa. Naoise, whom I had got to know by then, killed it for me and we all ate it, roasted over the fire, for supper.

We were at Wydfa for a long time, for months. The tent bleached in the sunshine as the summer wore on, and I lay on the short grass, smelling thyme and gorse, and all the summer smells, and felt happy. There were hares and rabbits in the mountains, carrots and even potatoes on the farms, everything you could think of in the shops of the village. I felt my face getting plumper, browner, and saw this happening to Mary too, although she was very thin otherwise. I liked, as well as all this, living in a tent. I liked to feel the sun heating the canvas in the morning when I woke up, or even to hear the rain pounding against it, as if it would wear it away with its beating. I liked to know that I could pull it up in a few minutes and pack it on my back and move. Although we did not move once we found the valley near Wydfa, and the band stayed there for a long long time, so long that the Welsh people came to know it and to call it the Valley of the Gwydellion.

Mary met the Ladies of Llangollen. Of course she did. She had heard about them at home. For weeks she had been trying to drag me to Llangollen to meet them. She hated the Gwydellion with a vengeance, hated them as much as the Welsh did, if not even more. And they hated her, too, because they were not stupid and could see her hatred. She was above them all, always thinking of her convent and our father's house and our family. She could not forget. If it had not been for me they would have thrown her out, or they would have starved her or maybe killed her.

She met one of the Ladies on the main street of the town less than an hour after we had arrived there. How did she know who it was? She knew because the lady was the richest-looking old woman walking along the main street on her own, and also because she was wearing trousers. A black coat, black trousers, a high stiff white collar. A man's black hat. Everyone knew that that's what the Ladies wore as soon as they got away from their families (before, in Ireland, they wore silk dresses, pink and yellow, ball gowns, lovely hats, just like all other fine ladies).

Was the Lady of Llangollen delighted to meet a sister Irishwoman? She was not. The country was crawling with them. 'Here is a halfpenny for you now,' she said to Mary, and turned away from her.

'I am not begging, yer hanner,' said Mary, speaking English. 'I am not a tinker at all but a respectable Irish girl looking for a place, yer hanner. I have read the Sixth Reader and was a monitor in my own school in Kilkenny.'

Mary said that because she knew the Ladies of Llangollen were from Kilkenny. She thought it would arouse some neighbourly sympathy, although we hadn't been neighbours, exactly, with the Butlers of Ormonde. Still, it worked. The lady in the black trousers invited Mary up to her house the next day. I went with her, at her insistence.

It was the strangest house I ever saw. It was perched like a bird's nest set on the side of a hill, shaded by big oak trees. The roof was thatched, high and pointed like a cock of hay, and it had tiny black windows set into it, like shiny black eyes. The doors were also black, and when you came close to them you could see they were carved all over with angels and devils and mermaids and foxes and birds and fishes. The walls of the house were white stone, crossed with thick oak beams like the cross on Calvary. Inside, the house was packed with things: furniture, books, ornaments, musical instruments, brass flowerpots. The walls were so thick with pictures that you could not see any wall at all. The furniture was made of the same kind of wood as the front door: black oak, heavy as lead, knotted and curled all over with engravings. Everything was as cluttered up as it possibly could be.

We sat in the kitchen, of course, and talked to the cook,

in Welsh—we had learned enough now to have a little conversation. The lady in the trousers came and talked to us in English and then we ate scones and jam and drank some coffee.

Naoise looked different from the others. All the other men looked the same to me, with their wild eyes and skin that looked as if a fine sack cloth had been draped across it, their hair sticking up like straw on their heads, or like bushes of gorse. Naoise had tidy hair, and his skin was clean and glossy, like an ordinary Irishman's, except that on the side of his face he had a birthmark. It was a small purple patch, between his cheekbone and his ear, shaped like a potato, a port wine stain.

The mark was small and you would hardly notice it but it is that that made him quiet and good. Even when he got drunk as they all did, from the Welsh beer, stolen from farms, as often as from their own *poitín*, he did not shout or swear or fight with his stick, but looked contented and became sleepy. Maybe he did not drink quite as much as most of them. He didn't beat his wife, not that I could see, but sat with her and talked to her, and sometimes he played with their baby, counting his toes and singing, 'This little piggy went to market', or carrying her on his shoulders as he walked about, showing her things.

When I needed pots I went to him rather than to anyone else, because he was the only man in the band I wasn't afraid of. He didn't mind helping me—I gave him some of the money I made, and bits of anything I got. I gave his wife some blue ribbons I stole from a stall in Betws-y-Coed once, and she took them, although she had not much to say to me. Jealous. Naoise and I were fond of one another, we all three knew it.

One night I caught him alone, behind the encampment, where I was fetching water from the stream. He stood still beside me while I filled the pandy and when I stood up he was right in front of me, his face close to my face, his stomach to my stomach. I put my free hand on his face and caressed it. I couldn't stop my hand going up to his face, he was so close to me, it was dark and silent in the middle of the mountains, so that I felt everything in the world had stopped moving. We kissed.

After that he didn't speak to me for a few weeks and made a show of being fond of his wife, putting his arm around her when I was near them. I let on I didn't care. His wife was pregnant again, yellow-skinned and dirty, with her clothes hanging off her, and smelly and old-looking. She was the way the tinker women are as soon as they are married any length of time at all. Scrap.

Poor thing, poor thing, poor scrap. He had kissed me for three minutes, hard, and his heat and his man's smells had gone right into me and stayed there.

We were scullery maids. They had a scullery maid already, a little Welsh girl called Gwynn, and they did not really need us but took us out of pity for Mary, who begged. Mary is a good beggar. We were to get our keep but no wages at all. Our bedroom was in a hayshed in the garden.

'It's better than that tinker camp,' Mary said, stretching in the straw.

Old dry dust tickled my nose and the straw scratched my skin. 'Oh yes indeed,' I said.

All day long we worked in the kitchen. Mary washed up, standing over the sink, scrubbing pots and dishes, glasses, cups and plates. I got up at six in the morning to light the fire and make the early morning tea for the cook and for the ladies. I scrubbed the front steps and the flagged floor of the kitchen. I brought the rubbish to the dump around the back and I emptied chamber pots from the bedrooms and I hung washing out to dry and brought it in. I gathered vegetables from the garden.

Most of the things I did were hard and unpleasant, the things none of the others wanted to do. But after a while I learned how to cook some things. I learned how to brew beer. I learned to spin flax and wool, and at night in the winter I sat by the fire with a candle burning and hemmed the linen sheets.

The scullery maid did not talk to us much. None of the maids did. The kitchen maids were Welsh and the upper maid was English. The English maid never talked to the Welsh ones, not because she did not know their language, but because she felt so high and mighty. And now the Welsh maids had someone to look down upon themselves. Us. It impressed them not a bit that we could speak some Welsh, as well as English and Irish. But it did impress the Ladies, a little.

'Why did you not go to the workhouse?'

'We tried to get into it but it was full. Hundreds of people were turned away, not just us.'

'You did not think of going to America?'

'We had not the price of the ticket. Maybe . . . ?'

But we would not get the price of the ticket from here either, since we never got a penny.

'Did your family die?'

'They all died.'

'Of the fever?'

'The fever, yes.'

'It is the fever that kills people, not the hunger, isn't it?'

'Yes, ma'am.'

We were hungry and that is why the fever got us. It would not have got us if we had had enough to eat. When we cut through the lumpy potatoes in July, through their browny-purple, warty skins, and saw them black and sticky inside, soft and sweet, we saw the fever. Their sweet sickening smell was the smell of the fever. The hunger and the fever were the same thing, although people like to think they were different.

Mary had let on we had had a good farm.

'The hunger was not bad in our village,' I said to the lady. 'Everyone had enough. There were a lot of fish in the river, and we had bread and milk, butter. We had corn. The people worked hard and had enough to eat. It was not like other places, in our village. It was the fever that killed people, not the hunger.'

She nodded, her blue eyes sparkling, her little glasses sparkling. 'Yes, yes, the fever is the tragedy. We sent what we could.'

The girls in the kitchen thought this was a joke. They thought the Ladies were a joke. You could tell this from the way they called them the Ladies of Llangollen when it was not necessary to do so.

'Ellen, go and empty the Ladies of Llangollen's pots,' the cook would say.

'The Ladies of Llangollen like their beef rare,' she laughed. 'Oh yes, they do. Rarer than any man, rare as rarebit.'

Mary got cross when this sort of thing went on. She got so cross that she cried, because she was so grateful to them for rescuing her from the tinkers. 'We could be dead,' she said. 'They have saved our lives.'

'Yes,' I said.

'Look at the food we get.'

'Yes.'

'And the dry place we have to live.'

'Yes.'

Mary thought she would be rewarded for her hard work by being promoted and getting paid. She thought she would become a lady's maid here in the cottage, and then become a lady's maid somewhere else, and live in a big house, with her own bedroom and her own sitting room. That was her dream. The cups and the plates gleamed, she polished them so much. They were like lakes in the summer sunshine, each white china plate, or like valleys full of hard snow. Every saucer shone on its shelf, shiny as a new dream.

The scullery maid told us the Ladies were not from Ireland at all. They were not the real Ladies of Llangollen.

'Who are they, then?' we asked.

'They are Englishwomen, queer Englishwomen, who have bought their house and wear their clothes. And carry on in the same way. The Irish ladies died long ago.'

We did not believe him. We thought they were saying it to annoy us, because we were Irish like the Ladies.

'And we are ladies, too,' Mary said. She said it when we were alone.

'Ladies, but not like them.'

'Why not?' she said, pretending not to know.

I blushed, inside anyway. The thought of what the Ladies did confused me completely. They had one bed in their dark, lovely, oaky room, where there was plenty of room for two.

'They are kind. They love one another. What's wrong with that?' Mary said.

At the back of the house was an orchard, with apples, pears, greengages and plums, and there were many fruit bushes and vegetables. I had never been near so much food, even in the convent. Every day we had chops or boiled mutton, bread and cheese, apples, plums, sweet cake, beer.

One day soon after we arrived the cook made summer pudding. I watched her doing it, because I had brought in the berries from the garden and because I wanted to see how she made something with a name like that. She put slices of bread into a bowl, then filled the bowl with blackcurrants, redcurrants, blackberries. Then she put more bread across the top of the bowl and weighed it down with a pound weight from the scales. She carried it to the coldest place in the house, the dairy, and left it there to cool, beside a basin of silent cream.

The next day she carried in the pudding to the big wooden table in the kitchen. When it was turned out on a plate it looked funny, white with red-purple blotches. She cut into the skin with a knife. Inside, it was black and purple, soft, sticky, sweet. She gave us each a slice and poured yellow cream over it from the blue jug.

It tasted like the sun on the white wall in the garden. It tasted like the smell of white cotton that has dried on the line. It tasted like Naoise. Not like his mouth, which was soft and salty, like all men's mouths, but like his name and like his face.

I closed my eyes and said to myself, 'Please, Naoise. Please.' I wished I had a salt herring to eat, so that I could dream of him. But there were no salt herrings in the house. I dreamt of him anyhow.

One of my jobs was to help the washerwoman who came on Mondays to boil the clothes. I helped her wring, in the hot steamy washroom, and I hung the clothes out for her. When they were dry I carried them into the kitchen and put them on the table and then someone from upstairs came and took them away.

I liked to be out in the yard where long lines were strung between trees, and I liked the feel of the clean cotton against my face. All the lovely white clothes, the nightgowns and frilly blouses, the aprons, the sheets and pillowslips, smelled of the wind, and of something else, grass maybe, or leaves. I let my nose into the heaps of white cloth, and let the sheets flap around me like clouds.

I was there in April. We had spent many months in Llangollen, autumn and winter, dark days in the hot kitchen. Mary was still washing up. Her hands were big and red, and the skin on her arms permanently puckered. I was still in the scullery, doing everything.

The garden was full of daffodils. They had thousands, all along the stone wall, under every tree. The sun danced. Soon it would be Easter. My arms were full of white clothes and I had a white apron on and a white cap.

Someone was standing by the wall, beside the green door leading onto the lane outside. A man, taller than a Welshman. He had a black soft hat, a black coat with tails, and a thick stick.

He was standing very still and quietly, looking at me. I knew he had been there for a while, because I had heard nothing at all except the wind rustling in the clothes on the line.

I put my heap of clothes on the damp grass and went over to him.

'I thought you were a goose,' he said, opening the gate.

I went out with him onto the road.

A man with gray curly hair and a tweed jacket, a gentleman, passed close to our tent.

'That is Father Toban,' Naoise said. This was the fourth day in Caer Gybi.

'How do you know?'

'I know by the cut of him. He wears that sort of coat. I will speak to him and see.'

Naoise spoke to him in Irish and he answered in Irish. He said: 'I am not Father Toban.'

'You are,' Naoise said. 'I know you are Father Toban. You will give us a blessing now before we sail for Ireland, since we do not know what is in store for us.'

'If I said I was not a priest but a Protestant and an Englishman, would you believe me?'

'I would not, Father.'

'If I said I could not bless you, would you hit me?'

'I might, Father.'

'If I said I would not give you my blessing, would you kill me with your big shillelagh?'

'I would, Father.'

'Kneel down there the three of you.'

I would not kneel for him. The little girl could not kneel, but Naoise held her in front of him so the blessing would land on her. I watched him, bowing his head and closing his eyes, to the man he believed was the priest.

My father said to me and Mary, the only ones left, after he, and everyone else in our parish, had lost their work on the relief: 'Kill me and eat me. I will die soon enough anyway.'

It was the beginning of July, hungry July, the beginning of summer. We had dug the first potatoes early. He knew it would be hungry July, hungry August, hungry winter. Again. Half the people in the village were dead. The landlord had sent others to Canada on a ship from Cork but we had heard terrible things about that journey, and about Canada.

'Get a passage to America,' he said, 'as soon as you can.'

I said yes. I knew I would not go to America, because I would never get the money for the fare together. I knew if I had half a crown I would get to Wales and the poorhouse there would feed me.

'*In nomine Patris et Filii et Spiritus Sancti. Vade in pace. Amen,*' the man in the tweed coat said.

We sailed that afternoon for home.

The Woman With the Fish

A NEW WOMAN HAD come to work in the English department, replacing Maggie, who was on maternity leave. Everybody was talking about her. There had been no new staff for ages and most people on it, apart from Maggie and the secretaries, were men. The new woman was small and fair-haired, and so far had worn the same thing every day: a blue jumper and blue jeans. This was not so interesting. What was interesting was that she also wore, when she came into the department in the morning and when she left at six o'clock, a large blue beret, made of thick stodgy felt and resembling a chanterelle in shape. In addition, she owned a pet fish. The fish lived in a glass bowl on top of her filing cabinet.

Michael noticed her the first day she came in, as he noticed all women who came to the department for any length of time. He was pleased that she had joined the staff. He told himself that she was probably a nice person, meaning that she was good-looking enough to be a pleasant companion and not too good-looking to be a threat. He made a mental note to befriend her at the earliest opportunity. This would be a kindness to her. He knew she would appreciate and no doubt need the friendship of a man like him, a nice man and a modern man, a man who was a supporter and lover of women, but never a womanizer: a man who, in his unique new way, was God's gift to women. He was one in a million.

But he did not talk to the new woman at all for a whole week. Once, on the Friday, he met her in the lift on the way down. She was going home, laden with her briefcase and the fishbowl, wearing the mushroom hat. He was slipping out to meet a friend for a drink, and planning to come back and finish the lecture he was working on later. When the lift hit ground he picked up her fishbowl, which she had laid on the floor, and handed it to her.

'Better not forget him!' he said, with a smile.

She returned the smile.

After that he did not talk to her for another week.

Michael had been working in the college for two years. He was employed as a tutor, and was working on a Ph.D. on Irish women poets of the nineteenth century. Before, he had been a schoolteacher, of English and Irish, but he had been delighted to give up teaching when the opportunity for different work arose. Lecturing seemed to him to be a more challenging and glamorous occupation. When someone asks you what you do, and the answer is 'I'm a lecturer', or 'A lecturer, actually', the response, Michael thought, was a nod of admiration, a silent What a clever and important fellow you must be; whereas when the answer was 'I'm a teacher', people thought, Oh good, someone who is as harmless and dull as me.

Ever since he had been a little boy, Michael had wanted to be considered a step above the run of the mill. He knew he was several steps above it. He knew, in his heart, that he was at the top, the match of kings and presidents, company directors and brain surgeons. But knowing in his heart was never enough. Others had to see it, too. And they wouldn't, while he was a teacher, especially a teacher of Irish, the language so many Irish people scorn and despise.

But Michael had loved teaching children, and so far his new dream was turning out to be very dull. Half the time he spent correcting other people's lousy English. It was astonishing how bad students were at writing, spelling, punctuation, or logical thinking. The rest of the time he spent trying to communicate the excitement and importance of literature to people who were less sensitive to the beauty of books than a cat is. Half the class never bothered to turn up to the lectures at all. Work on the

Ph.D. progressed at a snail's pace. Sometimes Michael despaired of ever finishing it.

He was barely forty. Already he had a teenage daughter and two boys aged ten and twelve. His wife had been in his year in college and the year they graduated she had suggested to him that they get married. He hadn't wanted to—young men didn't, according to custom, at that time. Marriage was an institution that women coerced men into, it was commonly believed. But he had been attracted to her, or in love with her, and he did not want to lose her or do the ignoble deed. Her parents expected him to do the right thing, since he had been going with her for three years. Wasting her time, they would have said. He would have been wasting her time on her, the time she should have been using to get a husband, just as she had used her time in college to get an education and then get a job. Whereas a man's time was somehow different. For him those three years would not have been wasted had he not got married. He would have scored a victory and totted up experience, and moved on to other things.

She—her name was Maureen—got pregnant on the night of their honeymoon. She never had a job herself. At the time it had seemed correct for her to stay at home and be pregnant and paint the flat, and then stay home and mind the baby, and then stay home and be pregnant again and mind the two children and then paint the house and make curtains and plant shrubs in the front. Michael had approved and had felt proud to be a breadwinner and a father.

Then. But times had changed. Now it was not fashionable for women to stay at home. The trendiest, best women had jobs and earned as much money as their husbands. Michael liked to be in the fashion where things like this were concerned. Maureen was now taking a Back to Work course. Too late, Michael sometimes thought. Like many women in their late thirties who have spent their lives in the gentle prison of the home, she was full of cheerful expectation. She did not realise the cruel realities of the business world. A plump, soft, faded prettiness was all the armour she possessed, along with her pathetic optimism. Even her clothes were subtly incorrect— too timid and too ladylike for the sharp-edged modern world, the world Michael inhabited. By now, Maureen and he seemed to belong to different generations. He felt himself to be much younger than her in mind and spirit, even in body, although in chronological terms she was his junior by almost a year.

He believed he loved her and always said so if she asked. But since he had come to work in the college he spent little time with her. He liked to come in at ten in the morning, to work on articles and his Ph.D. Nevertheless, he stayed very late. He found it difficult to finish any piece of work: he was a perfectionist. In consequence he seldom saw his family at all. His wife did not often accompany him to social functions. She had to stay home and babysit. In general he avoided events to which he would have to bring a partner. He claimed to dislike parties but the truth was he did not like to parade his wife in front of the other university wives, who were all size tens with glossy ashen coiffures. He liked his wife's body when he was at home, though. It was lovely to curl up on the sofa with her, or to curl up in bed. At home, look is not as important as feel. And Maureen felt good. Familiar and warm and reliable. He trusted her. She had always loved him and always would. She was more mature than him in character and was good at giving him advice and encouragement, praise and endorsement. Besides, she was an excellent cook.

He considered his marriage happy and liked to congratulate himself privately and not so privately on having made such a success of it. He had never been unfaithful to his wife, even though he was extremely fond of women. She was so understanding that she even understood this. It was a joke between them, in fact. She laughed when one of his friends phoned, when he spent hours chatting to them, or even when they called around on Sundays, the only day he was at home, to go for a walk with him.

When the woman with the fish, whose name was Anna Muller, had been working in the department for two weeks, he went to her room.

'I'm Michael,' he said. 'Remember, we met in the lift? How are you both settling in?'

'We're surviving.' She looked up from her computer.

'Well, I've been here for two years and I haven't cracked it yet. It takes time,' he said. 'By the way, I read that article on Forgotten Women. It was really good.'

'Thank you.'

'We need much more of that sort of thing in this college,' he pointed out. 'It's dreadful, the way women writers are simply ignored as a matter of course.'

Anna had heard this comment a thousand times. She had made it a thousand times herself. But Michael managed to make it sound fresh and original. He mentioned a book that had been published five years previously, and asked her if she'd read it.

'No, actually.'

'I've got a copy somewhere under the bed. I'll root it out and bring it in tomorrow if you like.'

'Thank you,' she said. 'That would be great.'

He gazed into her eyes for a minute as she said this. But before he left he stared for a while at the fish. His eyes and the silver glasses that framed them glinted. The fish, whose name was Anton and who was a big guppy, began to swim frantically around the bowl, as if it could feel itself being observed.

Michael did not come to Anna the next day. He was in. She saw him in the canteen. She kept thinking he would probably come over. But he did not. Nor did he come to see her on the following day. But on the third he came and handed her a paperback volume.

'Oh!'—she was overwhelmed with relief—'thank you so much.'

'No trouble,' he said. He did not mention the delay, but glanced at his watch. 'Found a good place to eat yet?'

'I go to the canteen. Or I bring a sandwich.'

'Me too. But today I've left them on the kitchen table. My wife just rang to tell me. I'm like that. Can't be let out on my own. Would you like to join me for a tomato soup in a pub outside?'

'Oh well,' said Anna. 'Why not?'

She put on her coat and mushroom hat.

'When do you feed him?'

'Anton? Just before I go in the evenings. Six o'clock. That's dinner time for him.'

'And weekends?'

'I bring him home. Or I have done so far. But now that he's settled in I might leave him. He'd be all right for a few days.'

'I could feed him for you if you like, at weekends. I'm always in on Saturdays.'

'That would be great.'

'Where do you keep his stuff?'

'Second drawer of the filing cabinet actually.'

Over lunch he found out that Anna was married too. Her husband was a businessman, working with a multinational computer company. She did not know precisely what he did, but he was away a lot, at least once a fortnight, in London or Boston, where the company headquarters were. She lived in Donnybrook—he made a note of the address. She'd worked in an American college in the past, and her ambition was to bring women's issues into prominence in this one.

He told her he was a feminist and was planning to teach a course on the suppressed female literature of de Valera's Ireland. He told her he believed women were better human beings than men, more intelligent and understanding and thoughtful. In particular, he had noticed how much better his daughter was than his sons. 'My daughter put her arms around me today and said, "Daddy, everything will be all right, don't you worry!" The boys wouldn't do that in a million years.'

'They are younger, aren't they?'

'It won't be different when they are older.'

Anna found herself having to defend the masculine sex in general, which she thought most amusing.

He asked her if she had children and she told him about her miscarriage. He wanted to know everything about it. When it happened? Where? How? How long she had spent in hospital and how many consultations she had had afterwards. Had she needed therapy, or any other form of treatment? He asked if she was trying to have another baby and she said yes. Yes. He told her that he was thinking of being sterilized, because his wife got pregnant every time he looked at her.

'Gosh!' was all Anna could say aloud, and the word she said in her mind was 'Yuck!' The very word 'sterilisation' nauseated her, although in general she approved of all modern developments in the area of contraception, as in all areas of life.

'You haven't . . . been done, yet?' she asked, trying to mask her consternation.

'No,' he replied drily, pulling back from her as he spoke and stiffening his back. 'Where do you go on your holidays?'

Three days later he had lunch with her again and on Friday asked if she'd like to go to the pub for a quick jar when she'd finished work. She would have liked to but she could not. She had to go to a reception with her husband.

'Drat!' he said. It was one of his strongest exclamations. He abhorred vulgar language. 'I'll see you on Monday then. I'll feed him for you tomorrow.'

'Goodnight,' she said softly, and sadly.

'Goodnight, love,' he said, even more softly.

Had she heard him correctly? She wasn't sure. But she hugged herself briefly when she got into the car. All evening a warm glow filled her, and her reception chatter was leavened with a vivacity which it usually lacked. Her husband complimented her on her good humour and appearance.

The next week Michael had lunch with her every day. After lunch he asked her to walk with him in Stephen's Green, and she did. On Friday he began to fret about the weekend. He asked her to telephone him in the department on Saturday, just to say hello, and she promised to do so. But she did not do this. Her husband never left her side, all day. At about four o'clock the phone rang. When she lifted it there was no one there. She knew it must be him and felt remorseful for letting him down. It was such a little thing to ask, one phone call, and she had failed to give it to him.

On the following Monday he kissed her. They were in the Green again, on the path that runs along the east side, from the Shelbourne corner to Earlsfort Terrace—it is the shadiest and quietest of the paths. He had checked beforehand to make sure the coast was clear.

'Do you know what is happening to us now?' he asked in his most serious tone.

'Yes,' said Anna, simply and firmly. She guessed he was about to declare his love.

'It's as if a sack has come down and covered our heads, isn't it?'

'Yes,' said Anna, in a darker voice. Her heart sank. She had no idea why and she did not know what he was talking about. It was a trick of his to use striking, concrete metaphors of that kind, which sometimes seemed brilliant and uniquely accurate and which sometimes seemed utterly meaningless.

The next day her husband went to London on one of his trips. She let Michael know he was away.

'Oh good,' he said cheerfully. 'I can ring you at home.'

'When will you ring?'

'Oh, about ten o'clock or so.' He smacked his lips at the close of the sentence, with a little sucking sound.

Anna supposed that he really would not ring at all, but would take the opportunity to call on her in person. She tidied the house and bought a bottle of white wine to put in the fridge. She also bought some cheese, French bread, and a fruitcake. She had noticed his liking for sweet things.

At half past ten he had not arrived.

She put a Mozart symphony on the CD player, guessing that he would arrive at any moment. She curled up on the sofa with her legs tucked under her and sipped a glass of wine.

At half past eleven she went to bed. She was crying and her stomach felt as if it had been kicked about by a rugby team. Her whole inside felt like that.

At ten to twelve the phone rang.

'Hi!' he said.

'Hello.' She sat up in bed. Her body slipped back to normal. It was as if it had been an object pressed into the wrong container, by accident, for a while. And now it had been taken out and put back on its own box.

'It's lovely to hear your voice,' he said in his caressing tone. 'Isn't the telephone marvellous?'

He did not mention the time, or the delay, but asked her many questions and let her talk on and on. He asked all kinds of silly, enjoyable little things. What was her favourite food? Did she like *Father Ted*? On what side of the house was her bedroom situated, the road or the back?

At lunch the next day he pressed his knee to hers all the time they were eating, and he kissed her in the porch of the pub, quickly but so passionately that they both shook afterwards and could hardly walk back to the college. Anna asked him to phone her at home again that night and he did. They talked for three hours in one of the most absorbing conversations Anna had ever had. This, she felt, was the essence of true communication.

This was the best talking experience she had ever enjoyed in her entire life.

The third night he came to see her.

He wanted to see everything in the house and examined objects closely, picking up books and ornaments and observing them in the light. He did not eat or drink anything, however, nor did he go to bed with Anna. Instead he sat with her on the sofa and kissed her for hours. She hadn't done anything like this since she was eighteen.

'What are we going to do?' she asked, at about three a.m.

'Do?' He patted his lips tenderly.

'About us.'

'What can we do?'

Anna considered it might be useful to go to bed, for one thing, or to find a flat and live together, for another. But she did not voice these thoughts, knowing that it is unwise to push a man in matters of love. She could see how deeply in love he was and knew that, given time, he would realise what they had to do.

He came down with a bad dose of influenza the next day. This Anna learned from the departmental secretary—he'd phoned in sick. She waited for him to telephone her but he didn't. Three days passed. Anna became frantic. She could not concentrate on her work, she could not sleep, she could not talk to anyone. It amazed her that nobody seemed to notice her turmoil, which threatened to swallow her up like a whirlpool. It became so overpowering that she phoned him at home. A woman who sounded young and vulnerable, childish, answered. Anna banged down the receiver, terrified.

The next week Michael did not come to college: term was well over and examinations already marked. On Tuesday he telephoned Anna. He told her he was on holiday in Mayo, and also that he had got a new job for next year, at another institution. It was not as prestigious as the one he was leaving but better paid, and he felt the work itself would be less demanding, leaving him more time for his own projects. He had not been ill at all last week, but negotiating and being interviewed. 'It's just as well, I think. Don't you agree?'

'You mean we won't see each other again?'

'What is the point in making one another miserable?'

Anna knew she could never be more miserable than she had been during the past ten days. But she felt beaten. She could not argue with him on the phone—the departmental secretary was sitting in her room. 'I suppose that's right,' she said. 'Good luck with the job.' There were no exclamation marks in her speech, on the occasion or for a long time afterwards.

Anton the fish died. He had been putting on weight, since Michael tended to overfeed him. Anna came in one morning and found him floating on the surface of the water. She threw him into the wastepaper basket and at lunch time went to the pet shop and bought a goldfish. It flashed like an amber gem in the water.

As he had anticipated, Michael found the new job easier. He taught only five or six hours a week and had plenty of time to read and write. 'The Hidden Ireland: Irish Women Poets of the Celtic Revival' was finally beginning to take shape. Michael worked hard at it. Anna he pushed to the back of his mind. As far as he was concerned, he would never see her again. She had been a nice friend, but no better than a dozen of other such friends he had had over the past several years. They all had to go, in the end. That was the way life was.

But after a month or so he began to think of Anna again. In particular, he remembered her house, which he had seen only once. He pictured her walking through its rooms, which were sparsely furnished and elegant. He saw her hoovering the plain white floors, or arranging white flowers in a vase of eggshell blue. He imagined her going to the fridge and taking out plates of cheese and caviar and wine and other delicacies, and putting them on the plain wooden table for that husband of hers. Muller. His grandfather had been German, she thought. Thought! She did not even know for sure. That was typical of her. She was so clever in some ways and in others so insecure. All her knowledge quivered and shook on its basis of sand. She was seldom sure of anything.

She had not telephoned. This surprised him. Usually when he dropped a woman in this way she plagued him with calls for a while. In such cases he would be friendly but indifferent, making and breaking appointments, feeding that woman a diet of uncertainties and disappointments until, eventually, she would abandon him in despair, sometimes after a very long time. But Anna had not phoned even once. He found himself wondering, quite irrationally, if she were still alive.

Six months passed. Now there was not a day when he did not think of Anna. He did not think of her all the time, of course. His work was very preoccupying. He was constantly talking to people and had made many new friends, including a few women friends. But the image of Anna popped into his mind many times every day. Anna in her blue beret. Anna with her fish. One evening he was drinking a pint of stout with his colleagues. Anna had been on his mind more often than usual that day and he had to talk about her.

'Did you see that piece by Anna Muller in *Hibernian Studies* last month? On the deconstruction of quotidian discourse among females.'

One of his companions, a medievalist, shook his head. The other, who specialized in Swift, said no.

'It was so original in its thinking. She's an excellent scholar, isn't she?'

'I love these salt and vinegar crisps,' said the Swift scholar. He munched loudly and the pungent smell of salt and vinegar and other crisp flavourings flooded the air. 'I've always loved them ever since they came out. Are you old enough to remember when there were no salt and vinegar crisps, just cheese and onion?'

'Not really.' Michael was, but he felt nauseated. He stood up. 'I'm off,' he said in his short voice. 'Got to get some sleep.'

The next morning the very first thing he did was to ring Anna. But she wasn't in. He left a message on her answering machine asking her to contact him at the earliest opportunity. She did not phone.

The following day he went back to his old university, and marched straight up to Anna's office. It was only half past nine when he got there, but she was in.

'Christ!' she exclaimed when she saw him. She wore a black skirt and jacket and looked thinner. Her hair was longer than before. 'What are you doing here?'

'I had to talk to you. Will you talk to me?'

'When?'

'Right now.'

'I'm sorry. I'm in the middle of something.'

'Will you have lunch with me?' His voice was wheedling like a little boy's.

'Yes,' she said, and sighed.

He smiled. They arranged a place and time.

'I missed you terribly,' he said, over his tomato soup. 'I just have to see you.'

'I missed you, too,' she said. 'I've been thinking of you all the time for months.'

'Will you see me again?' His face crumpled and his eyes were wet with tears.

'All right,' she said.

'Tomorrow?'

'All right,' she said.

They met at her house. Muller was in London again.

After kissing him Anna sat on the sofa and started to cry.

Michael stared at her, miserably. He decided to let her cry.

He knew what she was crying about: strength of her love for him, its clandestine nature, the need for lies and deceit to cover up something that seemed so good and beautiful.

'Don't cry,' he said, after a while. 'Don't cry, dear.'

He knew that at some time this love would end. But he did not know when this would happen and he did not think it would happen soon. There was no point in telling Anna this. She would not believe him. She was deeper in love with him than ever. She worshipped him—he could see this, without vanity, as a strange and frightening fact.

He moved towards her and caught sight of himself in the mirror. His hair had been falling out more rapidly than usual over the past week, thanks to the stress. It had receded noticeably, and the gray hairs were becoming very numerous. He looked at Anna, who was ten years his junior. She was slim and light and girlish, but soon she too would show signs of ageing. Her beauty would wither.

He pitied her profoundly. She loved him too much. He did not understand why women did this, women whom he simply wanted to befriend. They fell in love with him, or with some ideal of him to which he could never measure up. They needed him to be kind and gentle, understanding and warm. And when he failed them they continued to love him, like stupid goldfish. Indeed, they loved him even more, fondling his failings as they had fawned over his virtues. And he had never loved any of them. He had never loved even his own wife.

And now when his hair was receding and he was fat and forty he was in love for the first time. It seemed to him that he and Anna were soul mates. They were a perfect match. Their minds were one mind and their bodies fitted together like two sides of one fruit.

'Stop crying,' he said. 'Stop crying and let's talk. Let's talk about what we are going to do.'

'What are we going to do?'

'What can we do? There's Maureen and Muller and Nathan and Emily and Patrick.'

'And there's us. This is so good. It is so important.'

They sat on the sofa and talked about what they would like to do and what they could do and what they could not do.

It seemed to Anna that they were just on the brink of making a decision. And that decision would change their lives utterly and make them perfectly and wondrously happy. She could catch a glimpse of the new life just around the corner from the decision, a life of bliss, where physical and spiritual, temporal and eternal, blended into one simple being. The life there would be like a glass of clear cool water, unruffled, lovely.

And what Michael saw was that it would end. It would all have to end, and Anna would have to take the consequences. But the end was too far away to see and he was too deeply in love, at the moment, to look for it. All he knew was that the most complicated part was just beginning.

The Pale Gold of Alaska

SOON AFTER HER EIGHTEENTH birthday, Sophie left Donegal and went to America with her sister Sheila. They embarked at the port of Liverpool, and sailed as steerage passengers on a White Star liner called *Maid of Erin* to New York. The idea was that they would join their older sister, Winnie, who had provided the money for their fares, in Philadelphia as soon as they arrived. They were planning to get jobs as housemaids. Winnie, who was twelve years older than Sophie and eight years older than Sheila, had friends in Germantown where she had been working for six years. She would be able to fix them up in good situations without difficulty.

The plan was scuppered before the *Maid of Erin* was a hundred miles west of the Irish coast. On their second night at sea a storm blew up, whipping the sea into raging mountains and fathomless valleys: dark, terrifying—above all nauseating. Sheila, whose body was thick as a ploughman's, succumbed to seasickness, while delicate Sophie by some miracle remained unscathed. The ship was full of moaning, tortured people; it was sour with the smell of vomit, and jagged with the howls of bewildered children. Although the storm abated after a few hours, and for the rest of the voyage the ship glided over a buttermilk ocean between silvery blue skies, the illness lasted nearly as long in Sheila's case. She was not an easy patient, being both demanding and self-pitying. As often as Sophie could she abandoned her sister and sought the comfort of the lower deck to which steerage passengers had access at certain, limited times.

There, on her third day at sea, she met a weaver called Ned Burns, one of the few passengers besides herself who had

75

escaped sickness. Lighting his pipe in the shelter of his palm, he had spotted her over the ridge of his broad weaver's hand as she strolled slowly along the narrow gangway; he had smiled and asked her for the time of day. (A quarter past three—they were allowed to walk on the deck between three and four o'clock every afternoon.) By the time Sheila had got her sea legs Ned had shown Sophie how to elude the stewards and walk on deck whenever she felt like it. And by then it was too late to nip the relationship in the bud. Before the *Maid of Erin* had reached its destination, Ned had asked Sophie to marry him.

He was four years older than her, a tall, fair-skinned, curly-haired man, with a boyish face, and a thin mouth which in his case succeeded in looking vulnerable rather than mean. His manner was quiet, and this, coupled with the lips and his surprised-looking eyes, conveyed the impression that he was lacking in self-confidence, or weak. But he was neither of these things, as Sophie discovered very soon after meeting him. His eyes did not evade, but stared steadily into hers, as if pleading with her—for what she was unsure, but she believed she could give it to him, whatever it might be. Also, although he was not talkative in company, when alone with Sophie he had plenty to say, unlike any man or boy she had ever known before. What he said was often very amusing, usually in an acerbic way, he was always willing to be unkind or even cruel if that served his wit. He came from a village in south County Derry.

'Sure they're all like that in Derry,' Sheila had said, when Sophie had offered Ned's sense of humour as an excuse for her engagement to him. Why she had to offer excuses she did not know. But his good looks, his apparently trustworthy personality, would not seem sufficient motivation to Sheila. Probably nothing would.

'Well,' Sophie said as firmly as she could, 'I've said yes.'

'You'd never have got away with this sort of carry-on at home.' Sheila began to cry. Tears of frustration or annoyance, or jealousy or anger, rolled down her face, which was a round potato face, pocked with bumps and shadowy mistakes, not at all like Sophie's. Sophie's face reminded people of a glass of new milk, or a spray of thyme, or other things of that kind, redolent of nature at its most beguiling and benign. 'It's ridiculous, getting married at your age.'

It seemed no more ridiculous to Sophie than going to work as a maid in the house of a complete stranger in a foreign country. She said this, somewhat tactlessly, shouting it over the noise of the engines, which accompanied them all the time on board, a constant roar like that of an infuriated bull. They were watching the New York skyline as they conducted this final, decisive conversation. Night had fallen and some of the buildings of the city were lit, creating spots and pools of light, scattered haphazardly on an inky background like saffron-coloured flowers, flaming orange lilies in the sky.

Sheila paused before replying, to stare at the skyline and to allow her mind to flirt with the exoticism of her present situation.

Soon she would be in America.

'America'. It was a word she had carried in her head for a long time. A word, a dream and a hope, shining in her eyes, encouraging her heart.

But it was not something her mind could encompass, now that the moment of landing was drawing so close. America. The word becoming land and lights and buildings in front of her eyes. Too abruptly it had appeared, in the end, after all the voyaging and imagining. She felt as if she had awoken suddenly from a vivid dream. She tried, briefly, to cling on to it before it vanished completely, before reality rushed in and blotted out the picture she had carried in her head for most of her life. But she was not the sort to linger unnecessarily in the confusing borderlands of consciousness.

Turning her back on the land of the free she gave herself

to the sisterly spat. 'At least you'd get paid for it by a complete stranger,' she snapped. The dream was gone already. Petty details rushed into her head to replace what had borne her across the Atlantic on waves of nausea. Now all she could imagine was the lonely time ahead, the interviews with strange foreign rich women, women who might well be impatient and unkind; the days full of new, bewildering work. The shine was dulled, the hope inverted, all the sport drained out of the future by this new turn of events. Loneliness loomed, instead of promise. Everything, even her own body, seemed terrifying. The realisation of her homeliness hit her like a punch in the belly; no man would ever make an impulsive proposal to her. Probably no man would propose to her at all, even after long and careful consideration. No widower or fat old bachelor, no country bumpkin that better women would reject. She would live out her days in the kitchen of a stranger's house, slaving until she died, alone in this new hostile continent.

They were met in Philadelphia by their sister Winnie, who had jobs lined up and waiting for the two of them, for Sheila and Sophie. She was not pleased when she found out that Sophie's plans had changed. Now Sophie was not interested in working as a maid. She was going to be a married woman; she was going to live in a rented room with Ned.

'And how will you pay back your passage, may I ask?' Winnie twisted her long mouth and raised her thick black eyebrows.

'Never you fear, you'll get your money back,' Ned retorted. 'Sophie will be making more dollars than the pair of yez.'

How? wondered Sophie.

She would be working in a textile mill, that was how. It was not the future she had foreseen for herself, when she had agreed to marry Ned. But it would be her destiny, for a while, all the same.

Sophie and Ned got married almost immediately in St. Patrick's Chapel. Sheila and Winnie as well as several neighbours from their home in Donegal came to the wedding, and afterwards to a saloon owned by somebody from home. Lynch's was the name of the establishment. Ned drank quite a lot, the day of his wedding, but Sophie, Winnie and Sheila did not drink a thing. There was nothing available in Lynch's Saloon that wasn't alcoholic. They had never touched a drop of any kind of alcoholic drink in Ireland, and they were not about to start now.

Afterwards Ned and Sophie went to live in a room they would share with two cousins of Ned at the back of a row house in Moyamensing. The men worked in the cloth mills at Southwark where Ned and Sophie had been taken on. Ned drove a loom and she worked in the finishing room, where a machine rolled the interminable lengths of cloth on to giant spools, ready to go out to the shops. Her job was to check the cloth for broken threads, stains, bits of fluff, to remove what could be removed, and to stop the machine if the cloth needed to be cut. She had to keep eyes on her the cloth as it rolled through on the machine, never stopping, all the time. White, black, blue, gray, were the colours that came through, mainly. Occasionally red, green, yellow—the cloth was dyed every colour under the sun, with strong aniline dyes, brilliant colours she had never seen before. (Where she came from, cloth was blackish-brown, cream, or a rust colour obtained from lichens that grew on the rocks.) Sophie liked the colours. She continued to like them all the time she worked in the factory, even when her back was breaking and her eyes were itchy and red from looking at glaring colours for twelve hours at a stretch.

Ned called her 'Síoda na mBó', which means something like 'silken cow', when they were in the alcove that contained their bed, and which was concealed from the main part of the room by an old cream-coloured woollen blanket with faded blue stripes at one end, the end that touched the floor. They had to speak in soft voices there, so the cousins in their bed out in the room would not hear. 'Silky cow, silky little frisky heifer,' he whispered in her ear as they snuggled under the blankets in their corner—it was April, still quite cold, especially inside the damp old house. He pulled her blouse off and buried his face in her breasts. 'Silk blouse, silk skin, silk breast,' he whispered. She stroked his curls, which were not silky at all, but wiry and dry, completely different from her own smooth hair. She half listened to him, pleased at his compliments, if that is what they were. At the same time she got used to them. Soon it was as if they hardly applied to her at all, as if they were just words he said, the way women in Donegal say prayers. The same words over and over again, uttered in a sleepy singsong voice, uttered so often that the speakers do not even know what they are saying.

Maybe that was how Ned had learned to repeat himself, to chant an incantation over and over again? He liked to pray. Before he got into bed he knelt on the floor and buried his head in his hands, chanted five decades of the Rosary. Sophie had to join in although she had always found the Rosary dull and slightly repulsive. She did not like the sight of broad bottoms sticking out in the air above the bowed heads of their owners, the embarrassingly intimate smell of praying people, the monotonous sad sleepiness of their voices as they repeated the pious, superior words over and over and over and over again. Hail Mary full of grace. Fifty times a night. Holy Mary Mother of God. Pray for us sinners. Until she was half-dead from boredom.

Followed, maybe, by silken blouse, silken skin. Silken sinner. Not fifty times. Just as often as he felt like it.

Sophie, accustomed anyway to the admiration of men, took his laudatory litanies as her due. Kisses and words of admiration were what she mainly got from Ned, in bed, and that was not so different from what she had always received from other men, in the street and at dances, outside the chapel on Sunday—

admiration, expressed or tacit, but reliable and regular as the Rosary.

Soon, however, she began to learn that there were limits to Ned's admiration.

Ned wanted her to be neat, well-turned-out, pretty. Also he wanted her to work well and be popular at the mill. But it was important that none of this be taken too far. She should be a credit to him, but only up to a point. At first Sophie did not understand what was expected of her. She did not know that she could easily, without knowing it, step out of the field of Ned's admiration and into another area where he would despise her.

For a few months after they were married, he encouraged her, in every way, to do what she was good at: being attractive and sociable, working well. She made friends in the neighbourhood; she worked as conscientiously as she could; and, with her own money, she bought a new outfit for the summer in one of the big stores in town.

She wore this outfit, a tight black skirt, a white high-necked blouse, a small black and red hat, to Mass the first Sunday after buying it. As usual, it was clear to Sophie and to Ned that many people looked at her with pleasure. Kathleen Gallagher, a middle-aged woman who lived around the corner from them, said, 'That girl is the belle of Philadelphia', and her husband, Dan, nodded and said, 'Some have all the luck.' Ned stared at Sophie with his wide blue eyes, and said nothing whatsoever. On Sunday evenings they usually went for a walk together with her sisters, but that evening he said he was going to Lynch's.

'Can I come with you?' she asked.

'You wouldn't want to spoil your expensive rig-out,' he said. It was said in a voice she had not heard before, a dry, jealous voice, full of censure. He ate some bread and continued, in a gentler tone, 'Women don't come to Lynch's, anyway. You didn't like it at our wedding.' So now he was joking again. That was something he could do: move from complaining to joking in a few sentences. It was as if he had to complain, express his annoyance or anger or whatever it was that Sophie's success aroused in him, but that he regretted it almost before the words were out of his mouth.

After that, he took to going to the saloon every Sunday night. Sophie continued the custom of meeting Winnie and Sheila, on her own instead of with Ned. In a way it was easier like that and the sisters, who did not seem to like Ned much, certainly preferred it.

'Nothing stirring?' Winnie asked in September, when Sophie had been married for six months. Sophie was still slender and girlish. She had taken to doing her hair in a new style, pinning it up and letting some fair, wispy curls fall down over her forehead and around her small ears, neat as oyster shells. She tossed her head, dislodging a few more wisps, and did not answer the question.

'You'll have to get out of that factory soon,' Sheila said, with some satisfaction. She had become a parlour maid for an old couple in Germantown, and her life was considerably easier and more luxurious than Sophie's. 'You should get a baby for yourself and then Ned would have to find you a proper place to live.'

Two young men whistled after the sisters, saving Sophie the trouble of thinking of a response. Sheila raised her eyebrows disapprovingly at Winnie. Two old maids already, thought Sophie. That is what they were. Buxom, with their dense hair pinned to the backs of their heads in hard black balls, her sisters looked like women whose fate was sealed. Sealed by themselves: they lived in a city that was full of men, men from all over Ireland and Germany and Poland and Italy and other countries, looking desperately for women. But Sheila and Winnie never met any of them, any man at all, it seemed, except for old fellows who did the gardening or worked in the kitchen in their prim-and-proper houses. Men who were as old-maidish as themselves. They had shut themselves away from the world of men, the world Sophie inhabited. And by now they were afraid of them. If a young man whistled, they assumed the next thing was that he would do something unspeakable to them: the thing Sophie did several nights a week with Ned, the thing they could not— it seemed to her—even imagine. They equated that with being strangled or stabbed to death. Pleasure for Sheila and Winnie, Sophie thought, was having a cream waffle and a strong cup of tea in some rich woman's kitchen, their substantial bottoms positioned to catch the heat of the fire. Beyond that their desires did not seem to stretch. Could this be true?

The young men had been whistling at Sophie, of course, it was assumed by all. Sophie was wearing her Sunday rig-out, her belle-of-Philadelphia hat on top of her distracting hairstyle. She walked daintily, proud of herself, happy to flaunt her fine clothes when Ned was not around to put a damper on her tendency to show off.

Not that it was a question of clothes, or demeanour. Men whistled at her all the time, even when she was wearing her old patched factory dress. If Ned was not with her, they whistled. Maybe they whistled at all young women? Maybe it was the custom of the town?

'She's time enough.' Sheila responded on Sophie's behalf. 'Sure she's only a child herself.'

'People will be talking all the same,' Winnie said.

This was the sort of thing Sophie had to put up with. She was so used to listening to her sisters complaining about her that she hardly even heard it. She knew why she was not expecting, but was pleased with the situation. Time enough for all that. Walking along the dry, summer street under the shade trees, dressed in a snow-white blouse, seeing the crowds of people, was all she wanted. She did not want a baby to expand her waistline and limit her freedom. How could she have a baby in that room, anyhow, with nothing but a curtain dividing her bed from the two cousins?

The cousins were both in love with her. Sophie had known this might happen from the minute she heard about the arrangement from Ned, and she knew it would happen the minute she saw the cousins: they were Ned's age, but genuinely shy and awkward, unlike him. One of them had a girlfriend, a little girl with a sharp, pointed face who had come from Tipperary and who was not very good-humoured. She seemed to spend half her time not talking to the cousin, punishing him for various misdemeanours. He accepted this as normal. Chief among his many flaws was that he was in no hurry to get married. Sophie knew that in the end he would have to capitulate. He would marry this girl—her name was Agnes—whom he did not love, who was not beautiful, and who did not seem to like him very much. He would have to, if he did not find a replacement for her. At least he would know what his wife was like, before the wedding.

In the meantime he permitted himself the marginal amusement of being in love with Sophie. The mixed pleasure of this experience was enhanced, and even more confused, by the fact that his brother was also in love with her, and of course by the secret, silent nature of the emotion. It was never mentioned, by anyone. But anyone could sense it in the room, in the looks that the brothers gave to Sophie, lingering tender looks at her back, shy yearning looks at her face, amused looks or desperate looks at one another. It was obvious to Sophie, and she thought it must be so to everybody. She did not take it too seriously. Men and boys had been in love with her before, and had said nothing about it. As long as you said nothing you didn't need to do anything. It never seemed to do them much harm. They did not die of unrequited love, not at all. They got over it, they went away or they became involved with some other woman.

In a way she thought they might enjoy it, this secret, silent passion. It gave them something to think about when they were working—digging fields or footing turf, or standing all day at the huge loom, pushing the heavy shuttle to and fro, to and fro.

The rooming arrangement gave rise to plenty of comment in the factory and in the saloon, some of it ribald. People were careful not to pass remarks in Ned's hearing. He had already got a reputation for being belligerent.

But inevitably he heard something. A reference to Sophie's good looks, followed by a reference to Sophie's band of admirers, followed by a reference to Sophie's husbands. 'Sure she's got three husbands to look after her' was the comment. 'That should do her, with her blondie curls and her black hat' was what was said. It was considerably less offensive than remarks that had been going the rounds for months behind Ned's back.

But it turned out that Ned had not had the slightest suspicion of the emotion that filled the high, dark room. He had not even suspected that the arrangement would look odd, or scandalous, to neighbours. So innocent, or so wilfully blind, was he.

Sophie was to blame for the unfortunate state of affairs, in his opinion. He stopped talking to her. The same punishment that the girl from Tipperary gave to his cousin.

This went on for a week. It went into a second week. It seemed he would never open his mouth again. She could see he had it in him, was the sort of man who could close up inside his shell and never emerge again. Reluctantly, and with some trepidation, she asked him what was going on.

He found it hard to speak. But he did.

He told her she gave herself airs. 'What are you but a factory girl?' he said. 'You're making a fool of yourself, dressing up in fine rags and feathers.' He looked her up and down. 'It's not as if you're all that good-looking.' Then he laughed. So that last bit was a joke, not a criticism. He was back to being his normal fault-finding, joking self.

Not quite.

He led her to the alcove and did not bother drawing the curtain, even though it was broad daylight and the cousins might walk in at any moment. He pulled off all her clothes, the first time he had ever done this. She stood, naked, in the sunlight which fell in a narrow dusty bar across the wooden floor. Then he raised his hand and hit her.

She had never understood the expression 'he saw stars' before. Now she saw them, a galaxy flashing brilliantly in her head. She sat down on the bed, her face numb. He hit her again. Her nose bled a little. She did not scream or say anything. But she began to punch him—on the face, on the chest. Her hands pummelled him, hard, but it was like hitting a stone.

'Stop,' he cried. 'Stop.'

She didn't stop. Her hands flailed out, raining blows on him. He didn't reciprocate them and soon he started to laugh.

Sophie continued to hit him. But after a while she started to laugh too, although she did not know what she was laughing at. They both became infected with giggles, and rolled on the bed, unable to stop laughing.

Then he made love to her, and it was the first time the lovemaking worked, for Sophie. But afterwards he pulled away.

'I'm sorry,' he said, his voice so dry she could hardly hear.

She pulled a blanket around herself. He found her nightgown and threw it to her, drew on his own clothes and dropped to his knees at the side of the bed.

Soon after this, before winter set in, Ned suggested they move. Not to a new room, but to a new place. The west. Montana. There was copper mining going on there, silver and gold mining as well, and more money to be made than in the factories of the east. Also, more fresh air and more space for living. He and Sophie would have a house of their own immediately, instead of having to save in the building society and wait for years, as

would happen in Philadelphia. Their pale skins would get pink
and healthy; their lungs would breathe freely.

Sophie was unsure. Now that she knew Ned better, going
off with him alone, into the wilderness as it were, seemed
more dangerous than it had when she had first met him. She
knew he would not harm her seriously—the beating had not
been repeated, yet, and anyway it was not a beating in the
usual sense, the sense in which that word was used in Ireland,
and Philadelphia. She heard women shouting and screaming
sometimes, on Sunday nights, she saw black eyes and bruises,
sad shamed faces, which were not to be commented upon. She
did not think that Ned would do that to her again—he was not
a drunkard, he was not the sort of man who loses his temper
and lets fly. Maybe she could handle him, his attitude which
was after all a simple enough matter, of jealousy. She knew she
must not go too far. She must not expect too much praise, for
anything, from anyone, and above all she must not reveal to
him if she got it. That was all that was required, really, to keep
him happy. He loved her because she was beautiful, and clever,
and sensible, and neat. But she must never carry any of these
desirable attributes to what he considered to be excess. That
was all. It should be easy enough. She would have to do that
anyway, even if she stayed in Philadelphia. She would have to
do that as long as she stayed with Ned.

There was the matter of leaving her sisters, and her friends.
But she had made friends easily in the factory. There was
no reason to suppose that she would not make new ones in
Montana. Leaving her job would not be a sacrifice. It was
enjoyable to work with other people—ready-made friends, in
their scores—but the hours were too long. Having Sunday free
no longer seemed like enough when you worked for eleven
hours every other day. In Montana, she would not have to have
a job. Ned would make enough money for the two of them, or
more of them if necessary. She would be a real wife, and mother

she hoped, at home in her own house, doing whatever she liked, while he was off in the mines digging for silver, for money, for the two of them.

They travelled to Butte by train, a journey of three days. Sophie sat alone on a wooden seat in a third-class carriage, as a concession to her femininity. Ned went in the luggage van, in the coal van, in the cattle truck, as necessity obliged, thus saving the price of one fare. It was the way the Irish did things. Any man would have considered it madness to waste money on a railway ticket. Tickets for transatlantic ships had to be bought. Stowing away on board ship was too risky. But once you landed in America you never paid for travel again, if you could possibly help it. 'The land of the free,' Ned said, climbing on to the roof of the guard's van.

Missoula, where they ended up, was a town of dirt streets and low wooden buildings. A boardwalk, constructed from two planks laid side by side, provided a footpath. High pine trees grew everywhere, on lots between the houses, on the side of the street. There were general stores, hardware stores, draperies. Several saloons, a hotel. Also three churches, Catholic, Presbyterian and Anglican, the Catholic being the biggest.

The mines were to the north of the town, and Sophie and Ned went there, to a smaller village higher in the Rockies, called Greenough. Ned staked out about a half-acre of land just outside the village, close to a settlement of people who had converged on this place from half the countries in Europe. He did not sign for the land—it wasn't necessary to do that, according to some Irishmen who lived there. First come first served. Did it belong to nobody? Sophie asked, surprised. They laughed and pointed to the high, rugged silver peaks behind them. *Na Fir Dearga.* The red men. They've moved up the mountains. It belongs to us now.

Ned's land was on the edge of a forest, mainly fir and pine. Sophie walked into it between the tall, bare trunks of the fir trees. The sun came slanting through them in thin gold lines and the trunks stretched like telegraph poles towards the sky. The passages between them were like the aisle of the big church in Philadelphia.

Not for long. Ned, with help from two of the other Irishmen, chopped down dozens of the tall trees, a lot more than he needed. With some of the logs thus gained he built a cabin, and the rest they stockpiled for firewood. The cabin consisted of two big rooms plus a porch (this was Ned's personal addition, his poetic touch). He furnished the rooms with a bed, a table, two chairs. The fire was an open fire, on a stone hearth at one side of the kitchen. Later they would get a stove, and other luxuries.

Ned started work in the silver mines as soon as he had finished the cabin; he apprenticed himself to an experienced miner, who would pay him well while teaching him the miner's trade. Ned worked deep in the earth, all day and sometimes long into the night. Sophie was left alone in the cabin for very long periods. She had never in her life spent so much time on her own. In fact she had never spent any time alone—her parents' house in Ireland was always full of people. Then all there had been was the ship, and the room in Philadelphia.

She got to know some of the other women in the hamlet. There were very few of them—most of the men who came to the mines were single. During the day, the village was inhabited only by these few women and their children. There was no school for the children so their noise was to be heard all day as they played around the cabins, or ran in and out of the forest.

There was work to be done. Getting food, preparing it. They ate meat mostly: venison and wild mutton. There were elk, goats, and sheep in the mountains—also bears and mountain lions. Ned learned how to set traps; he hunted when he had free time, bagging easily what they needed. She had to skin animals, peeling the pelts from their cold bodies with a sharp knife. Then they had to be butchered, hacked into pieces, dried or cooked over the fire. Flour they could buy in Greenough, and transport on a cart to the cabin. She had a big sack in the corner of the room, and every day she baked loaves of bread. In the summer, berries grew richly on the floor of the forest. She gathered perfumed raspberries, bloody blueberries, honeycoloured huckleberries, bitter cranberries. She made three varieties of jam, spending hours tending the pots of viciously bubbling, stickily smelling, viscous messes, watching the chemical colour change: she poured berries of pink or yellow or green or blue from her bowl into the pot. But by the time they were boiled and set they were all a dark, carmine red.

When they had been a few months in the area they bought a cow. Then there was milking to do all summer, morning and evening, the hot flank of the beast on her cheek, the teats tough and testing between her fingers, the heavy odour of the cow dung, cow body, churning through her body night and morning, morning and night. Churning once a week in a barrel made by Ned. Come butter come butter come butter come, the rhythmical turning of the handle like a fast violent reel, her back breaking with the effort of it, her complexion pink as a hot summer rose, her wrist thickening. Butter in golden pats lined up on the table. A neighbour, a Swedish woman, taught her how to sour the milk and make a thick, creamy liquid which tasted sweet and sour at once, which enhanced the flavour of huckleberries, even of bread. She showed her how to make cheese.

Sophie loved the cabin. It was different from the house in Donegal, which she had found stuffy and crowded, and from the room in the city. The wooden walls emitted a pungent, resinous smell. The fire burned wood all the time, adding to the spicy atmosphere. On the walls, she hung animal skins: a thick brown bear skin which they had got for a few dollars in Greenough, beaver skins, a rough buffalo skin. On the floor were deer skins, red and silver, snowy white. She loved the various textures of the furs in the fine silky deer skins, the thick shag of the bear like scutch grass, the dense velvet of the beaver. The shapes of the skins too she liked; they were like flat maps of animals. Alone in the cabin she felt the company of the creatures who had once inhabited the skins.

In September, before winter came, Ned bought her a coat made of sealskin which someone who had come down the river from Canada sold him for a few dollars. The sealskin was thick but flat, silvery gray and silvery white, shimmering like ice or seawater, gleaming like the animal from which it had come. When she wrapped herself in it she felt she was a different person. She did not feel human at all, but part of the huge animal world which surrounded her now on all sides, which was with her inside and outside her cabin. She felt like the animals she did not see but heard in the depth of the night, barking or screaming in the forest and the mountain.

Outside her cabin, close to her front door, was the forest. The high dark green trees, secreting a world of animals, of berries, of strangely shaped fungal growths, some of which they learned to eat, fascinated her. Behind the forest the great mountains loomed, purple or silver, golden or flame-coloured, black or stone, depending on the light. Never had she lived among such high mountains, so close to a vast forest. A clear sweet river— they called it a creek—ran at the end of their clearing, forming a border between it and the forest. In this creek she washed her clothes. In this creek she washed herself, when Ned was away and nobody was looking.

They were not always alone. On Sundays, there was Mass in the morning, and then the saloon. The mores of Philadelphia did not apply here. Women went to the saloon as well as men. They even drank alcohol. Stout was the drink, or whiskey, both from Ireland, with Irish names on the labels. Tullamore Dew. Black Bush. Also a light beer which the Germans liked.

Sophie took to drinking port wine. She sat at a table with a woman called Kathleen Sullivan, drinking this and chatting. The men drank whiskey and played cards. Twenty-one, forty-four, poker. One man had a fiddle. He held it straight under his chin, the way they do in Donegal, and played Irish tunes. Jigs and reels. Old slow songs that brought tears to Sophie's eyes, although she did not know why. Not because they reminded her of home. She was glad to be here, glad to be away. It was much better than Ireland.

There were not enough women.

Men stared at her constantly, even when Ned was present. He didn't like it but did nothing about it, attributing it to the shortage of women rather than to any intrinsic worth of Sophie's. She was careful to maintain her distance with all of them, which was easy enough. They were rough diamonds, not the kind who knew how to talk to a woman. Except on Sundays, when the whiskey and music softened them, their minds were focused on one thing only: money.

Ned was preoccupied with money as well. He spent so much of his time underground, in the dark cold earth, chipping away at the rocks for silver. His pay was good, but he experienced danger for it, as well as backbreaking work. None of the silver he retrieved was his: it belonged to the owner of the mine, who paid him by the hour. He began to work longer and longer hours, greedy for the dollars which were mounting up, slowly, in a bag he kept under the bed in the cabin.

Burglary was a threat.

Anyone was a potential robber. Everyone knew who was earning, who was likely to have money stashed away, who used the bank. Your best friend might rob you. In this community, assembled of people from all over Europe, none of whom intended to stay there permanently, nobody was entirely trustworthy. But you had to hope for the best, trust some sort of moral bond or sense of interdependence that would prevent your workmate or neighbour from breaking into your house and relieving you of every penny you'd got.

You could not hope for that as far as the Indians were concerned.

Sophie was warned to stay indoors as much as possible, both to keep an eye on the house and to protect herself from being snatched away by one of the red men who sometimes roamed around Greenough, looking curiously at the people who had so recently relieved them of their territory. Some of these men were known in the town. They sold skins to the store, they bought whiskey at Clancy's. None of them worked in the mine, however. 'How do they live?' Sophie asked. 'Them fellas?' said Ned. 'Hunting. Fishing. They grow maize.' They used to grow maize in the valley at the foot of the Bitterroot Hills, on the plains. They would settle in a place and cultivate the rough, dry land until it yielded the maize, beans, and the peyote they used as a medicine and a drug. Their women knew how to make the roughest land fertile. But as soon as they succeeded in transforming scrubland to fertile soil, the army moved them on. Now they were pushed into the hills, higher even than the silver mines. They were often starving: the women came down to Greenough carrying their babies in baskets strapped to their backs, and scavenged in the bins for leftovers, scraps of meat or bread the miners had thrown out. 'They'd eat anything,' Mrs Sullivan said disdainfully. 'They're not like us. They have no sense of cleanliness. Ugh.' All the women in Greenough hated the Indians.

One day, Sophie walked up from the river, carrying a bucket of ice. It was November. The ground was covered with snow and the air was so cold that it seemed to freeze in her nostrils as she breathed. At the mine, the men had to melt the seams with fires and blowtorches before they could begin to dig. Sophie had to put ice in a pot on the fire to get water.

From the eaves of the cabin, hunks of venison and mutton, legs and shoulders, hung, coated with white ice crystals. Whole rabbits, half a deer. Trapping was easy in the winter. And you could take all the meat you could get. There was no danger of it going off, so you could kill more than you needed. All you had to do was skin it and hang it outside the house in the cold, to freeze. When Sophie needed some, she brought it inside and let it thaw out before cooking it.

She was wearing her sealskin coat, which almost kept her warm and which had a huge hood. The hood gave her blinkered vision: she could only see what was in front of her eyes: the river, the spiky trees weighted with snow, the path back to the cabin.

She went into the cabin and put the bucket on the floor, near the fire. She stretched her numb hands to the flames, to thaw the fingers before taking off her coat.

A cold hand, heavy as a falling tree, clamped her mouth.

Another hand gripped her stomach.

So this was it.

What she felt was—nothing. Not fright, not terror. Nothing. It was as if every smidgeon of herself, even her capacity to be afraid, had vanished.

Not for long.

She had heard stories. Terrible stories. They seeped into her consciousness. What they would do to you. First all the men of the tribe would rape you. Then you might undergo unspeakable tortures. Not so unspeakable that every child in Greenough did not know what they were—that Sophie did not know what they were. Hadn't Mrs Sullivan regaled her with accounts, whispered over a glass in the saloon, as part of the Sunday night entertainment? Stories to make your hair stand on end. Burnings, in the worst places. Cuts at the most female, intimate parts of you. Finally you would be scalped—after your death if you were lucky.

Now the burden of stories flooded Sophie's head. A deluge of imaginings annihilated her, blacked her out. When she came to, she was lying on her own bed. The Indian was standing beside her. He had a mug of water in his hand. He handed it to her and she drank a few drops of the ice-cold liquid.'

He smiled.

Sophie did not return the smile. But she felt less afraid now. Instead she felt limp and helpless, as if her body had been squeezed in a mangle and all the feeling had been wrung out of it. Or as if her mind and her eyes were outside her body, hovering somewhere over her head like a dragonfly staring down at herself. It was not an unpleasant sensation.

'I need some meat,' he said. His English was slow and all his words were spoken with exactly the same emphasis, like a row of stiff pegs on a clothesline. In this his English was not so different from the English of most people in Greenough. Sophie and Ned spoke Irish usually when they were alone, or among other Irish people. Almost all the settlers had some language that was their own—German or Swedish or Icelandic or French—and their English was for use with outsiders. So what language did the Blackfeet speak? That he could speak at all, like other human beings, was a surprise for Sophie. The women who scavenged on the rubbish heaps of Greenough were as silent as trees.

'Take it,' said Sophie, not looking at him.

'Goodbye,' he said.

That was all. He left the cabin, unhooking a side of deer from the eaves outside. Then he walked away. She got up and watched him from the little window as he moved into the forest, disappearing from her view more quickly than he should have. Maybe, she thought, he was not real. Maybe he was some sort of ghost.

Kathleen—that is, Mrs Sullivan—complained that her children were driving her mad.

'Don't they play in the snow?' Sophie asked. She had been married for two years. The idea of children increasingly embarrassed her. Even looking at them embarrassed her. She did not envy Kathleen her brood, not at all. But she was always conscious that envy was the emotion Kathleen, and everyone else, attributed to her. Poor little Mrs Burns. Childless, God help her.

'They play in the snow. They slide on the lake. They ski down the slopes on those wooden yokes their father made for them. But it's dark most of the time and they have to be inside.'

'Why isn't there a school for them?'

'There's nobody to teach a school here,' Kathleen said.

'I could teach them to read and write,' Sophie said. 'If I had some books I could.'

Kathleen thought it was a good idea.

Ned did not agree. 'You can hardly read or write yourself,' he said.

What about the letter she wrote every month to her sister? What about the local newspaper she read aloud to him once a week? What about that?

'It's one thing being able to write a letter to your sister and another teaching children to write or to read.'

What would he know about it? Ned Burns, who'd been brought up in the bad end of County Derry, who'd seldom darkened the door of any school.

'Teachers go to school till they're eighteen years of age. Then they have to be apprenticed to a master teacher for six years. That's how long it takes to be a teacher.'

His scorn was so immense that she believed he must be right. But Kathleen was sceptical. 'Apprenticed for six years? I never heard tell of that,' she said. 'Anyway, what odds? You know more than the children anyhow,' she said. 'And more than most of us.' She did not say 'more than Ned' but that's what she meant. Ned could read a bit, and sign his name. But he could not read a newspaper. He couldn't be bothered, the small print hurt his eyes. And he had never written a letter.

'I suppose they get some sort of training,' Sophie said.

'We're not going to get a trained teacher out here in the back of nowhere,' said Kathleen. 'There aren't many like you here, either.'

'What do you mean?' Sophie was not being entirely disingenuous.

'A girl like you. A fine-looking girl who can read and write. Nobody knows what you're doing here.'

'I'm here because I'm married to Ned,' Sophie protested.

'Aye,' Kathleen said, looking curiously at her. 'Well . . . '

'I'm fine,' Sophie said. 'I like it here.'

'Well, that's grand,' Kathleen said. 'But you could spare a thought for the children.'

'If you can't have a child of your own I don't think you should interfere with other people's' was Ned's rejoinder to that. 'You think you're so clever but . . . ' He did not finish the sentence.

The sun shone on the snow, and it was warm in front of the cabin. Light scattered across the trees. Sophie was inside, writing a letter to her sister. She told her about the attempt to teach, and, in a watered-down way, about Ned's reaction. Then she tore up that letter and started another one which made no reference to the incident. Sheila would probably agree with Ned. Or else she would use the information as ammunition against the marriage.

A knock on the door.

The Blackfoot again.

'What do you want?'

'Flour, please,' he said.

'I haven't got much,' she said, thinking, that's the trouble.

You give in once and then they keep coming back. All beggars were the same.

'We have none,' he said.

'All right,' she said. 'But this is the last time.'

He handed her a small basket made of bark. She went to her flour sack, and scooped two scoops of the crunchy yellow flour into the basket. When she turned, he had come into the kitchen and closed the door behind him.

'It is so cold,' he said, by way of explanation.

'Do you go to other cabins? Like this?'

He shook his head, and smiled at her.

She smiled as well.

Then it started to happen. What should not have been possible, with a man like this, a man who was not real, who was a sort of animal. Blackfeet. Red men. Savages. She felt her heart change inside her. It changed so that she could feel it, she could feel her whole mind and body and soul begin to change, to ignite, and she felt this change as her heart tossing around inside her like a lump of butter in a churn and her muscles shivering. His brown eyes stared at her, as if he knew what was happening to her. But he couldn't have.

'Here is your flour,' she said, handing it to him and speaking in a cold, neutral voice. 'You'd better go now.'

'Thank you,' he said.

She wondered, later, where he had learned his English. Just hanging around the town? Or in some other way? There was nobody she could ask. She had no business talking to someone like him at all. The correct thing for a woman to do, when confronted by an Indian, was to scream her head off and run as fast as she could away from him. If Ned knew this had happened, he would probably strangle her.

She still read the paper. She read it on Saturday nights after she had come home from the store, when Ned was bathing his feet in a tub of hot water. His toes were almost frozen off sometimes, with the cold of the mine.

'Gold discovered in Yukon,' she read. 'Gold has been discovered in the Klondike region of the Yukon Territory in northern Canada. Already hundreds of eager prospectors have arrived in Dawson City, with a view to bettering themselves. The seams, which have been found close to the junction of the Klondike and Yukon rivers, are said to be exceptionally rich . . . '

'Gold,' Ned said. 'Gold is better than silver.'

'The Klondike must be an awful place,' Sophie said. 'Up there in the north. Haven't you heard of fools' gold?'

'You're such a fool you wouldn't know the difference between gold and silver,' he said. And he laughed. But she did not laugh this time, and let him go to the saloon on his own. When he came home he was very drunk. She pretended to be asleep. But he woke her up to tell her that several men from the village were planning to set off for the Yukon as soon as the ice melted. They hadn't needed to read about the gold in the paper. Already, somehow, word had reached Butte that there was more gold up there than had ever been found in the whole of North America before. 'It's for the taking,' he said. Sophie knew it could not be so simple, but nodded and pretended to agree.

Blackfoot looked about twenty years of age to Sophie, who was now twenty-two herself. His image was in her mind most of the time as she went about her tasks or lay in bed before falling asleep. (Ned seldom kissed her, or caressed her, any more. He was too tired, most of the time, after the work at the mine. When he came home at night all he did was eat his dinner, say the Rosary, and flop into bed.) It was a disturbing image, and she tried to dislodge it from her head, but couldn't. His tall, strong body clad in its beaver skins. His bronze face with its pools of dark eyes, its polished cheekbones. His hair fell to his shoulders, thick and opaque, unlike any hair she had seen. She felt her fingers itch to touch it just to find out what it felt like.

If he had not been able to speak English this would not have happened to her, she thought. Or if she had not been able to speak English, but only the Irish she had spoken at home, and still spoke with Ned. If he had only spoken his savage's language, and she her own, she would have kept away from him.

By now, four years after Ned had started his apprenticeship to the silver miner, he had learned all there was to know about the trade. He could locate a mine, he could drill and blast. He could identify different kinds of minerals. He could evaluate them.

'The value of silver has dropped,' he told Sophie. 'It's gone from eighty cents an ounce to forty cents.'

At first, Sophie did not understand how this had happened. 'President Jackson did it,' Ned said, neutrally. 'He devalued silver.' How could a man, even if he were the President, have enough power to change something like the value of silver? Apparently that is just what he had been able to do, by simply ordering it to be so. It sounded to Sophie like the wedding feast at Cana.

'Gold is the thing,' Ned said. 'We'll never get anywhere if we don't mine that.'

Then it struck Sophie that gold could change its value too. It struck her that it had no value. 'Why is gold valuable?' is what she asked.

'What?' Ned was incredulous.

'Can't its value change? If President Jackson changes his mind?'

Ned didn't appear to think so. Anyway he didn't give her an answer. His mind was made up. Already he had planned every inch of his journey, from Missoula to the Klondike. He would take a paddle steamer most of the way. Then he would walk from the Yukon fork to Dawson City. That was where the best gold was: clear, bright yellow, the most valuable kind.

'Why? It's nice to look at, but it's no use.'

'Of course it's use,' he said.

'What use is it?' Sophie persisted, as her mind wrapped itself around this idea. What use is silver? More use than gold. Silver knives and forks, silver cups and bowls. They last and last. They shine and can be shone up again, clean and bright as water.

'It's use,' he said. 'Don't be stupid. There's so much you don't understand.'

'I suppose so,' Sophie said. But she wondered. Gold. Why did they want it so much?

'Because it looks like the sun,' North Wind said.

'That's probably it,' said Sophie, although she wondered. Did it have some properties she was unaware of? Could it cure some pain?

Could it endure for ever, like—perhaps—a man's lineage?

North Wind. That was his name, in English, but for a long time Sophie could not say it. It sounded so silly. What does Sophie mean?' he asked.

'It doesn't mean anything.' Sophie said. 'Names don't have a meaning.' He looked sceptical and as she said this she wondered if it was true. Edward. How could a sound like 'Edward' mean anything? It was not a proper word, just a name.

North Wind came to the cabin again and again, as the winter turned to spring. Ned had moved away, not to the Yukon, but higher into the mountains behind Greenough, the Bitterroot Mountains, where he was digging for gold.

'Do your people use it?' she asked North Wind.

'No,' he said. 'We use instead beads made from shells. Wampum.'

'The same thing!' said Sophie.

No, it was not the same thing. The shells lay everywhere, on the shoreline of the lake. On beaches at the foot of the high cliffs that fall into the Blackfoot river. The Indians did not blow up the mountains in order to get them. The earth gave them the shells, for nothing.

He came to the cabin for meat and bread. They both knew that was why he was coming. It was for no other reason. To him, she looked old and pale. Paleskin, and she was very pale, even now with her fair hair, her white peaky skin. Even her eyes were colourless, by comparison with his. Black hair, bronze skin, dark brown eyes. He was the colour of a dark forest animal, a fox, a bear, while she looked like an urban aberration.

He told her things. The names of the months. The month of the melting snow. The month of the greening grass. The month of the rutting stag. He told her about the animals in the mountains: the great brown bears, the thin mountain lions. One had come and taken a child away from the camp where he lived with his tribe before the snow melted. The lions were short of food—and he blamed this, like almost every misfortune, on the white settlers. He told her about the Great Spirit that inhabits the whole earth, that owns the forest, the mountains, the plains, the waters, the animals.

The Great Spirit sounded to Sophie like God. But she did not say this to the Blackfoot, who would have scorned her. He thought everything about the white settlers was stupid.

'Our land is more valuable than your dollars,' he said. 'It will last for ever. It belongs to the Great Spirit and white men cannot buy it, although they think they can. If they cut down the forest and blow up the mountain, the Great Spirit will punish them.'

But he did not know how the Great Spirit would go about this. In fact most of the punishment going seemed to be meted out not to the white men, but to the Blackfeet. They were half-starved on their cold encampment. Several of them had died during the winter—the miners had taken the lion's share of the game on offer from the Great Spirit, apparently.

'You have more guns' was the explanation he had for this. Guns, dynamite, steam engines: the Great Spirit was no match for these weapons. Yet.

Ned found gold. He came down from the mine and showed it to Sophie: nuggets of rich, dark, solid gold. He said fifteen decades of the Rosary in thanksgiving. Sophie's knees were worn out by the time he'd finished. Then he drank half a bottle of whiskey and tried to make love to her, but fell asleep before he could.

One of his colleagues took the nuggets to Butte to sell them. 'Our fortune is made!' said Ned.

Sophie had been excited when she held the rough, heavy lumps of gold in her hand. They glittered like the water in the lake when the sun shone on it in the middle of summer, sparkling it with a million diamonds. It was like holding that sparkle of sunshine in your hands. The darkness of the gold reminded her of the dark eyes and dark skin of the Blackfoot. Indian gold.

But she was not so sure about the fortune. 'What will we do then?' she asked uncertainly.

'Go somewhere,' said Ned. 'Out of this hellhole. Back east. Back to Ireland.'

When she walked in the forest she did not see the Great Spirit. But she heard the trees talking to her. She watched the light seeping through the high roof of the fir needles as she moved along the aisles. She watched the rich green and carmine carpet of berries sprouting around her toes.

Wrapped in her sealskin, she felt she was a seal. She felt she was a tree.

Naked, bathing in the deep dark pool of the creek, she felt she was a fish. A slippery salmon, fat and juicy, its skin the same colour as the shingle on the banks of the river.

North Wind came to the cabin while Ned was there, during the week of waiting for his fortune to be brought back from Butte. North Wind knocked on the door and Ned answered it. When he saw the Indian standing there, dressed at this time—it was the month of the long sun—in very little, he hit him on the jaw. Then he turned and picked up his rifle. By the time he had got back to the door North Wind had vanished.

'Fucking bastard,' said Ned. He was so angry that for a while he did not think to ask what North Wind was doing there. But later he remembered. Had Indians ever come to the cabin before? No, said Sophie, wondering if this lie were wise or foolish. No. Sometimes the women come, searching in the bins.

'Shoot them if they come here,' said Ned. His voice grew tender. 'You shouldn't be here on your own.'

'I'm used to it now,' said Sophie, as nonchalantly as she could.

'At least you won't have to be alone here again,' he said.

But the news from Butte was bad. The gold was not valuable. It was too dark.

'What?' Sophie could not believe this. 'It's still gold, isn't it?'

'It's gold. But it's gold that's no more valuable than silver.'

So it was true, Sophie thought. Gold was not always precious. Some of it was and some of it wasn't. Maybe it was not precious if you could find it too near home, if you came upon it too easily? Was that it? Or was it that someone decided, some powerful man sitting in Washington, that some kinds of gold were important and some were not?

'No no.' Ned would not hear of it. 'That's not why. It's the colour that's wrong. It's too dark. It's redskin gold, it's nigger gold.' Too dark. Only the white light blond gold of the Snowy Arctic would be good enough for America. The gold of the Klondike.

'I'll stay here,' Sophie said, when Ned announced that he would go there, drawn to it as the bees to clover. Once you started on this road there was no turning back.

'You can't,' he said. 'It's too dangerous.'

'More dangerous than the Klondike?'

It seemed that her life had become a balancing act as she moved from east to west, choosing the lesser of two evils all the time. Ned was better than Sheila and housework in Philadelphia. Being alone in a cabin in Montana was better than working in a factory in Philadelphia. Now going to the Klondike with Ned was supposed to be better than staying in the cabin here. But her judgment was faltering. She could no longer weigh up one choice against another and see, quickly, which was the best. North Wind had skewed her power to do that, had taken away her ability to distinguish black from white, silver from gold, bad from good, good from better.

'There isn't enough money. You can't stay here.'

'If I taught the children they'd give me food and fuel,' Sophie protested weakly, but knowing as she said the words that they were true. She could stay here on her own and survive.

'Don't be silly,' he said firmly. 'You can't teach anyone.'

'What if the gold in the Klondike also turns out to be the wrong kind?'

'It's the right kind. And I'm going to get it,' he said. In spite of his experiences, Ned had not changed. He was still always convinced that he knew exactly the right thing to do.

When Ned had been on Granite Mountain, mining the dark and useless gold, this had happened. North Wind had come to the cabin when Sophie was washing clothes. She washed them, during the summer, in the creek, rubbing the hard soap on them and scrubbing them on her washboard. She liked to watch the suds dancing off downstream in the sunlight.

'You should not do that.' North Wind was suddenly there beside her. You never heard him coming.

'Why?' She smiled up at him.

'It poisons the water,' he said.

Of course. That was what she would never think of. 'It's just a tiny bit of soap.' She watched the white, lovely suds.

'Yes,' he said. 'But if all the white women do it, it is a lot of soap. Then, no fish.' He helped her fill a tub with water. Then he helped her wash.

'Do you do this at the camp?'

He laughed. 'No,' he said. 'Never.'

'Have you a wife?' she asked suddenly, out of the blue. Did they have wives? Not in the sense that she was Ned's wife. Not in the sense of a priest and Mass and signing your name in a book. A real marriage.

He did not answer.

She touched him then. He was kneeling at her big wooden tub, splashing some shirt around in the soapy water. She touched his slippery hand under the surface of the water. He took out both their hands and pulled her towards him, kissing her. He led her to the forest and laid her on the soft old needles. First he dealt with her nipples, kissing them until she twitched with desire. Then he turned her on her stomach, so that the pungent needles tickled her skin, teased her belly and her thighs. He slid into her from behind. This time what she felt was not the twittering of birds, but an overwhelming delight which encompassed every inch of her body, back and front and in and out, which seemed to wrap her and him and the forest and the sky together. America. Gold. Heaven.

Ned had to go to Missoula to get some supplies for the journey.

Soon after he was gone North Wind came in.

They made love on her bed.

'We are going away,' she said afterwards, the languor the lovemaking had given her body blunting the pain of what she was saying.

'Why?' He looked curious rather than dismayed.

'Ned wants to go to the Klondike, north of here.'

'I know where it is,' he said, patiently.

'Sorry. Well, you know why we're going then.'

'Gold fever.'

'Yes.'

'You will get rich.' He laughed. 'There's plenty of gold up there.'

'I will die, maybe.' She realised this was true.

'You will be all right in your sealskin coat. You will be at home.'

'I am at home here.' She realised this was true too. She had been here for five years. Ireland was a dim, unpleasant memory. When her mind moved to the Klondike, she saw endless snow. The snow was beautiful but even here she had learned what an enemy it could be, how imprisoning, how threatening of starvation and isolation. And here the snow lasted for about five or six months. Half the time the earth was green. There was hot, very hot sun. The water in the pools was warm, so that bathing was like bathing in a tub. Up there, the snow would last for much longer. Maybe it never melted? There would be no food apart from meat and fish.

'We move all the time.' North Wind had been on the move since the moment he was born—the year of Little Bighorn. He had moved farther away from home, if home was the sowing fields, the winter hunting grounds. He had moved to the badlands.

'Yes. But we don't have to. We were doing well here.'

North Wind shrugged.

'He wants gold because he does not have a child,' she said.

'If he had a child he would need gold for another reason,' North Wind said.

'How many children have you?' she asked him, blushing suddenly and feeling weak.

'None,' he said. 'I have no wife.'

Her heart leaped. 'Why not?' she asked, smiling.

'I am young. Twenty-two.'

She had assumed they would mate as soon as they could,

like cats or dogs. Everything she assumed about the Indians was
turning out to be wrong.

'Would you like to be my wife?' he asked.

'I'm Ned's wife,' she said.

'Among the Blackfeet, if you get tired of one husband you
can take another.'

'I'm a Catholic,' Sophie said. 'I couldn't do that.'

'If I kidnapped you, you would have no choice!' He laughed
and gently pushed her down again, stroking her so that she
laughed for joy.

They were ready to go. The mining tools were packed in one
backpack, and food in another. All the clothes were in a lighter
pack, which Sophie would have to carry. The cabin was ready to
be closed up and abandoned. Somebody might come and take
it over while they were gone. No arrangement was made, one
way or the other.

'We might come back here,' said Sophie.

'Aye surely,' said Ned.

He went to Clancy's to have one for the road, the night
before they were to set off for the steampaddle at Missoula.

When North Wind came, he was not alone, but accompanied
by four other men. He did that to make it look like an authen-
tic raid. He could see the headline in the newspaper: redskins
capture white woman. It would absolve Sophie from blame, at
the risk of starting a war, but it was so easy to give rise to a war
that the risk hardly counted. A battle could start over a stolen
sheep just as easily, or a frightened child. In addition, it would
help to assimilate Sophie to the tribe. Abduction of a white
woman they would understand.

The men were painted, black and red and blue stripes on
their faces and bodies. One of them wore a war bonnet and the
other three had feathers sticking out of their loose black hair.

They carried machetes.

Sophie hardly recognised North Wind. She knew his voice, but apart from that he did not at all resemble the man she had got to know, taken to bed with her. He looked like a redskin. He looked like a savage.

She did what white women did, in these circumstances. As he carried her away on his horse—a mangy, underfed nag—she screamed loudly.

He clapped his hand over her mouth.

Already Kathleen Sullivan and all the little Sullivans were out. They were also screaming, at the tops of their voices, in their Kerry-Montana accents.

The Blackfeet did not know what to do with her.

'I'm happy now,' she said to North Wind. They were on the move again, moving to somewhere new where the Greenough gang would not find them.

But before they could dismantle the teepees and get out, Ned and Mick Sullivan, Mossie Fitzgerald and Miley Gallagher, Fritz Zumpfe and Jon Johannsen, and several others, converged on the camp. They carried shotguns, pikes, shovels, axes, anything they had available.

'Fucking savages.' Ned's voice was heard above the others. 'I'll rip them apart. Fuckers.'

Nobody was hurt.

A miracle.

The Blackfeet had run away, all of them. They were packed and ready to go anyway as Ned and his friends came upon them.

'Brave braves!' Ned said sarcastically. 'As soon as they sniff a real man, off they run.'

Sophie looked at him, neutrally.

'I'd like to strip their skin off and roast them skinless,' Ned said. 'Did they do you any harm?'

She did not answer.

'The poor wee woman's not right after it. No wonder,' said Miley Gallagher. 'Give her time. She'll tell you what happened when she's had time to let it all sink in.'

'Aye,' Ned said.

They went to the Klondike three days later.

Sophie had a baby, up there in the north, sometime the following spring. The baby was fine, a small light-skinned boy with black straight hair, not like Ned's or Sophie's. They called him Teddy. People often said to Ned, 'He's the image of you.'

Sophie loved her child. She fed him with her own milk, she wrapped him in furs, she sang to him and told him stories about Ireland, about the mountains, about the creek that ran sweetly outside her cabin in Montana.

Before Christmas, Ned hit gold—the pale gold of Alaska, which was the most valuable kind. His joy was boundless. 'By summer we'll be rich enough to go back home. We'll buy a good big farm in Derry and live like gentry.'

After Christmas the baby caught a cold. For two days the sound of his small cough racked the cabin and then, unable to get his breath, he died.

After that, the black sickness descended on Sophie, immured in her cold cabin in a land of ice. It descended on her mind and her heart like a blanket of black frost, blotting out every song and every flower that grew there, snuffing her flame.

Nothing ignited it again.

Ned prayed for her, night after night, in long litanies of supplication to his beloved Virgin. Mother Most Merciful, Mother Most Pure, Mother Most Renowned, pray for her.

After a while Sophie, who had not been one for praying before, began to join him in his prayers. Morning Star, Help of the Sick, Comfort of the Afflicted. Pray for Us. She recited them not only in the evenings, kneeling at the rough wooden chairs in the cabin before bedtime, but all day long. Mother of God, Star of the Sea. She walked around the shanty town, wrapped in her sealskin coat, chanting these incantations, without cease. To the litany she added an epithet of her own. North Wind, North Wind, North Wind. Nobody noticed that it broke the rhythm of the song, or that it was in any other way extraneous. Nobody would have commented if they had.

It was generally thought, among the Irishmen, pious or secular, sensible or wild, who were hitting gold with Ned, that Sophie's ordeal in Missoula at the hands of the Indians had affected her brain, and that she was not quite right in the head.

The Day Elvis Presley Died

PAT AND DOUGLAS ARE STAYING in the house—meaning the enormous gray stone pile that sits on the hill overlooking the lake. Jim and Margaret, Douglas's parents, have another residence, referred to as 'our own place', close to the edge of the wood. From the window of her narrow room Pat can see 'our own place': it is a log cabin, one of a cluster of such cabins, all nestling cosily into a backdrop of rich dark green spruce, fir, pine—whatever. To her all evergreen trees look the same. But she likes the look of them, always has: maybe what appeals is their association with Christmas, with snowy mountains and tinkling sleighbells, or with mountain walks, the idea of hiking groups of cheerful young people. Or maybe it is just their reliable colour and contours.

'Settled in?' Douglas asks. Pat has been in her room for five minutes. She has opened her big suitcase but has not removed any of the mountain of clothes from it. The bare boards of the room, the painted wooden wardrobe with its clatter of wire hangers, remind her of rooms in convents where she went on spiritual retreats as a schoolgirl. That such old, shabby, well-used rooms exist in the United States comes as a surprise to her. In Douglas's house, south of here, in Delaware, everything is plushly soft, deeply comfortable.

'Yes,' Pat says. She looks out the window. It's so beautiful. She means the long blue lake, sheltered by spiky evergreens, the gray and black and silver mountains, the hundreds of wooded islands; those things, and the clipped lawns sweeping down to the edge of the lake. The wooden docks, the canoes gliding along the calm water. The clear summer sky. She does

112

not mean the room, which disappoints her, although already some Americans might think this sort of worn-down austerity special and charming. Douglas does, apparently. 'It's not bad,' he says, glancing around at the bare cream walls. Maybe he's pretending not to understand Pat? She regards him with suspicion. She knows he hates her enthusiasm, her exuberant praise of landscape, her sentimental overstatements—the trite, unconsidered verbiage that flows out of her in her soft, excessively pleasant voice.

Pat is too eager, too eager to please and to be pleased. That is what he thinks. She is too readily effusive about almost everything. What a wonderful view, what a wonderful dessert, what a lovely carpet, what magnificent houses! She is exclaiming every five minutes. How can you believe a single thing such a person says?

Pat knows what she's doing wrong but can't help it. Everything she has seen since she came to America has seemed amazing to her. The words at her disposal, lovely, gorgeous, beautiful, seem the only ones suited to describe all this loveliness, of tree and landscape, of architecture and interior decoration. Of people. Of food.

What surprises her most is that America is both shockingly familiar and stunningly novel. For instance, the America Douglas belongs to, exactly resembles the America she has seen on television for most of her life. She walked into his living room and felt instantly at home. She'd been there so often as a child. On *The Donna Reed Show* and *The Lucy Show. The Honeymooners.* Real life is better than the sitcoms, because in it you see not just the living room, the staircase and the front door, but all the other rooms as well, the upstairs and the outside. You see the painted wooden gingerbread exteriors, you see the generous unfenced gardens, the clean, flower-edged winding suburban roads. You see the malls and the turnpikes and the highways. All that before you come to the mountains and see this: scenery more

splendid than anything Ireland can offer. That also came as a
surprise to Pat. She has not travelled very widely and has always
been taught that Ireland is the most beautiful country in the
world, without qualification. That is what her mother had told
her. Her mother, her teachers, the Irish Tourist Board. Ireland,
in compensation for its economic and social failures, was Miss
World in the International Beautiful Places Competition—a
dumb, and virtuous, blond among smarter but uglier nations.
That's why everyone in the world should take an Irish holiday.
That's why millions of Irish emigrants weep and sing tearful
songs about their homeland, remembering the unsurpassable
natural beauty they have left behind them. But what's the fuss
about? The truth is that America is not just a place where you
can get a job. The truth is that it also looks nicer than Ireland.
It is more beautiful, and sunnier, and there is so much more
of it. You can drive for hundreds of miles through dramatic
mountains, or deep forests. The sun doesn't disappear after half
an hour, and the good scenery doesn't give way to flat boring
stuff after half a mile. You do not have to anticipate a change,
often for the worse, every five minutes.

America has been a stunning experience, for Pat. And
Douglas doesn't like that. He wants her to appreciate America—
his country. But he doesn't want her to go overboard with this
appreciation. He wishes she knew when to stop. He wishes she
could be less childish, more studied, and cool. Maybe he wishes
she could be less Irish?

Douglas sighs and looks at her, his eyes ironic, but not really
unkind. Suddenly he puts his arms around her. Their warmth,
through the thin cotton of her blouse, abruptly seduces her
emotions, so that she feels tears springing up behind her eyes—
gratitude, though, rather than desire, is her overwhelming
feeling. So much of the time he is impatient with her. The
tension sears his forehead, tortures his face, and is to be heard
in the dry, irritated tones of his voice. Then come the spurts of

forgiveness, like a sudden pouring of warm sweet rain during a drought. She soaks up those rare moments like a withering flower, a browning scrap of sheep's bit, desperately clinging to the rock. She buries her head against his chest, trying to take every drop of kindness from him, as if that could sustain her for the next period of deprivation.

He kisses her. His mouth is warmer than hers. He has everything in abundance. He is a cornucopia, a fountain of gifts, for her, if only she could manage to take them. If she could find the way into him, for more than five minutes at a stretch, happiness, joy without end, would be hers. If only she could learn how to make her way through to him, there is no end to the bliss which he can give her. This is what she believes.

They hold the embrace for a couple of minutes: for several weeks, they have not had much of a chance to kiss in comfort. First, because they were separated: Pat was in Ireland, Douglas was here in America with his family. For the past week they have been together but in his parents' house. It's not that it is small. And they have often enough been left discreetly alone in the den. But even there, tucked underneath the house, on the wide old comfortable sofa, Pat has felt inhibited. At any moment, she feels, Douglas's mother or worse, father might walk through the door and discover them. So just at the times when he wanted to be tender she has been anxious and resistant. She has kissed and hugged with one eye on the door. When she had her chance to love him and take his love, she ruined it all.

Now the bolt is shot on the door and Douglas's parents are far away, in their cabin. There is no reason, no logical reason, to be wary. Douglas, not releasing his lips entirely, nuzzling her hair, her neck, pushes her gently enough to the bed. It is a plain, narrow bed and the mattress is firm. It does not give under Pat's weight. But she maneuvers her head on to the spongy pillow. She sighs, and gives herself, at last, to his kiss.

There is a kitchenette in the log cabin, where you can cook or make coffee. Jim and Margaret will eat their meals in the dining room, down in the big house, but they have this extra facility should they require it. When she has unpacked her clothes—a couple of white blouses, cotton flowered skirts, a light-blue silk shirtwaister for the banquet that will occur on the final night— Margaret makes a cup of herbal tea. She calls to Jim: 'Would you like some tea?' He answers immediately, in his round booming voice, 'No thank you, dear.' She doesn't take it as any sort of snub: they'll go to dinner in half an hour, and he seldom takes cups of tea or coffee, snacks between meals. 'I'm going to drink mine on the porch,' she says cheerfully. 'I'll join you in a minute,' he calls back equally cheerful. She can tell from the tug of his voice that he is shaving his upper lip, stretching his mouth to make a smooth surface of skin.

Margaret goes out and sits on one of the sunchairs on the porch. It is a substantial porch. There are four wooden chairs on it, as well as a low table suitable for cups or glasses. The porch has the same view, more or less, as Pat's room, namely the lake. All the cabins, and most of the occupied rooms, have this view. Only staff sleep in rooms that look backwards to the yards where the dustbins are stored, and to the wall of forested mountain.

Margaret surveys the scene and feels a great sense of relief. She it was who invited Douglas and Pat to share a week of the holiday with them. She wanted to give Douglas a break, and she wanted to show Pat this beloved place, the resort she had been coming to for forty years—as a child her parents had brought her here, driving up from Delaware in their big Studebaker, taking the train during the war (when Jim, already her boyfriend, was fighting in the navy). They had stayed in the house then; these cabins, although they look old, were built only ten years ago. But although she is glad she had had the bright, if expensive, idea, she was also glad she had decided to book them rooms in the big house (also an expensive idea). There is plenty of room in the cabin for the four of them. But she had believed that the young people would value some privacy. What she had not realised, not so consciously, was that she would value hers so much—that she would be so glad to be free of Pat. She is not sure what to make of Pat: she is a polite girl, and she looks all right, if not as pretty as Margaret would have liked, for Douglas. The neighbours who have met her have described her, to Margaret, as 'sweet': she has good hair, fair and waving, and long. And she has quite nice blue eyes, but there is something wrong with her teeth—they are uneven and turned slightly inward, like a shark's—they spoil her appearance, which is a pity, especially since they could have been corrected if her parents had looked after them in time. That might not matter if she were a livelier, wittier girl. But it is difficult to drag conversation out of her. She admires the scenery and the surroundings. That is gratifying, although sometimes Margaret has wondered if all the admiration is sincere. She also answers questions, but she seldom asks any apart from the most general. And she never proffers any information about herself. She is cheerful, but secretive. You never know what she is really thinking. Being in the company of such a person all day is a strain.

Now, however, thanks to her own kindness and foresight, Margaret can forget about Pat for a while. For a full ten minutes she allows her holiday mood to course through her as she sits in the evening sun. It is a most definite, tangible feeling, her holiday mood: a happiness which is a mixture of childhood memories, of the smell of the Norway spruce and the giddy glitter of sun on the water, of the excitement of the long drive up the tree-lined Northway Route to the lake. Even though the temperature is in the high seventies, there is a freshness, a crispness in the air here at all times. The air at home, where the temperature is in the high eighties, is leaden and humid.

If the air-conditioning is off for half an hour, you drip with perspiration. A walk along the sidewalk to the corner store leaves you washed-out, flaccid.

But up here, the outdoors is exhilarating.

'Ah, it's exhilarating,' beams Jim. He has changed into a check shirt and khaki shorts. His legs are tanned—it's late July, he's been swimming and sailing for months on the little lake at home. His stomach is protuberant in the shorts, but in a healthy way – it almost looks as if it is a firm extension of his toned, muscular body, rather than a flabby mess of a belly. He looks like a man who is well looked after, content with his lot. That is what he looks like, Margaret thinks, and a lot of that is thanks to her.

He ruffles her hair—blond, a light fluffy bob—and drops a peck of a kiss on her forehead. 'Well?' he asks. 'Settled in yet?

'Isn't it wonderful?' Margaret gazes at the lake. Her happiness is still welling up inside her, like hot water in a geyser. She knows happiness of this quality cannot last for long and she is making the most of it.

'Not bad,' says Jim. His voice is warm and kind. Margaret smiles, hearing the tone rather than the words. He sits down and opens a book, a book about golf. 'Not bad at all.'

What does he think about Pat, Margaret wonders, idly, and then answers the question herself. He probably doesn't think about her at all.

Douglas is the handsomest boy Pat has ever seen. It sounds like a preposterous boast, but it is really true. The first time she saw him, in a room in the college they both attended as graduate students in Dublin, she could hardly believe he was real. Real, and studying in this college, in the humanities faculty, where the boys were thin on the ground and usually smaller than the girls, much shorter than Pat, who is five foot eight. (The big sporty boys tended to select such subjects as engineering, medicine, or law.) Douglas was about six and a half feet tall. He towered over everybody. His face was classically handsome, his teeth white and perfect, his eyes a clean mid-palette blue. He had brown-ish-fairish hair, thick and wavy, falling in an undulating lock over his high forehead. Apart from a few spots, a sign of mascu-linity at his age, there was nothing the matter with him at all, as far as looks were concerned. If you were designing a blueprint for the perfect man, this would be it. So Pat thought.

She did not get to know him for quite a while. He spent little time in college, and seemed cool and distant with most people. It was generally assumed that he had a better and more glamorous life to lead elsewhere, that he was concerned only with what he was learning and, for obvious reasons, would not be interested in making friends with any of the ordinary students. Besides, Pat had a boyfriend already, a medical student whom she had been seeing for almost two years. Terry was the medical student's name. He was tall, but not as tall as Douglas. And he was handsome, but had a reddish, spotty complexion which detracted from his good looks. Douglas managed to be tall and well-built, with the solidity of a full-grown man, even though he was at most twenty-two. Terry, the same age, looked as if he was half-grown. It was not at all clear how he would finally turn out, although you could guess he would age well, if you were prepared to be patient.

When Douglas had been around for six months, somebody from class held a party. She was an American girl called Rain. (Her father was Irish; he called her after the most typical natural attribute of the old country.) Rain might have been holding this party especially to get off with somebody—quite possibly with Douglas. Or she might have decided to have the party for fun, or from a sense of social obligation—she was the sort of girl who might act altruistically, without self-interest, because she was both generous and rich. So it was rumoured among the Irish students, who were all, in varying degrees, poor, like most Irish people in those days. Rain had a Fulbright scholarship, which was rumoured to be very large, and also a very large flat and a very old car. She had perfect teeth and a perfect complexion. Also serious ideals about her education and her subject, which was Medieval History.

Her flat was full of medieval reproductions—delicate blue and gold illustrations from books of hours, sculptures based on the Lindisfarne Gospels or the Book of Kells, a long tapestry which was a copy of a section of the Bayeux Tapestry, depicting small Viking boats on a smoky-blue stormy sea. She had bought these things, as well as records of medieval songs, plainchant and madrigals and carols, at museums and libraries around Europe: she'd been to Lindisfarne, to Iona, to Bayeux, to Clairvaux, to Chartres, to the museum of Cluny, to Canterbury. She'd been everywhere that mattered in the Middle Ages, even to Southwark on the London underground. To her, the Middle Ages were more than just a subject. They were interior decoration. They were blouses and dresses, long-playing records, and a hairstyle.

'She looks medieval,' Pat said to Douglas, at a certain stage in the party. 'Doesn't she?' It was a bitchy comment but it was true. Rain's plump high-breasted body, her soft oval face with its strawberries-and-cream complexion, her long ringlet of hazel hair, might have stepped out of the pages of Marie de France. Not Guinevere, nothing as hard and calculating. Not one of the wise beautiful fairy women, a Circe who bewitched men and trapped them in their apple-blossomed lairs. But one of the young, soft girls, the daughter in the Lai de Frêne maybe, whose mother locks her in a tower and spanks her daily as a punishment for her sexual misdemeanours, is what she looks like. Vulnerable, nubile, fated. Of course she plays it up, this look, with a velvet dress, wide batwing sleeves, dangling earrings: everything dripping, droopy, silkily soft. Summer rain.

Douglas laughed, and looked at Pat with admiration. Pat felt glad that she had managed to win this look for herself, diverting it from Rain. She elaborated. She trotted out the Lai de Frêne analogy and he took her hand, gazing as he did so over at Rain, who was frolicking with two of the lecturers, her large rump outlined against the flimsy velvet of her dress, and her round breasts showing their cleavage. Douglas had had about a bottle of red plonk to drink, at this stage—even Rain bought plonk. It was the mid-seventies; you could get only bad wine in Dublin then. Two-litre bottles called Nicolas or Hirondelle. Pat had had half a bottle already, which was enough to make her giddy. She smiled all the time when she was drunk, and burst into giggles on the tiniest provocation.

They went home together in a taxi. Home to Douglas's bedsitter, a room about one-twentieth the size of Rain's flat, about the size of a bathroom. They did not have sex. But they lay on top of the covers, kissing and wrestling, for whatever was left of the night. Pat drank Douglas's kisses as if they were spring water and she a camel who had plodded for weeks across the Sahara. She had not realised how serious her longing for real kisses was, until she tumbled into his arms and felt, for the first time ever, the urgency and energy of desire.

Meals at the lake are eaten in a big high dining hall, the walls and ceiling of which are panelled with dark wood. It is the sort of dining hall you associate with old universities. In such places, you usually sit at long narrow wooden tables, and are served by elderly Jeeves-like men in black jackets, or women who look as if they might have had an injury such as a blow to the head, or a baby who was taken away for adoption, in their youth and have never recovered from it.

But it is not like that here. The tables are suited to small groups, four or six, and are covered with cheerful gingham cloths, blue and white. A little bud vase holding a few daisies or a bit of yellow broom sits in the middle of each. At breakfast and lunch the dining room is self-service. At dinner, the waitresses are young, very pretty girls dressed in T-shirts and jeans. They are known as Muffins. The Muffins are the children of families who have been coming on holiday to this resort for years or for generations. Their reward now in their young adulthood is to be allowed to wait on table, wash dishes, clean bedrooms, and be paid for it, in the camp. Some of them look cheerful and happy with their work and others look disgruntled and incompetent, sulky sophomores dishing up baked potatoes, thick steaks, broccoli, creamed mushrooms.

Pat, Douglas, Margaret and Jim always eat dinner together, and usually lunch as well. At breakfast they sometimes miss each other: Douglas and Pat get up earlier than his parents, or get to the dining room quicker. It is, after all, in the house where they sleep.

Now they are eating dinner. It is the end of the second day of the holiday. They are summing it up. Jim wants to do this. Or maybe it is just a way of keeping the conversation going.

'The art class was good. I enjoyed it,' Pat says. She had spent the morning painting a bunch of broom stuck in a pottery jug, with a lot of other people, most of them old-age pensioners. Douglas had done this too, out of loyalty to her, although he has no interest even in the idea of painting. Pat, however, is devoted to the idea of many activities: painting, ballet, playing the piano, horse riding, mountaineering, sailing—activities which she did not get a chance to practice in her youth and which she thinks would be fun to try now. And apparently it's not too late. Look at the old women—and men—valiantly daubing at their easels, struggling with the jug of airy broom.

'Your picture was fine. It has something—a sense of movement.' Jim speaks not seriously, but with an air of conviction. Douglas glances at Pat with a glow of admiration and Pat feels inordinately grateful to Jim for winning this bonus for her.

'Yes it was lovely,' Margaret agrees. She is still happy. The day has gone off well, so far. All three of her charges seem content, which is all she asks for. 'Anyone like some orange squash?'

'Thank you, Mags, I'll have some.'

Douglas says, a bit surly, that he'll help himself. One of the things that irritates him is the way his mother is so helpful, just as it irritates him that Pat is eager to please. He thinks his mother treats him, and all of them, as if they were babies. Pat, on the other hand, likes having her squash poured for her, she likes to hear Margaret being solicitous about her health, her well-being, her happiness. At lunchtime Margaret insisted on buying Pat a tube of suntan lotion, and told her to rub it into her skin before going out again. Pat has not been mothered for a very long time.

'And how was the pony trekking?' Margaret asks.

'OK,' says Douglas.

'Go far?' asks Jim.

'No, not far,' Douglas says.

'We spent a lot of time learning how to sit on the horse and hold the reins,' Pat explains eagerly. 'So we didn't really go for a trek. She said we might go into the forest tomorrow.'

'Sometimes she goes right up and onto the ridge. You can see the riders from our kitchen window: strung out along the ridge, silhouetted against the sunset. It's quite a sight,' says Jim.

'Oh yes it is.' Margaret nods and smiles.

'I hate that damn horse,' says Douglas. 'A broken-down nag. I'm not riding her again if you pay me to do it.'

'Looks like you'll have to trek alone,' says Jim, cheerily, to Pat.

Pat smiles uneasily.

'Look.' Margaret is not deliberately trying to change the subject. But she has noticed one that is more interesting.

Pat sees it and her heart sinks.

A young woman so slim, so smooth, so lovely, that she seems to belong to a different species from all the other women and girls in the room. Star quality: perhaps what Princess Diana (now about fifteen and not a princess) had. Or Jacqueline Kennedy. Some film stars. Women who have style, class, sexiness, beauty. Pat feels like a worthless lump as soon as she sets eyes on this creature, who is clad in a simple white shift dress, sleeveless, the better to reveal her long brown arms, and short, to reveal her similar legs.

'Amy Brownlee,' Margaret whispers.

'She's the hostess this year,' Jim says. 'Yep. I met her dad last night. This is their twenty-fifth year at the lake.'

'Still haven't done as many years as me,' Margaret says. But although her tone is as ringing, as bright, as usual, her face is shadowed. Pat knows what she is feeling, if not thinking. She is feeling that Amy is a more fitting partner for Douglas than Pat is. It is what she feels, and Pat feels it too. But it is a feeling too frightening to be formed into a thought, much less a communication.

'Nobody can ever do that!' Jim says, pushing away his plate firmly. 'Did you know, Pat, that Margaret first came to the lake when she was four years old?'

Pat does, because all of them have told her so more than once. But of course she pretends she hasn't. Jim and Margaret between them repeat the story, or the linked stories, of Margaret's first visits to the lake. Douglas concentrates on his dinner, much too fiercely it seems to Pat. The furrow between his heavy eyebrows deepens.

Later when they are taking a long walk along by the lake she asks him about Amy. They know her parents, Douglas says. He picks up a stone and skims it across the water. It's black now, shiny: there is a half-moon hovering over the trees, a sprinkle of stars. Pat knows she has to wait and hope that he decides to offer more information. He picks up another stone and skims it before doing this.

'We went to the same college, me and old Amy.' Pat smiles, as she is meant to do, relieved to hear her denigrated in this Way. Old Amy. So there's something wrong with her too. Maybe she isn't clever enough? That would irritate Douglas, just as it irritates him that Pat isn't beautiful enough. He needs a girl who is both very bright and very beautiful. Until he finds such a girl, he is going to feel short-changed. He is going to sulk and wonder why he is unhappy. This is not something he has realised yet. Pat is learning to realise it, against her will, against everything she wants to know. It will be a long, tough lesson for her as it will be for Douglas, when the time comes to let the truth sink in. 'We went out a few times.'

'When?'

'Sophomore year. Second year.'

'And didn't you . . . like her?'

'She's OK.'

'Don't you think she's attractive?'

'She's OK,' says Douglas. There are many things he can't acknowledge, to Pat or to himself. He adds with a dry laugh, 'And her dad's a millionaire. They were all hoping we'd get it together.'

Pat says nothing, but she's grateful to him for his tact, for pretending that the important thing about Amy is that her dad is a millionaire—how that information diminishes her!

Douglas stops throwing stones. He links her arm companionably and they walk for a stretch, easy and happy almost as they used to be a year ago, when they first fell in love and when it didn't matter that Pat wasn't beautiful enough to compete with the smooth-skinned girls of America. They walk until the path ends and they are at the wood. Pat would like to go on but he won't let her. 'Poison ivy,' he says. 'We won't see it in the dark.' They have to watch out for poison ivy every time they come to the forest. It prevents them going most places. Pat finds it hard to believe in poison ivy. She can't believe that a substance so treacherous could grow everywhere, waiting, constantly, to trap the unwary. And they have never actually seen any: whenever she asks Douglas to show her some, he can't find examples. 'And then there's the snakes,' he adds, knowing she is terrified of them, like all Irish people.

'I'd like to walk back to the other end then,' Pat says. The meal she has eaten is still lodging heavily in her stomach, and there is nothing to do at the camp after dinner except go for a walk or go to the soda fountain and eat ice cream, or go to your room and kiss. It's only ten o'clock. Many of the campers, especially the young ones, will get up at six for an organised early-morning swim in the lake, so it makes sense to go to bed early. But Pat doesn't feel like it, not after that dinner.

Pat did not tell Terry that she had fallen in love with Douglas for a while. At first, anyway, she wasn't sure if this had really happened. Although she knew she enjoyed being with him more than she enjoyed being with Terry and she knew she enjoyed kissing him more than she enjoyed kissing Terry, it wasn't clear if this were enough. Terry she didn't like kissing at all, and she was impatient and often bored with him. On the other hand she liked him and trusted him. He was gentle, soft-hearted, reliable. And she knew that he loved her absolutely and completely, although she did not know why. He was like a devoted dog.

That, she thought, was the trouble. He loved her too much. No matter how cool and standoffish she was, he went right on being in love with her. A dog, and he made her feel like a fox being chased by a dog. A mean nasty cold and cunning fox, being chased by a kindly, tail-wagging dog who only wanted to play and lick her all over.

It had not always been so. Initially she had wanted him as much as he wanted her, loving his large blue eyes, his gentle manners. But very soon all that had changed, perhaps because he was too good, perhaps because he gave too much? Now all she felt was guilt. Guilt, pity, remorse. Why did she stay with him? Not from motives of charity. She stayed because she needed a young man, a boyfriend, in the background of her life. She needed someone to mind her, to love her, in the absence of a mother. (Her mother had not died. But she was in a psychiatric hospital, suffering from severe depression, so it was said. This had been going on since Pat was twelve years of age.) Terry had filled the role for a few years. He was there, to take her to movies and parties at the weekends, to be her escort when she needed one. She could talk to him about most things that concerned her—her studies, her exams, her father. She never talked to anyone about her mother. With him as a companion she had become self-assured and seemingly independent. She concentrated on her work and had become good at it. She had been able to streamline herself into an efficient, focused career woman. It was thanks to Terry that she was a graduate student, doing a Ph.D. Thanks to him she had been able to concentrate on her studies, and do well at them, because she didn't have to waste time worrying about matters of the heart. Terry was there for her.

She knew that he was the kind of comfortable, safe man any girl or woman should aim to have in her life. Looking around, it seemed that many of her friends had opted for relationships with men like Terry—certainly the girls who were not among the most lively, the most beautiful, the most sought-after. But how could you know this? How could you know anything about other couples' feelings for one another? Maybe dull, uninspired pairs were fired by hidden passions, invisible to the eyes of their friends? Or maybe many people felt no need for any sort of passion?

She could hardly say that what she felt for Douglas was passion: he kept it at bay, and anyway she was still too terrified of sexuality to allow herself true passion. But he presented her with a challenge. She knew she felt happy in his arms, satisfied with his kisses and caresses. To spend a night with him, locked in those arms, was not the trial it would have been with Terry. Far from it. She never wanted to leave him when the long sessions were over. (And he didn't want her to leave either. Not at the beginning. They would linger, drawing out their farewells, taking one last kiss, one last taste of the other's skin or hair, their bodies unwilling to separate until the moment when one of them, usually Pat, jumped up, as a lazy sleeper jumps from bed, breaking off the dream abruptly in mid-flight, and pulled herself away.)

Weighing the two relationships, the two men, in the balance, Pat did not know which was better. Sex or faithful companionship? Which was she supposed to choose? Which of these was true love? While she wondered, Pat continued to see Terry at weekends, and Douglas during the week.

After a while the problem seemed to solve itself. Gradually, perhaps through force of habit, Pat and Douglas became inseparable—they became one of the college couples that went everywhere together. (There were couples, it was said, who even went to the toilet at the same time, one—the boy usually—waiting outside the Ladies until the girl was finished and ready to move back to the library or wherever they had been.) They read together, they had lunch together, they went to parties and to plays together. The barrier Douglas had erected around himself had broken down and Pat was admitted to his circle, the magic circle of Douglas and Pat. (What she did not know was that such a barrier can always be put up again, quite easily, by a man who has one to begin with.) Love. There was no longer any doubt about it. Pat and Douglas, Douglas and Pat. They were in love, they knew one another. Pat couldn't be apart from Douglas for long without suffering something that felt like real pain.

That is when she found out what love is and that is when she had to tell Terry—Terry who already knew, all too well, what it was, at least in its terrifying, unrequited or half-requited, form.

Pat would learn about that, too, in time.

Margaret and Jim are lying side by side in their double bed. They
have just had sex, easy-going and pleasurable. Jim is in a joking
mood, a more joking mood than usual. 'That wasn't bad,' he
says, yawning. 'I think I can get to sleep now.'

'Thank you,' Margaret says, turning on her side to her
bedside lamp and her novel. She is not being ironic: it is a habit
she has, to thank him for this ritual.

'Do you ever think . . . ' she begins. Then she stops.

'What?' He is alert. She can tell from the sharp rise in his
voice that he thinks she is going to make some interesting
revelation.

'Ah nothing,' she says then.

'Go on! It's not fair, starting on something like that. What
is it?'

Margaret had been going to say, do you ever think how
different all this is when you are young and in love? How there
is less fun, in a sense, but much more joy? Do you ever yearn to
be back there? Or to have that again? But she says, 'I wonder if
Douglas and that girl will stay together?'

'Pat?' he says. He gets out of bed to get a sandwich: he is
naked. That is another reason why Margaret decided to take
a separate house from Douglas and Pat, that it is part of Jim's
holiday to sleep naked and walk around the room and the house
naked as much as he can. Margaret herself is always clothed,
just now in a pale pink cotton shortie nightgown. She is thin
enough to get away with it. 'Who knows?' he says.

'She's a nice girl,' says Margaret.

'Meaning?' He is in the kitchen getting bread and cheese
from the refrigerator: they have laid in some simple supplies.

'Meaning just that.'

'Meaning but. What's the but?'

'I don't know. I just wonder.'

They seem to get along together all right.

'Oh yes!' Margaret says, brightly.

'She's white. She's not a drug addict.'

'She doesn't even smoke cigarettes.' Margaret thinks it might be better if she did.

'But she drinks.' Jim laughs and wags his finger in the air.

'She drinks? How do you know?' Margaret feels puzzled.

'Did you ever meet an Irish person who didn't?'

There is a snake on the wall in front of the house. It is a thick, long snake, grayish with yellow marks, and it is coiled like a Danish pastry on a flat slab of stone, apparently asleep. Pat sees it and screams. Douglas is not as scathing as he might be.

'It's probably just a copperhead,' he says. 'But we'll report it.'

'What are the dangerous ones?' Pat asks.

'Rattlesnakes.' He tells her what these look like. Pat doesn't take it in. The sight of the snake on the wall fascinates her. She had visualised the local snakes as small and thin, sly wormy creatures sliding secretly in the wet grass, under the pine needles. But this is as big as any of the snakes she has seen in the zoo in Dublin, although their skin, as she remembers it, tends to be more yellow and brown, speckled like leopards. Or maybe she is thinking of 'The Speckled Band.' It looks like a gray, lumpy-skinned eel, except for its round desperate eyes, which it opens as she watches. It begins to flick its tongue lazily at flies.

Douglas is not afraid of the snake, but he is surprised by it. He stands in the hot lunchtime sun and gazes for a few minutes with Pat, his arm loosely hooked around her waist. She can feel his appreciation of her discovery. Quite by accident, she has measured up to his expectations. It can happen so easily. But it has to happen effortlessly, by accident. How can she figure out how to control a situation while not worrying about it? If she could only master that trick, she'd be all right. Douglas would love her again.

They go to talk to an official in the reception office of the camp, a well-spoken man wearing an outfit that looks like a combat suit. Her luck holds. They are the first to report the news. The man strolls out and looks at the snake with an expert eye. Not dangerous, he says, winking at Douglas. It's just an old water snake. But we'll remove it straight away. It'll scare the children.

So the snake is not vicious or poisonous after all, in spite of its terrible looks. It's just a fat harmless snake that came out of the lake to lie in the sun.

That there are snakes in the lake is unpleasant news to Pat, though. She had felt safe there until now, in the surprisingly cold water.

Terry asked Pat to continue to see him. They had been together for two years, and she had only known Douglas for a few months.

'How could I do that?' She was genuinely puzzled, even though she had in fact been seeing both men for the few months in question.

'Why not?' He looked cross, at this stage, rather than angry or upset. His face was very white under his reddish hair.

'I don't know. It just seems odd, that's all.' Pat was bored. That was one of her main feelings during this meeting, which took place in a public house on Suffolk Street. It was not as inappropriate as it sounds: they met at seven o'clock and had the upstairs lounge bar to themselves. The barman watched television discreetly in the corner, leaning against the shelves of jewel-coloured bottles.

'Relationships don't have to be so exclusive' was one of the things he said next. It seemed he had a theory about the situation, a compromise solution to which he had given some rational, sensible thought.

This took Pat by surprise. It simply hadn't occurred to her, ever. Relationships with men do not have to be so exclusive, when you are twenty years of age. You are not married to anyone.

You can have more than one friend who is male, more than one at a time.

Is that what Terry was trying to say?

If so, it seemed to Pat that this was the most interesting thing he had said about anything in all the time she had known him. He was clever, he was supposed to be a good judge of situations and character, he was a good rugby player. In addition he was good-humoured. But Pat had never had even one conversation with him that riveted her, or even one conversation that had interested her in any way. And she still believed and hoped that such conversations were possible, that they were waiting there to happen, somewhere in her brilliant future. She still believed that, in the right company, she would be a lively participant in a brilliant, intellectual, sparkling conversation that would illuminate aspects of life, literature, philosophy, history. That for some reason no such conversation had ever come her way in twenty years she attributed to bad luck, lack of the right company. But one of the things she felt, sitting in this pub where wedges of silver dust danced in the evening sun, was that if Terry could provide her with even a hint of the sort of conversation she craved, they'd be all right. They could certainly go on being friends. But then, she thought, if he had done that she would never have 'gone off' with Douglas. He didn't make brilliant conversation, either. But he had so much else to compensate for that lack.

'I don't think it would work,' Pat said, drearily. Suddenly the smell of cigarette ash and beer weighed heavily on her. The seediness that all pubs carry within themselves, no matter how cosy or glamorous they pretend to be, became overwhelmingly obvious. Both she and Terry were drinking Cokes. But they had spent many many hours drinking other things in this pub and others.

'Can't I see you at all?' His face was weighed down with something else. Desperation, disbelief. Guilt struck Pat, but from afar: she heard its waves breaking on a distant shore. That she was the cause of this she did not really believe. That was a real illumination. It was not her fault that he was in love with her. She was the love object, that was all. He thought he loved her to distraction but how could he? In a way all his love was in his imagination and had nothing to do with her.

'What's the point?' Pat had an overwhelming desire to get away. She felt selfish, guilty, mean, horrible. But also cheated. She had done what she believed was wise and right for a girl: she had allowed herself to be loved. She had had a nice safe relationship with someone who was safe and reliable, someone who needed her more than she needed him. In so far as any advice on relationships had come her way, the gist of it had been that Terry was the kind of man to choose. She had taken that advice. She had done what was wise and right and look what was happening now. Disaster, for that nice reliable person. A broken heart for him and a guilty conscience for her.

A guilty conscience, and emotional danger.

Immediately after the encounter with Terry, she went to Douglas for comfort. At that time he was living in a tiny room on Camden Street. It was dark, its one small window looking out into a damp, mossed-over area. She came to him, walking, from the pub. It was summer then too, the summer before this one on the lake. She walked briskly along the empty, sunlit streets. Her head, her body were shadowed by uncomfortable, messy feelings. But above them floated a certainty that she had been brave. She had been loyal to Douglas, and straight with Terry, instead of duplicitous and self-interested. From Douglas she wanted praise for her good behaviour.

But what he said was 'It's your own business.' All her confusion, all her triumph and hope, were deflated. He was telling her then that he was not involved in the plot of her life, whatever she chose to imagine.

She heard him, and understood what he was saying. But she

went on imagining another story for herself, in which Douglas played the leading role.

And they never spoke about Terry again.

When Margaret had started coming to the lake, as a child, the resort had been much smaller than it now is, and more overtly religious. There is still grace before meals (usually the hostess says it in a low voice that does not carry well). There is church on Sunday and no alcohol. But in the old days there was a prayer meeting every morning, and Bible discussion groups in the evening after supper. Both were voluntary, of course, but many people, especially women, attended them. Margaret had attended them, with her mother and aunt.

That is where Jim had seen her, in the little wooden chapel, which is at the end of the village of log cabins. He saw her there one Sunday: he did not go to church on weekdays and he did not go to Bible discussion groups at all.

He saw her on three Sundays, spread over two years, in church. She would have been wearing a floppy muslin or silk dress, with a sailor collar, and a white boater hat, white gloves at the end of bare brown arms. The fashion of the thirties. Her hair was shoulder length, waved like Veronica Lake's, although not that brassy colour, a colour you would usually only achieve with chemical assistance. Margaret's hair was reddish then, what was called sandy. (Now it is the colour of Veronica Lake's, although its texture is different.) Her best feature was her mouth. It was wide and her teeth were perfect and perfectly white.

Jim saw her at other places as well. In the dining hall, of course, and walking around the lake. He must have seen her in the boats, since she went for a row with some girlfriends every evening. He had no doubt noticed her on the beach, in her puckered red satin bathing suit, with its skirt of spotted muslin half-covering her thighs. But he never approached her and she did not notice him at all, until her father told her he had had a note from a young man asking if he could ask her for a date.

A note from a young man!

Even her parents thought it was a little formal and old-fashioned. This was the year 1938.

'Well,' her mother gasped, smothering the suggestion of a sharp, ridiculing laugh. 'I . . . ' She had been about to say 'I never!' Something like that. But she looked at Margaret, eating cornflakes, and stopped. Margaret was clearly impressed. So her mother said, 'Well, what do you think, dear? Will you go on a date with him?'

'James Henryson,' said her father, consulting the note.

'Yes,' said Margaret.

'OK!' Her father shrugged. 'What am I supposed to do next?'

'You'll have to write back to him and say that she will,' said her mother, having trouble suppressing her laughter this time. 'Tell him she will be honoured.'

Margaret stepped in and overruled this. 'I'll write to him,' she said. 'Give me that note.'

She had seen Jim. She had seen him on the golf course where she walked, along the edges of the fairways, with her friend Alison, spying on the young men who played there. She had seen him on the beach, and in the water, where he was a strong swimmer although not better than she was. She had seen him diving from Diver's Rock, a cliff about fifty feet high at the far side of the lake, where the boys went to show off during the afternoons while the girls sewed under the trees by the lakeside or discussed the meaning of the Song of Solomon or Noah's Ark with Miss Simpson and Miss Benson, the two old ladies who organised these events. Some of the girls, though, including Margaret, sometimes skipped these classes They used the time gained to row across the lake to a tiny cove at the back of Diver's Rock. They docked there, and climbed to a stand of trees where they could conceal themselves while watching the young men run and jump from the edge of the cliff. Naked. Jim was one of the very best-looking of those who thus displayed themselves —he looked then very much as Douglas looked now: one of the stars. In men this is not as important, as excluding, as it is among women. I you have the luck to attract such a man, he is not necessarily danger, but a prize you can take if you want it.

Margaret sat there reading his note to her father and feeling, if not thinking, these thoughts. His handwriting was enigmatic: it was elliptical, with long under- and over-strokes. The individual words were hard to decipher, but the overall effect was both very neat and very stylish. It was the most grown-up, the most sophisticated, handwriting she had ever noticed. Her own hand was rounded and clear, a childish style which seemed to betoken simplicity, willingness to communicate, honesty. What Jim's hand told her was that he was self-reliant and determined. She felt she would probably marry him.

The room, Pat's rather than Douglas's, although they are both side by side, continues to be their private meeting place. They do not have real sex, because Pat is not on the pill. This is another problem for them.

'I'll go to the clinic when I go home,' she promises.

He's not pressuring her. But it seems odd to him that they do not make love, make love properly, though they have been together for a long time. Pat is not sure whether it is odd or not. Her feelings about this most intimate of matters are influenced by outside forces. She has left the Catholic Church behind her, already sensing that it is consistently operating against her interests, against all women's interests. But she is not free. Social mores, convention, even the law, exert a considerable influence over her sexual life.

This is still a time when you would not be sure, in Ireland, what other people were doing, as far as sex was concerned. You think you know what people do in England and the Continent and America. They go for it. So Philip Larkin said in his poem.

It began in 1963, bout fifteen years ago. But in Ireland fifteen years isn't long—even if it's a whole childhood—and you couldn't be quite sure how long a fashion would take to catch on. The official line is clear: sex is wrong. The law forbids it, more, or less. Contraception has just stopped being illegal for married people, so they are now permitted by the government to engage in sex whenever they like. But it is still illegal for unmarried people. You can't, for example, buy a condom in a shop or in a chemist's, still less in a machine in a student cloakroom. 'Going to the clinic' means going to an illicit clinic, operating subversively in a cellar in some quiet back street, run by feminists or perhaps English people. It does not mean going to the ordinary doctor. The ordinary doctor is not supposed to prescribe the pill to women who are not married.

On the other hand, everything one reads or sees in the movies or hears in popular music suggest that you ought to be sexually active. All these sources indicate that not having sex is abnormal—a crime against nature. So there are two diametrically opposite attitudes in the air. You can sin against the state, or you can sin against nature. In such circumstances, it is difficult to figure out what real people actually do. Which voice do they listen to? Pat is the sort of girl who wants to do what everyone else is doing—the right thing. But she isn't the sort of girl who would ask them what that is. What could she do anyway? Conduct a survey? Even if you could, the chances are most people would lie about it.

Douglas can be protective of Pat. She is his protégée, here in this strange land, in America. He knows what she is coming from—smallness, complexity, absurdity. Primitiveness. He knows but already he occasionally forgets that other world. Pat herself forgets it: the unheated house with its cheap rickety furniture, the ten-year-old car, the endless obsession with money. The father who is increasingly unable to function effectively even in the world he inhabits, whose old, uneducated country ways don't equip him to understand the mechanics of the modernising urban society he finds himself in. Her mentally ill mother. When Pat arrived in Delaware, a week ago, she and Douglas immediately understood that in Delaware, in America, she would never even have met someone like Douglas. The social gap would have kept them segregated at least until she had firmly lifted herself, by her own efforts, far out of her own sphere. The degrees from the unglamorous Dublin university and her illusions, her dreams, would not have accomplished that lift, as they did, or as she imagined they did, in Ireland. White trash, she probably was, in these people's estimation. Douglas knew it, the day she arrived, for a few days afterwards. It made him tender. He had selected her; he had brought her here. 'At least she's white!' It was a joke, but it was almost the only point in Pat's favour in middle America.

But after a few days they slipped back to their old roles. They forgot that Pat was poor and Irish. She became what she was in Ireland, in college: anybody's equal, Douglas's equal. His classmate in Medieval Studies. His girlfriend. His lover. His enemy.

Amy is at the beach for the early morning swim. A group of boys and girls gathers on the tiny stretch of shingle, laughing and exchanging greetings, like a flock of beautiful seabirds. Army is the most attractive, and she is dressed in an all-in-one, modest, classy white swimsuit. Her tanned limbs show up very nicely against its pristine snowiness. Her hair is tightly wrapped against her head, encased in a rubber swimming cap shaped like a black turban.

Pat glances at Douglas, big and muscular and pale, in his swim trunks which are really shorts. He is not looking at Amy at all. He is looking at the lake, a pale gray in the morning light: it is 6.30 a.m. 'Taking the plunge?' he asks.

'Sure!' Pat has already begun to talk like an American: this process had started before she ever set foot in the country, thanks to Douglas's influence. For the rest of her life she will say 'sure' in the American way, and 'movie' and 'necktie.' It will not be noticed. So many Irish people have picked up Americanisms anyway, from television. Pat seldom watches much television, but who is to know that?

She places one hand in a position to hide the hairs which are showing, horribly, at the edges of her very skimpy brown bikini (the only bikini on this beach), and runs with Douglas to the edge of the water, and then into the water. She is not surprised by how cold it is, having swum in it already, but it is still a shock to the body. Douglas races out a couple of yards, then plunges and starts to swim. Pat would like to walk around, spend ages getting used to the cold, but since she has to do what people do here, and also hide those springy, sexual-looking hairs, she follows Douglas and immerses herself in the cold saltless water.

It is not as cold as it seems at first, and within a few minutes she is comfortable. Douglas is a strong swimmer, he has swum out towards the middle of the lake. The water is now full of swimmers. Everyone is in, ducking and plunging, playing or swimming in a long line like a plane going through the sky towards some invisible destination out in the water. Amy's black turban is bobbing along like a cormorant, making a beeline for—it seems to Pat—Douglas. By now he is a few hundred yards away. There is no question of Pat pursuing him. She will not swim out so far. She has always been taught to swim in towards the shore or parallel to it, and that is what she is doing now. Amy's black turban, other swimming hats, red and yellow and blue, are making their way after Douglas, out to the middle of the lake. She can see out there, far away, a kayak. She guesses that is what he has picked as his destination.

The caps, and the sleek short back-and-sides of the boys make their way to the kayak. Hardly any swimmers are left near the shore, with Pat. She watches Douglas, a speck now, and the other specks in pursuit.

She feels very light, like a leaf falling from a tree. Her head is clearer than the crystal lake water. Gloriously clear, glass, holy water. Light and free.

She swims to the narrow beach, steps up the rough, cutting shingle to the rock where her big white towel (camp property, and so appropriately pure and thick) lies draped. She wraps herself in it, slips her feet into her sandals, and makes her way back to her room.

Just now she feels free. She doesn't care what happens.

In her room she showers, dresses, dries her hair and brushes it more slowly and carefully than usual, backcombing it until it is a glossy crest of gold around her head. She cleanses her face with a tube of cream she bought at the airport, scrubbing the corners of her eyes, the crease of her chin, meticulously. For days she has neglected herself, meaning her skin, her body. Giving herself over to the novelty of the holiday has been more than enough to use up all her resources of energy. Giving herself up to her concern about Douglas, about holding on to him or making him pay attention to her, has been enough. The carelessness shows, at least slightly, in freckles, spots where she didn't even bother to cleanse off makeup at night before going to bed, in the wild frizz of her hair, which is dry and needs conditioning if it is not to go mad. But she is not performing these rituals of cleaning and creaming, of brushing and polishing, in order to make herself more attractive to Douglas. Not really. What she is doing now is what women or girls do from time to time. She is pampering herself. She is restoring her own relationship with her real self, pulling away from that slightly crazed, neurotic creature who has no time for anything, for anything in the world, except one man. Applying a cream called Royal Jelly Face and Neck Moisturizer to her skin may not be the most profound or permanent path to her inner self, but it is faster than any other way she can think of right now.

By the time Douglas arrives back in the house she is sitting against the white pillow of her bed, neat and clean, reading a book.

'What happened?' Douglas has a white towel draped across his shoulders. Water drips to the wooden floor.

'I got tired. I came back.'

'You could've told me!' He speaks angrily but looks concerned.

'You were too far away. I can't swim as far out as you.'

'I was looking everywhere for you. I thought you'd drowned.'

He comes over to the bed and sits on the edge, in his wet swimming shorts. Pat puts her book on the floor and looks at him. She pats his hand, which is still cold from the lake.

'I'm sorry,' she says. 'I thought you'd have guessed.'

He shakes his head in mock disbelief. 'You thought I'd have guessed,' he says in a sarcastic voice. A sarcastic but relieved and friendly voice. Whatever it was Douglas thought he is not going to say, openly, to Pat. Just as he is not going to tell her what he thinks about Amy, or his mother, or anything much. Americans are reputed be open and frank. Innocent, even. But they are no more open and frank than anyone else.

He gives her a warm, wet hug. Then they hurry off to breakfast in the big, beamed hall. Waffles, maple syrup, ham and eggs and sausages and hash browns, French toast and ordinary toast, orange juice and pink grapefruit juice and cranberry juice, cereals, cream, coffee, tea, muffins, bagels. What is on offer every morning. The atmosphere is buoyant at breakfast. The big hall hums with low chat, the sounds of people embarking on a hopeful summer day at the lake.

What Pat remembers is always the same. The name of the lake, which is stiff and upright, old-fashioned, the name of an English king. It is not the only name this lake has. Before it got its very English name, it had an equally unsuitable, very French name, which it had been given by Jesuit priests from Canada. A very

Catholic name. And since the lake was clearly in place before those priests arrived here, it must have had another name too, an Indian name, rough-hewn and exotic as the names of the mountains that encircle it. The Adirondacks. It must have had such a name, given by the Iroquois, meaning something to them or perhaps not. Perhaps a name so ancient that nobody, no scholar, can discover its meaning. For so it is, often, with the names of lakes, and rivers. They have been there much longer than the languages that are spoken on their shores. And the people who lived on their shores had a name for the lake centuries and millennia ago. Those names, lake names, are the oldest words there are in human language, often sticking to the lake, surviving successive linguistic changes. But not so this great beautiful lake stretching from New York State to Lake Champlain. For some reason it has been named at least three times—maybe because it is big and strategic, and successive waves of settlers have needed to claim it as their own.

The name. And the high, stiff dark green trees, fir trees or pine, she still could not tell the difference, that grow all around its long dagger-shaped shore. The higher rocky mountains that strut up into the sky behind the trees. Then the big outcrop of the camp, the old brownish crumbly-looking house with its tendrils of outbuildings

Only after all that does she recall the water, the lake itself—blue glittering, calm. The blue sky overhead. The sun shines all the time she is at this lake, one glorious day succeeds another, and yet the air is fresh, the temperature hot but eminently bearable. She knows that occasionally there must be less perfect conditions here. Maybe it rains sometimes, is cold. But she can't believe that it is so, not really. She has seen the lake only in this amazing light and remembers it as a perfect place, unblemished by meteorological flaws.

It is dinner time. Douglas, Pat and his parents are at their usual table, looking at their small plates of melon balls with mint, a starter which they will eat as soon as the bell rings and grace is said, by Amy. Amy is still in position near the door of the hall, dressed in blue this evening, welcoming the tardy campers with a smile and a nod, nothing in her expression or demeanour indicating that they are holding up the proceedings. That lack of expression expresses more disapproval than any pout or word could, anyway, to those who have the tendency to feel guilty.

Pat keeps glancing over at Amy, when she gets a chance in the gaps in the conversation that is going on, which is mainly a description of an outing Jim and Margaret have made to a museum in the mountains. The Adirondack Museum. Pat will have to go there, Margaret says. She will find the Native American artifacts, the illustrated history of the mountain area, fascinating. It includes a replica of a big Indian lodge, and several kinds of totem pole. Charcoal burners' huts, trappers' cabins and their tools. There is a film giving an account of the history of the lake region from the earliest times to the present day,

Jim talks about Davy Crockett. Or is it Daniel Boone? Pat gets the impression that Davy Crockett lived in the Adirondack Mountains, because he was a trapper who fought the Indians, like a lot of people here. (Later Douglas, complaining about his father, lets her know that Davy Crockett came from Tennessee and died in Mexico, at the Battle of the Alamo, fighting Mexicans with his bare hands.) Jim is not interested in the historical facts anyway, but in the stories. He tells a tall tale, the kind of tale associated most closely with Davy Crockett. It is a story about an encounter between a grizzly bear and Davy Crockett. He is telling this because he thinks Pat would be interested in it, and also because he is himself amused by these stories, which his own grandfather, the person he loved and admired most in the world, used to tell to him when he was a child. He does not tell Pat this, thinking it is less important than the stories themselves, as far as she is concerned. There he is wrong, of course. It is what surrounds these tales, which are somehow silly, that would ignite some interest in her. As it is she smiles politely, laughs unconvincingly, as she tries to think of some suitable response 'That's a really good story,' she says sometimes, weakly. Or else she asks for clarification of some point, some clarification that she does not need. Were there a lot of bears hereabouts? Are they still there? Questions to which she knows the answers perfectly well.

Jim has not got to the end of his story when a commotion breaks out at the door, or what passes as a commotion in this intensely polite environment. A strange man has entered the hall. He is dressed in shorts. Nothing unusual there. Every man in the room is dressed in shorts, even now, for dinner. But his are different, crumpled and dirty, and instead of wearing the plain white or blue or lemon polo shirts that all the other men wear on top he is wearing nothing at all. On his head, nevertheless, is a baseball cap, back to front, which he does not bother to remove.

In addition, he is black. He is the first black person Pat has seen in the camp, she realises, although without much of a jolt—she has hardly seen any black people at all since she came to America, after the first half-hour at the airport.

As soon as they see this person Jim and Margaret cast down their eyes and start to eat their melon balls. The bell has not been rung, grace has not been said, but they do this anyway. Pat starts to eat to obediently, but Douglas doesn't.

The man is saying something to Amy, who looks flustered. But within seconds other men, men who clearly have some management function in the camp but who are usually invisible, have moved up to the door and are engaged in conversation with him. Amy has disappeared—not disappeared, she is at her table at the head of the room, chatting animatedly to her

companions. It is obvious from the way she is talking that she
has something vitally interesting to say.

Before the main course is served they find out.

'They've found it,' Jim says to Douglas.

'What?' Pat has no idea what they are talking about.

'Oh nothing,' Margaret says. 'Some body.'

Meaning a corpse. It was found not in the lake but in the
forest. A girl had vanished ten days ago, one of the Muffins. The
black man—he was soon followed by some state troopers—had
found her corpse when he was picking blueberries in a stretch
of forest up the lake earlier in the afternoon. She wasn't buried,
just covered by some branches and pine needles.

Pat asked Douglas if he had known about this, and why he
hadn't mentioned it.

'We didn't want to worry you' is the first answer he gives.
Then he shrugs and says, 'Anyway what's the point in talking
about it? It's one those things.'

One of those things the Henrysons didn't talk about.

While Douglas was home in the States, during the first month
of the summer, and Pat was still in Ireland, she had gone to a
barbecue on a beach near Dublin. The barbecue had been set
up in the marram grass and camomile that grew at the back
of the beach, and a camp fire had been lit on the beach itself,
on the rough-grained, silvery sand. Many people Pat had been
friendly with before she had met Douglas were at this party.
They were either friendly in a distant way, chatting briefly to
her but looking suspicious, or overly hearty. 'Long time no see'
was something three different people said, at different times.
'Howdy stranger' was what the girl who had thrown the party
said. In general there were no hard feelings. They were young,
optimistic, forgiving. Not competitive. Grudges had not had
time to take hold and harden, as they would later.

Terry was at the party. He came late. Pat had already drunk

quite a lot of beer, and eaten several sausages and burned, delicious hamburgers, when he appeared on the path that ran behind the grass. It was almost dark at that stage. She was listening to a girl strumming a guitar and singing a song called 'Happiness Runs', a song with just these two words which she repeated hundreds of times in her high, tuneful voice. The words were rolling across the sand down to the waves breaking softly, but in a strangely abrupt way, on the shingle. Beyond the sea was spreading a milky, mild, darkening blue. A floating lighthouse flashed on the horizon every few minutes. The fire flames flickered.

Terry saw Pat before she saw him—in fact he had been tipped off by the hostess, if that's what she was. She had rung him and asked if he minded, she had asked Pat. He, being Terry, said he did not mind. But he wondered if it might have been more tactful of her to have asked him first, before she had already issued the invitation to Pat, instead of warning him not to come if he didn't want to risk seeing her.

He did not seek her out. He did not sit beside her. Instead he went and joined another group, a group that had congregated around the steel barbecue. They were somewhat noisier, drunker, than the people at the fire. They sat on the prickly grass and threw sausages at one another.

When Pat went to get another burger, she saw Terry. All he did was nod and smile. He did not even say hello. She returned to her spot by the fire, feeling chastened.

Something was happening in her relationship with Douglas at this time, even though he was not in Ireland. What was happening was that he was not writing to her, or telephoning. He had been gone for five weeks and in that time she had had one letter, although she had written several.

She was supposed to be going out to have a holiday with him in August, two weeks from now. Her ticket was paid for. This gave her a sense of security. How could he turn her away after encouraging her to buy a ticket? But although she believed a ticket so expensive would have to be used, could not be cancelled, she was apprehensive. He would have to get in touch with her before she left for America. He would have to confirm that he still wanted her out there, make arrangements about collecting her from the airport. Even if he did write to deal with these issues, what was going to await her when she got to America?

She sat at the fire and thought of this problem.

Later, she went and talked to Terry. He was talkative, as talkative as he had ever been, and not angry or in any way upset. It was as if nothing had happened. They had never had an intimate conversational style, there were no codes, no private jokes, between them: somehow their lack of common ground, their mutual lack of imagination or initiative, ensured that. Their lack of chemistry ensured it. He was like one of the many boys and men she knew slightly, her friends' boyfriends, her classmates, people she had known for years but with whom she could never have a real conversation. So far, in her experience, the only boys she could have a serious conversation with were boys she had at some stage been attracted to. With all others, some sort of barrier to conversational intimacy existed. With Terry that barrier still existed.

Why, then, did she put her arm around him, invite him to kiss her?

Habit, probably. And probably to test him, to find out if he was still there for her, if all failed with Douglas.

That was something she had not told Douglas about. The party at the beach. The fire, the mild sea. Her attempt to seduce Terry, to test him, just in case. Terry had returned the kiss, but then had walked away and had not come back at all.

Douglas told her a bit more about the murdered girl after they had said goodbye to his parents, and were driving back to Delaware in his big car—a Buick or an Oldsmobile, some car like that, bigger than any Pat had ever been in.

'She was a Muffin. Kelly Guildford. She was raped and then strangled.'

'By whom?' Pat is still interested in this story. Her interest seems, even to herself, prurient and vulgar. But it's there. And it seems to be inspired not so much by a curiosity about the details of the crime itself—which are, after all, fairly commonplace, and anyway not the kind of thing she takes any interest in—as by the circumstances. It seems so impossible that a Muffin could be assaulted in any way in this puritanical, sweet, precious, protected place.

'They think maybe the guy who found her.'

'The black guy?'

'Yeah.'

'Why would he report the thing?'

'I don't know. How could I know? It's what they're saying.'

'Who is saying?'

'The guys at the camp. My father. Amy. All that lot.'

Amy. But she doesn't care any more about Amy, who is stuck at the camp until the end of August and who lives in Washington, DC. She is still more interested in the dead Muffin.

'How did she get into that forest? Did she go there herself?'

'I just don't know,' Douglas snaps, gritting his teeth. His face is tight, strained to breaking point by his impatience with Pat and with everything about this holiday. 'What does it matter? She's dead.'

Pat wants to know. She wants to know how something as cruel and passionate as a murder, rape and strangling, could have occurred in such a sanitised, genteel place. There is something she does not know about that resort, she feels now. There are aspects to it that have been kept hidden from her, by Douglas and Margaret and Jim. They have all pulled the wool over her eyes.

Margaret goes for a walk in the woods. She goes alone, early in the morning before Jim wakes up, before the young people, Amy and that lot, are out for their swim. The sun has just risen over the mountains, and the lake is spangled, black and gold and red. The hush of the forest is deeper, cooler than usual, a dewy chill under the trees. She moves along through them, through the pines which are high and bare as telegraph poles, long long pines, the foliage high above her head. Occasionally she hears a shuffle, a flurry, as something flies or runs.

She walks far into the forest, as far as the place where Keli Guildford was found. She finds the spot where she was buried, or covered—it is marked by a little rope barrier, red flags. The police and the forensic people haven't finished their investigations.

It is not different from other parts of the forest. You can see that the soil has been disturbed a bit, the pine needles brushed or moved to make a heap. Otherwise there is nothing, apart from the signs by the police, that anything unusual has happened in this place. Once the flags are removed, there will be no sign at all.

'Where were you?' Jim is on the veranda, drinking coffee, when she comes back.

'I went for a walk,' she says brightly. 'By the lake?' He looks at her curiously.

'Yes. I saw the sunrise,' she says. He gives her coffee, and they sit in their rattan chairs, looking at the lake.

'I don't think they will stay together,' Margaret says abruptly, without preamble, as she bites a muffin.

'No,' says Jim, unconcernedly. 'I guess not.'

'He's not in love with her,' Margaret says, calmly. 'I don't know why he invited her over, really. Poor thing.'

'Well, these things happen,' Jim says. 'It'll all work out.'

'I'm glad we were able to do this for her. Give her a holiday here, at the lake.' Margaret smiles, genuinely pleased.

'See Lake George and die,' says Jim.

Pat sees her and Douglas as tied by an elastic band. A longish elastic band, wrapped around them like a cat's cradle. It stretches this way, it stretches that way. He pulls away, stretching it to a taut rubber wire, ready to snap unless she moves forward. It is her job to keep that band flexible. It is her job, because Douglas does not even know it is there, he does not see it at all. That is what it means to be a young man. He is a young man of definite preferences, a deliberate, careful, pure man, the only kind Pat could feel anything for. But that means he has other things to do, he has no time to watch the progress of his relationship, to analyse and prod and test and know, and to remain silent. The watchful one will have to be Pat. That is the price she would have to pay to keep the connection going. She would have to be eternally vigilant.

She did not immediately know she cared about Douglas, even after the party at Rain's flat, and the kiss. A thing like that could happen. You could kiss someone and no more need come of it. That is what Douglas himself anticipated, and the thought relieved him but made him gloomy. He was very lonely then, alone and friendless, spending long evenings, weekends, alone in his gloomy flat while people in college believed he was going to hunt balls. Rain had said to Pat that she knew his type. 'He knows his cocktails,' she said, with a shrewd grimace. She told Pat that he went hunting in Kildare at weekends and was on terms of friendship with the aristocracy of Ireland, people the college crowd hardly knew existed. But she was wrong, they all were. Douglas was so isolated and beaten down that he did not believe that even Pat would stick with him.

A few weeks after Rain's party there was another party, hosted by the English department for its postgraduates. Douglas was not invited, since he didn't do English. He was sitting in the library, working, while the party was going on. But many of those who belonged to Rain's crowd were present. They drank wine in the common room and talked to the lecturers and professors, something they considered to be a treat. Somebody started talking about love, as people were wont to do. It was the subject that interested all of them more than any other. It was indeed the subject of many of the lectures, the courses, they attended. The study of medieval literature was the study of love. Some of those present in the room believed that romantic love had been invented in the Middle Ages (they were the ones who did French).

But even those who would question a theory that so limited the spontaneity of humanity were interested in the topic of love.

Soul mates. In the corner they were talking about soul mates.

'Of course,' one of the professors said. 'Fine. But my soul mate could be somewhere in South America. What use is that to me?'

The man who said that looked old and thin and disappointed. His wife was at his side, and did not react to his remark.

My soul mate could be in South America.

Pat saw, in her head, Douglas, sitting at his table in the postgraduates' library. She saw him, his head bowed over his books, engaged in the slow, painstaking work they all did: translating Insular Latin or Old English, checking every word, mind bent to the rigours of the task—the arduous, noble, old-fashioned task of learning an old language that most people in the world didn't care tuppence for. He gave himself to that hard work, as she did, without knowing why. They had risked a lot for old languages and literatures, just because they loved them. That they had in common. And now she knew he was there, alone and lonely, when she was enjoying herself, drinking wine with the professors, talking about soul mates.

A huge wave of longing, a wave of pity, overcame her.

Her soul mate.

Abruptly, she left the party, and ran along the long, dark corridors to the graduates' room.

He was there. It was ten o'clock and the whole vast college was empty. But he had waited, hoping someone—she?—would come.

Douglas's thesis is written. He has finished it more quickly than had been expected, during the summer. Already he has sent it to Dublin. He will come back to take a viva in September. But after that there will be no reason for him to remain in Ireland.

He tells Pat this now, on the way home from the lake.

'What are you going to do then?' She wants him to tell her everything. What he is going to do then, and then, and then. She wants to know. That he is going to ask her to come with him to America. (It would have to be a marriage proposal. She is not going leave home for less. They both know it.)

But he tells her nothing.

And she can't ask. You can't ask a man like Douglas about the future. You could hear something very upsetting.

They are driving down the Northway Route, on the way back to Delaware. The lake is behind them—for ever or maybe until next year, until a few years down the line. She realises something about the camp. Temperance.

'Is it a temperance camp?'

'I suppose so, something like that.'

Something like that. It's not Methodist, it's temperance. That's what united all of those nice people. Jim and Margaret and Amy. An aversion to, a lack of interest in, alcohol. Pat had noticed no drinks but had not thought about it. She already knew the only cocktails his family drank were eggnog, cranberry juice with soda. At the resort, the word 'temperance' had never been used. Why should it be? Maybe in America you are more aware of the strategies people use to insist that their own culture is the norm than you are in Ireland where most of the population colludes to shut out everything that seems alien?

They have the radio on in the car.

Rich music floats out into the crystal air, the dark green forest. Dory Previn is singing a song about a man she knows—probably André Previn. 'I know I know I know I know,' she sings, tragically. I know his face and his hands and his eyes. I know him out, I know him in. I know his lies. I know I know I know I know.

Pat in the passenger seat, Douglas driving, the music floating around them, the dark pointed evergreens. She loves this. This where she wants to be. In the passenger seat, zipping along a wide blue highway, listening to a song that seems to her unbelievably true, a song she feels she could have written herself. The song of a woman who has given herself to love.

Suddenly the song is stopped. The fruity voice of an announcer breaks in.

Elvis has died.

He died this morning, this very morning. News has just come in.

Douglas and Pat are too young to have known Elvis as a star for themselves, if they ever would have listened anyway. The Beatles, they have experienced, just about. Douglas likes Peter, Paul and Mary. The Byrds. Joni Mitchell. Pat likes Simon and Garfunkel.

Still. They know what he looks like.

An icon for their age, or the age before this one.

A diversion.

Pat observes Douglas's worried face, and feels a momentary relief. That he is shocked by the death of Elvis bodes well for her, she thinks. She does not know why, but she feels that it gives her some leeway. He will be easier on her for a while now, because of this tragedy. Tragedy that will be talked about. Talked about a lot, if they listen to the radio, watch television when they get home. It will divert his attention, and make him feel that having a woman in love with him is not the worst thing that could befall a man. Maybe he will understand what Pat needs? Maybe he will forgive her for not being good enough, perfect enough? Tell her what his plans are, that they include her? Maybe all the mistakes that surround them, soon may overwhelm and destroy them, will somehow vanish in the light of the greater tragedy, in the sticky sweetness of the Elvis songs?

The radio plays Elvis songs all the rest of the way to Delaware.

Long after this summer, when Douglas has disappeared from her life for ever, Pat meets Rain at a conference in Ottawa, where Rain has become a professor of Medieval History. She is very plump now, but still has a youthful, striking face. She is sharper than she was as a girl, and more impatient. Pat is still very thin. Her hair is fuzzy rather than wavy now, and is dyed a mixture of blond and brown. Her teeth are still crooked but they are her own. She became a schoolteacher in the end, and teaches English, but has kept up her medieval studies, writing occasional articles and belonging to some learned societies. She did not get married and neither did Rain.

She talks to Rain about Douglas, and asks her if she has met him since they were all students together. Rain hesitates before she lies. Pat waits, wondering what sensational report is in store—Douglas has been in a coma for ten years? Douglas is on death row? Douglas is dead?

'He's a professor,' says Rain eventually, and names an Ivy League university. 'He did well. I'm surprised you haven't come across him.'

Pat, annoyed, mutters that she has lost touch with the academic grapevine. She reverts to the safety of the past, and tells Rain about the summer at the lake.

'Well, you probably had a lucky escape,' Rain says, in her

husky, mellow, comforting voice. 'It would never have worked out.'

Of course it would, thinks Pat, even more irritated. How can an intelligent woman like Rain utter such a flaccid banality? Pat firmly believes that if she had handled things differently, if she had manipulated the situation subtly instead of clumsily, she would still be with Douglas. The people who get what they want are those whose controlling touch is so light as to be undetectable to the innocent, not those who are themselves genuinely innocent.

'And you're happy anyway, aren't you?' Rain asks, with an uneasy crooked smile.

Now it is Pat's turn to hesitate. She pauses, and in the pause, she remembers everything that matters: the snake, thick and roughly scaled, coiled like a cake on the hot wall. (By now she knows it was a rattlesnake, one of America's most dangerous reptiles, not a water snake at all.) She remembers painting the bunch of broom, and feeling pleased because, entirely without effort, she had managed to give her picture life and flow and energy. She remembers the flowers on their long swaying rough stems, the paint wet on the thin paper, the old teacher in her flowery smock encouraging the motley crew ranged before her. Old men and women, Douglas and Pat, side by side, concentrating on their pictures. The pine trees, the silvery lake, a backdrop to the jug of yellow blossom. The morning sun hot on the nape of her neck.

'I am quite happy,' she says, realising that it is true. Nothing in her life has worked out according to her original plan. She did not marry Douglas, or Terry, or anyone. She abandoned her academic career as soon as it began. She is not rich, or powerful, or important. But in the mysterious borderland that separates dream and reality, the gap called 'anyway,' she is happy—more or less.

The Banana Boat

WE'D BEEN ON HOLIDAY for a week, in a summer cottage in west Kerry. The weather had been glorious. Every day the sun shone, blessing the landscape. I had been sunbathing on golden strands, swimming in clear blue water with views on each side of moss-green hills rolling into the ocean, or walking along lanes lined with flower-studded ditches—purple self-heal, blue sheep's bit, everywhere the brilliant yellow of dandelion and buttercup. The typical outdoor sound had been the buzzing of bees. It had been a honeyed landscape and a honeyed holiday.

Our two teenage boys had not been enjoying it much, however. John was sixteen now, and Ruan fourteen. John was only happy when on the golf course. He would play thirty-six holes, on his own, staying away from morning until dinner time, coming home pale and exhausted under his tan. He refused to play with Ruan, claiming that his game was not good enough. Ruan denied this but in fact he had other fish to fry: computer games. All day he would spend close to the television set, controlling a hand-held pad and watching cartoon figures jerk around the screen to the sound of a monotonous tune. We had a constant struggle to get him away from the games, to encourage him to spend some time outdoors. The struggle dominated the holiday. He did not want to go for a walk, he did not want to go for a swim. We, of course, had bought the machine that seemed to control his life, but we blamed him for his addiction. How could we have foreseen that it would lead to this?

One thing was clear: this would be one of our last holidays as a family. Next year they would probably refuse to come with us.

After a week the weather forecast promised a break. We

would have a showery day. Usually when the RTÉ meteorologists forecast a showery day it meant heavy rain where we were, out on the southernmost tip of the Dingle Peninsula. Mists were always rolling in from the Atlantic, hitting the hills of our parish and falling on us as rain, even when the rest of the country enjoyed sunshine or at least sunny spells. I suggested we go on an outing to Tralee, where the weather is often better than it is out here and where there is a big swimming centre, with pools and slides and all kinds of amusements. The response was not exactly enthusiastic, but eventually both boys agreed to come.

The weather forecast was wrong: next day dawned bright and sunny, just the kind of day we had grown used to. The swallows were fluttering around, chirping, high above the meadow in front of our house, and the island lay in a pale blue sea like a basking whale, complacent and enormous.

'It's a good day for golf,' John said sleepily, turning in his untidy bed. 'Do we have to go?' Yes. We have to go.

John insisted that he wouldn't go for a swim. I thought he might change his mind when we got to Tralee, and packed his swimming togs along with everyone else's. We piled into the car, lightly dressed, and set off, me driving as usual. At some stage in the past ten years this had become normal, although when I had married I did not know how to drive and Niall did.

There is bickering in the back of the car. John continues to insist that he won't go for a swim, and Ruan retaliates by saying that he won't go if John doesn't. 'OK OK!' I say, since there is nothing else to say. But this begs the question of why we are going to Tralee at all.

'We can go to the heritage centre,' I say, 'You haven't been there, Ruan, have you?'

'I hate heritage centres,' he says.

'It's got a little train that takes you on a trip through history,' I continue. 'Tralee through the ages.'

'For fuck's sake he's fourteen years old,' says John.

'Must you use that word?' Niall sighs deeply and switches on the radio.

Veteran of family holidays, I just switch off my ears and concentrate on the road.

I love driving along the narrow roads, with the fuchsia branches dripping onto the sides of the car. There is a lovely, lustrous light falling on everything—hazy blue hills across Ventry Bay, olive green hills closer. It is so beautiful, in this sunshine, that you could believe it was real. It surprises me, in a way, that the boys seem so uninfluenced by the surroundings. But as far as one could tell nature has absolutely no effect on their moods. If anything, it annoys them. They don't seem to see scenery in the way I do. So what are they seeing, as they stare out the windows, scowling?

'Did you turn off the oven?' Niall asks.

'Yes,' I say confidently. But of course how can I be sure? 'I think so anyway.'

Why should he ask? I remember then that two years ago we left the house—the same house—and came back two hours later to find the kitchen filled with thick black smoke and the oven on the point of bursting into flames. We managed to put it out and since then a new cooker has been installed.

'I don't think it would matter anyway,' I say. 'This one wouldn't go on fire even if it were left on. That old oven was filthy and covered with grease. Plus it always overheated—the thermostat didn't work.'

I believe this and I have absolutely no reason to suspect that I have left on the cooker or the oven. I'd been washing up—we have an optimistically planned washing-up roster and today is my day—and had been close to the oven for long after we'd finished cooking Ruan's breakfast fry. Still, the question makes me uneasy. And it opens up uneasinesses that are never far from my mind.

The holiday has been working fairly well, so far, but nevertheless I have often been assailed by worries. Niall believes this happens because I am a compulsive worrier, but I believe this happens because there is plenty to worry about. I worry about my job, back in Dublin. I worry about what is going on in my absence, things I have forgotten to do, things I have done—this always happens on holidays, especially on holidays in Ireland where there is not enough going on to blot out the memories of work. The details of the worries vary from time to time but the anxiety remains the same. I worry about money, pensions, the future. I worry about my elderly mother. I worry about Niall, who is also elderly, or getting there, older than me. That he could become ill, that he could die, is always an idea conducive to a good old worry.

Sometimes, I think that this must be the root of all the worries, and is the reason why I cannot be quite at peace. We are having a wonderful life together, just as we are having a wonderful holiday (when we forget that the boys are hating every minute of it). But I am somehow conscious of the threat of mortality putting an end to it all. Death hovers somewhere around, lurking in the corners like the mists that are always somewhere out there on the Atlantic, sweeping towards us on the wind. Maybe it is because of this that I am always afraid that the rug of my joy can be pulled from under me, that the whole delicate edifice of my domestic happiness will suddenly disappear. The structure of our secure, contented life seems to be held together by some magical charm. But I worry that at any moment that charm may lose its subtle, intangible power.

Maybe that is it. Or maybe it's much simpler. That I'm premenstrual, or premenopausal. I'm never quite sure if my worries are rational, or simply the result of some physical imbalance. Mind, body, reality: worries are thoughts but they are not like plain, unemotional thoughts. Emotional thoughts, they can have their origins in various places, or in more than one simultaneously. Stop worrying, men say. Niall says. The boys even say this. Nothing is going to happen. Everything is going to be all right. They do not believe in God, but they believe in the steadfastness of the spell that protects ordinary lives, whereas I believe in nothing. Or perhaps it is not that, but that as males they are naturally brave, naturally carefree, naturally insouciant. 'You have nothing to fear but fear itself' is one of Niall's mantras. 'The coward dies a thousand times, the brave man once' is another. These sayings always encourage me for a while, and then they lose their power.

Niall wants to buy a table for the bedroom, so that he or I can sit there, at the window, and write, while the children watch television in the living room. As we drive down from the Connor Pass I suggest that we turn off at Castlegregory, where there is a furniture store. Once, years ago, we bought a little suite of Dutch furniture there, big chunky wooden armchairs with wide squat armrests, covered with dull purple velvet. The memory of that suite of furniture does not attract me to the store, but I know that Niall will jump at the chance to visit it. I guess that his desire for the workable will outweigh even his innate dislike of digression and changes of plan. And I'm right.

'What a good idea,' he says cheerfully, smiling across the gearbox.

'What?' snaps Ruan from the back of the car, more alert than one might imagine. 'We're turning off at Castlegregory?'

'Maybe we could go for a swim there later?' I suggest wildly. 'We could rent out boats and things at that water sports centre.'

'But I don't want to rent out boats and things,' says Ruan, not unpredictably.

'Me neither!' John chimes in automatically. At this stage his grumpiness has become lukewarm. His dismay at the way the day is developing is so immense that even his normal supply of negative energy has diminished.

A certain amount of half-hearted, uninformed complaining about the articles for hire at Castlegregory water sports centre goes on in the back seat, as we drive along the flat road between small fields and gardens overflowing with flowers: nasturtiums, geraniums, roses tumbling abundantly over lawns and fences, a horticultural counterpoint to the abundant wild flowers of the landscape. Before I have actually turned off the main road for the village of Castlegregory, however, Ruan has performed one of those miraculous U-turns of which he is still capable, at fourteen. He has decided that he might like to go for a swim at Castlegregory. Probably he remembers previous swims during previous summers—the water around here, in the flat sandy stretches of the Maharees, tends to be considerably warmer than on the other, more rugged side of the peninsula. Maybe that is what has caused his change of mind, or maybe it is something else that he has remembered, or spotted on the roadside. One never knows but is grateful for even the slightest co-operation.

The village of Castlegregory is pretty in the way of Dingle, with pastel stuccoed houses and plenty of windowboxes on its three narrow winding streets. But the hordes of tourists who swarm up and down the streets of Dingle are lacking here. Two women wearing shorts and T-shirts, bronzed to the colour of toffee, stroll along the footpath dangling plastic bags of shopping. Otherwise the village seems as deserted as an off-beat Italian hill village at midday. You might assume, if you did not know otherwise, that the natives were all taking a siesta or a long leisurely lunch, and that come four o'clock the village would buzz with life.

We see a pub, painted pink, with a lot of geraniums dangling outside and a sign saying 'Seafood. Pub Grub'. It's called the Natterjack Inn. Inside, it is pleasantly furnished with pine and súgán, and the menu looks right. Like the village the pub is deserted.

We sit in a large conservatory, open on two sides to let plenty of air in, and furnished in a higgledy-piggledy way with old wooden tables, benches, some comfortable straw-seated súgán chairs. There are flowers and potted plants dotted around it in an odd assortment of tubs and skillets and pots. In one corner is a pool table. The boys' eyes light up when they see it. They get some coins. The balls crash out. They are happy for a while.

There are crab claws on the menu and Niall and I order them, while for the boys there are chicken nuggets and chips. I get a glass of white wine and Niall a beer. We sit and sip these drinks, the sun shining through the perspex roof. We talk about the natterjack toad. The barman tells us that yes, Castlegregory is one of its few remaining habitats in Ireland. If you walk down the lane opposite the pub until you come to a lake, you can hear the toads and even see them sometimes, at eleven o'clock at night. The barman has often done this. We wonder if it is worth coming back at eleven o'clock some evening just to hear the croaking of an endangered toad. As I sip the wine and feel extraordinarily happy, I think that it probably is. But I do not make a plan, knowing I might be forced to stick to it if I do. Even in my mildly inebriated state, I am not optimistic enough to hope that John and Ruan will put the natterjack toad high on their list of holiday priorities.

When the crabs come they are great: the biggest crab claws we have ever seen. They taste quite good too. Not perfect, but, given the sunshine, the flowers, the happy chatter of the boys, the wine, I am more willing than usual to pretend that they are perfect. For the price, which is low, it is a fantastically good lunch. We sit and munch and sip, and I feel that this is what a holiday should be: a family enjoying lunch in a sunny conservatory, with a colony of natterjack toads within walking distance and the wine cool and good.

At night, Niall and I go for walks sometimes, just to escape from the noise of the television, which tends to fill the house.

Last night we walked down to the graveyard, which was cleaned up by some youth employment scheme a year ago. We recalled that when we had last been in it the long grass had been treated with some weedkiller which had turned it straw-coloured and had created an eerie effect: long drooping hay draped over stones and walls and everything, like a surrealist vision of Golgotha. Morbid grass.

This year, all that is gone. The grass has grown back, and already it is long—apparently the employment scheme does not extend to ongoing maintenance. The old sign outside warning that the ground is uneven and that the graveyard contains ruins is still there. We went inside and looked at the first, most elaborate grave, which is that of Tomás O Criomthain, the Islandman. *Ní bheidh ár leithéid arís ann*, his most-quoted sentence, is engraved on the headstone, which stands sturdy and tall against the backdrop of the island where he lived, whose inhabitants he was referring to. Our like will not be found again. In the quiet of the graveyard the words regain some of their meaning, which has been diluted by overuse outside (you hear this saying everywhere, you read it on T-shirts in Dingle; if there is one sentence every Irish speaker knows, it is this one.) There in the graveyard, however, I accept the truth of what he said, looking at the other, older, more poignant graves. Seán O Dálaigh OS. Died 1944. He was a writer who used the pseudonym Common Noun. His son was Niall's best friend in the parish. We often went out on Sunday nights with him and his wife Peig. Both of them are now dead. Almost all the natives of this parish are dead, although not in these graves. The valley is full of houses, but mainly they are summer houses, populated by people like us from Dublin or Cork, from Germany or America. The houses are busy for a few weeks, a few months, of the year. The rest of the time, empty. There must be more empty houses in this valley than anywhere else in Ireland—and still the sign SITE FOR SALE is ubiquitous; still the builders are busy making new white houses, the well-drillers steadily boring into the rock for water.

The graveyard has been improved. You can walk through all of it now, which you usen't be able to do. We passed the Islandman's grave, and Common Noun's, and turned the corner at the back—it is a tiny graveyard, containing only about thirty stones. Down at the back the ground is uneven, and pocked with holes. I looked into one of these—morbidly, wondering if indeed I would see what one might expect to see. And yes, I did. There were some sticks that might have been bones. I stepped back and got a better view. Then I saw the skull, framed by a V-shaped bit of stone—not stone, wood, the V-shape being the surviving bit of coffin. Everything else had rotted away, apart from a little cowl to shelter the head. Even most of the bones of this skeleton's body seemed to have disintegrated, or to have mingled with the dust that once covered him or her—there was no headstone so we didn't find out who it was.

Close to this grave is the grave of Bride Liath, with its sad, sentimental lines: 'Is anseo a luíonn Bride Liath, an cailín is gleoite agus is deise a mhair riamh ar an saol seo'—*Here lies the most beautiful, virtuous girl that ever walked the path of life.* A famine victim. There is a story about her, burying her three little children and then her husband, one after the other. Then dying herself, of starvation.

After lunch Niall and I leave the boys playing pool and walk to the furniture store. It is farther away than we think, since previously we have driven there. We get a good look at the village of Castlegregory, and wonder again at its beauty and its neglect by the tourist industry, which is capricious, unjust, and in a way not very intelligent—unless it is that everyone wants to be where the crowd is, which be the case. When we eventually reach the shop a sign informs us that it is, surprisingly, closed on Fridays. Today is a Friday.

We decide, more or less by a mutual consent possible thanks to the pleasures of the Natterjack Inn, that we won't bother going

to Tralee, but simply have a swim here and then go home. We
drive out to the beach, one of the flat, sandy beaches of this area,
backed by dunes and caravan parks. It always seems very light-
hearted and gay to me, and indeed it is the sort of place where
families with small children come for a beach holiday: the sky is
wide and blue, cotton clouds floating around airily over the pale
green rushes and marram grass and clipped grass of the caravan
parks, and places to park the car.

'It's nice, isn't it?' I ask.

'Yes, if it weren't for that strange building down on the
beach,' says Niall. 'What on earth is it?'

That's where we're going. It's the water sports centre. It's not
a building, it's a collection of paddle boats and surfboards, water
bicycles and banana boats, canoes and bodyboards—all the sort
of thing that makes my heart sing, maybe because I longed for
such playthings during a childhood of summer holidays but
only read about them in children's books. These things look
attractive to me and to Ruan and John, but I suppose if you did
not know what they were they would constitute a blot on the
landscape, and look like some sort of exceptionally offensive
fish farm.

We park and go down to the beach. The tide is in and there
is only a narrow stretch of sand, with plenty of people already
sitting on it—plenty by Irish standards, that is, where having
the whole beach to yourself is not unusual. We find a place
close to the rocks and settle in. John says, 'I might go for a swim
later.' Niall reads the newspaper. Ruan puts on his togs—which
this year consist of shorts and a T-shirt, and look exactly the
same as what he wears all the time anyway—and says, 'Give
me some money. I want to rent out a surf bike.' I am delighted
that he is interested enough to do this. I give him a few pounds
and he runs off. I am pleased that he is old enough to take care
himself of the transaction involved—he can make the enquiries,
do the hiring, go off surfing. All I have to do is provide the cash
and take it easy.

I put on my own swimsuit, and think about getting in. John doesn't change his clothes, but sits and stares moodily out to sea. A so-called banana boat is taking half a dozen children on a ride. They sit astride a longish banana-shaped tube, and are pulled by a motorboat which goes increasingly fast. When the boat makes a sudden turn all the children fall off the banana into the water; we can hear their screams of joy or whatever, their laughs as they scramble out of the water and try to regain their seats on the banana.

Where is Ruan?

'There he is,' I say. The part of the beach where the windsurfing and water biking goes on is separated from the part where we are by a string of buoys and a sign saying 'NO PLEASURE CRAFT BEYOND THIS POINT'. It is not too far away but much too far to distinguish an individual's face or even clothing. There are lots of pleasure craft bobbing around there—thirty or forty at least, it seems, several with children on them, peddling or paddling or surfing. I am pretty sure I can distinguish Ruan, however. I can tell the shape of his body, or perhaps it is the way he holds himself; rather stiffly and determinedly, his back straight and his head down. He is making a beeline for the horizon, which also figures—he probably thinks he is a bit old, at fourteen, to mingle with the smaller children who cycle up and down by the shoreline. Actually the bay curves out in a semicircle so that even as you go out to sea the shoreline is not too far away—I discovered this when Ruan did the same thing, i.e. went out too far, a year or two ago. I ran along that semicircle shouting at him to come back in. I feel he is old enough now to take care of himself. Anyway, there are lots of paddle boats and surfers around where he is. After a while he turns and makes back for the shore and then he goes out again towards the mouth of the bay, and back again.

I sunbathe for a while and then, having observed an older man (older than me, I mean) swimming with obvious pleasure,

I go down to the sea. There is a fringe of brown seaweed on the edge of the tide, and I realise that there is no hope of getting John to come in. That brown fringe will deter him, if nothing else does. He is unafraid to die, but he is squeamish about squelchy substances. I wade through the soft obnoxious stuff, thinking, as I always do when I walk in seaweed, of a working holiday I spent on the Frisian Islands when I was a student. They are situated in a shallow, sandy zone (Erskine Childers wrote his novel *The Riddle of the Sands* about that area—I think I should try and read that novel sometime) and people walk on the flats in their bare feet for the sake of their health. *Wattlaufen*, the activity was called—something like that. The theory is that the oils or the vitamins from the seaweed sink into the soles of your feet and do you good. I suppose the seaweed baths at Ballybunion—which I experienced last year—are based on the same idea. Anyway these reflections take me through the brown mess which certainly looks rather unattractive, and into the clear greenish water.

It feels colder than I remember it, not any warmer than the sea at Ventry or Smerwick, where I have been swimming recently. Maybe this is related somehow to the tide. But it is not painfully cold, and this is the test for me now. If my feet don't ache from the cold I know the water temperature is reasonable. I plunge in immediately, and start swimming. It still surprises me that I am doing this. All my life I have been one of those swimmers who waits for a long time, walking around and paddling the water with my hands, before getting down to it. I was like this as a child and continued until now, when I am forty-five. I remember being amazed at John who, when he still went for swims, ran in and started swimming straight away, not making even a break between his run down the beach and his first strokes in the water. In fact I can see him running down this beach and doing just that, as I sat on the towel at the rocks where I can see him now, reading the newspaper. Niall seems to have fallen asleep. He is hardly visible because he is wearing green trousers and a beige and brown shirt. Camouflage. They are his favourite colours. He always blends in easily with nature, and there he is now, no more obtrusive than a clump of grass or a bramble bush. John in his turquoise shirt is easier to spot.

I get accustomed to the water very quickly and as usual I have a wonderful swim. The broad bay is rimmed with mountains— greeny lilac mountains, Binn Os Gaoith, Cathair Chon Roí, the Sliabh Mis range. I remember a poet telling some story about Mis at a conference I attended earlier in the year. Mis, some goddess or poetess, some mythical creature, lived in these mountains. I couldn't remember the story. I didn't like the name Mis, either. It sounded sneaky, and perhaps sexual, it sounded like an Irish word for some soft, secret enclave of the female body. Soft seaweed.

The water is clear as glass. I swim along, looking through the water ripples at the rippled sand beneath. Ripple, lap, plash, paddle. Back and forth I go, looking up occasionally at the rim of mountains, at the umbrella of blue and white sky, looking in at my husband and son on the beach, looking over to Ruan, still peddling furiously in and out, in and out, peddling away all the anger of the holiday and his teenagerhood.

I stay in for about a quarter of an hour or twenty minutes, then plod through the seaweed and back to the towels. I spread one out and lie down to dry in the sun.

Some women have taken the next spot. I can hear them talking as I lie there. What I catch is the end of a recipe, cooked recently for some party or celebration.

'I did a bake,' the voice says. 'You know, courgettes and peppers and everything with breadcrumbs and cheese on top.'

'Mm, sounds lovely,' another voice says.

I wonder what they had with it. The conversation fragments. 'That green top you had on looks lovely on you,' I hear. There is some discussion as to which green top is meant. 'I went home and watched a video for three hours last night, until three o'clock in the morning.' I wonder where. Was it one of those caravans back up behind the beach? Or a rented house? Or a summer house, like ours? 'That fellow from *ER* was in it.' George Clooney? John Carter, my favourite, young and noble-looking, standoffish?

There is a summer house on the coast visible from the window of our summer house. Even now if I stretch a little I can see it. Gray walls with a touch of blue—the woodwork, a lovely faded blue, the blue of the summer house in the garden in *A Passage to India*. A slated roof, sloping in four slopes over the house, rather than the usual two back and front. Hip-roofed, that is the term. It is a beautifully proportioned house, perching, as it seems, right on the edge of the coast, with nothing behind it but the sound and the hunk of the island. There are no other houses on that side of the road. You can't get planning permission to build there. But the bungalow—it is always called 'the bungalow', as the island is always called 'the island' - was built before that rule came in, perhaps before there was any such thing as planning legislation. It was the first summer house in the valley, which is now chock-a-block with them. Built in the twenties or the thirties, it is a reminder of more gracious times.

But although it looks perfect from a distance of about half a mile, the bungalow is really a ruin. The roof is beginning to cave in, every window is broken. Nobody has stayed in it for forty years.

Once it rang with laughter. Or quarrels. Or songs. Niall remembers visiting there in the 1950s on his first trip to the valley. He remembers a little girl—she now lives in America, and owns her own summer house in this valley—reciting 'The Owl and the Pussycat' in the middle of the kitchen. He remembers helping a local farmer to tie straw on to the seat of a chair, helping him to pull the rope taut. He thinks the house was beautiful inside, simple and rustic, with lots of books. It belonged to a professor of Irish and Greek, and his family and extended family spent long summers there long ago.

It is the oldest summer house. But it did not survive beyond a single generation—a long generation, it is true. Is this the fate of summer houses? People build their own, bring their children, come faithfully to their house for forty or fifty years—ours is already thirty years old. And what then?

The people of Long Island or Martha's Vineyard, of the Frisian Islands, of the Swedish archipelagos, could probably tell us. They have had a summer-house culture for hundreds of years. But I don't know. There is only one old summer house in our valley, and there it stands, a gracious ruin.

I look over at the pleasureboat enclosure. We've been here for about an hour. It's half past four. Niall stirs and asks if we will go home soon.

I look over at the boats. At first I can't see Ruan. Then I catch sight of him. He is moving out again. He seems to be cycling faster than previously and soon he is going out farther than he went before as well. He passes the last of the big paddle boats, and is out among the wind surfers. Then he passes them. He is beyond the mouth of the bay, well past the curve of the beach. He is out, alone in the sea, on his surf bike, still moving quite quickly.

'Look at him, he's heading for Tralee!' I say, a bit anxiously. I can see Fenit far away, miles across the water.

'Stupid eejit,' says John.

'Do you think he's all right?' I ask Niall. Niall can't see him at all.

'Of course he's all right,' he says. 'But it's time he came back. I want to go home.'

I keep my eye on Ruan—on what I think is Ruan. He gets smaller and smaller. Then he disappears—the banana boat is moored out there, about a kilometre out, a speck from here, and he seems to be behind that.

I give in to my anxiety and run to the lifeguard who is sitting in front of a hut close by.

'I think my child has got carried out to sea,' I shout at him. He seems unalarmed. But he asks me if I see him and I show him what I think is Ruan—a far-off speck in the bay. It could be just an empty boat, or a lifebuoy, or any of the many objects that are bobbing about on the water. He looks through his binoculars and says, 'He's on the banana boat. You should go to Johnnie over there'—he indicates the sports centre hut—'and ask him to do something. He could send out a boat.'

I run along the beach, passing the families sunning themselves, making sand castles, picnicking. When I get to Johnnie's I am quite alarmed. But the woman there is calm. 'There's a strong offshore,' she says. I am impressed by the professional abbreviation. 'Don't worry. The boat has already gone out to pick him up. There's a few of them out there. The offshore takes them out on days like this but we keep an eye on them.'

I see a small orange dinghy out at the banana boat. It takes a long time to do whatever it is doing—utterly invisible from where I am. But I feel relieved. Everything is being taken care of.

'What's his name?' the girl asks—she is a cheerful, competent-looking young woman with a kind face, and a mobile phone.

'Ruan,' I say. She repeats it and then asks someone on the phone if the boy in the boat is called Ruan.

'He's not?' I hear her saying. I feel real fear then. 'What does he look like?' she asks me. I tell her. Blond. Blue eyes. Smallish. As I say these things I realise how useless they are as a description. The description could apply to almost every boy on this beach. What should I say. Nose a little flat and broad, like mine only smaller? Mischievous grin—no that wouldn't do. They all have that and he probably isn't grinning mischievously now anyway. Crooked teeth—I should get him to an orthodontist very soon. If . . .

I realise right now that there are two ends to the story, two ends to the story of my day and the story of my life. I think of Mary Lavin's story about the widow's son, which I have recently seen told dramatically and well by a professional storyteller. In one version, Packy is killed as he collides with a startled hen as he cycles home from school with the good news that he won a scholarship (the equivalent of the lottery for bright children in those days. I remembered, even as I stood on the sunny beach wondering if my child were . . . all right, the day I got my own results from that scholarship exam). In the second version of the story, Packy is not killed but the hen is. Packy's mother nags him so much about the killing of that hen, which was her prize hen, or perhaps it was a prize cockerel, that he leaves home in anger and disgust a few weeks later and is never heard of again. The message of the story is that the loss you suffer through no fault of your own is much easier to bear than the one you bring about by your actions.

But it's going to be more ambiguous than that.

I should perhaps have come here with Ruan, booked his bike, warned him not to go out too far. I thought he was wise enough, at fourteen, to take care of himself. But I had misjudged him. I had misjudged the situation—the offshore wind, the vigilance of the water sports centre. I had misjudged everything.

'Where do you think he is?' the woman asks the man on the phone. I can see him nowhere. I think he is the boy on the banana boat, the boy who is now in the rescue boat. That is the boy I had my eye on, the stiff-backed, determined body that I think is my own body replicated, and also Niall's body. But if he is not Ruan, as they say, I have no idea where Ruan is. He could already be far out at sea. He could be at the bottom of the sea.

She talks to a young man who has suddenly appeared beside us. 'Tell him to find Ruan,' she is telling him urgently.

I am not shaking. I am suspended in a sort of jelly. The water is full of happy children and fathers (mostly it has to be said) paddling around, laughing and having a good time. The beach is golden, with its holiday-makers, its bronzed boys and girls, its bikini clad-mothers passing on recipes for vegetable bake, its toddlers making sand castles. Normal life. And I am part of it still, but only just. I am on the edge of a cliff. In a minute I could tumble off and fall into another kind of life altogether. A life of pain and tragedy. Loss and mourning. Funeral arrangements. If . . . The long aftermath of life without Ruan. Unimaginable.

It happens.

On Friday a girl was drowned in a swimming pool in France. An Irish girl I mean. Aged fourteen.

Yesterday a man was drowned in Bray, near where we live in Dublin. On our beach in Dublin.

Piet Sayers lost several sons to the sea. Everyone on the island did. A commonplace tragedy then, not so commonplace now but it happens. It happens all the time.

One moment a family is cocooned in the happiness of normal life. The next it is elsewhere, in another land or another ocean. It happens in a few moments.

Those are the few moments I am in, the liminal time between ordinariness and tragedy (also of an ordinary kind; to others it will be so, ordinary and instantly forgettable. While for me it will be *the* tragedy—the raw edge of the unimaginably terrible. Parents never get over it. I have seen it. I have heard it. I know it).

'So who have you in the boat?' The young man is on the mobile phone. 'Well ask him, John. Ask him for Christ's sake. Ruan. Ruan. Ask him to tell you his name.'

There is a pause. In that pause I see in my mind's eye the small stiff determined figure making his way to the banana boat. In that second.

'His name is Ruan,' the young man exclaims. 'You gobshite, John!'

The young man turns to me. 'You're all right. He's in the boat. You should have called him some ordinary name like John or Michael for Christ's sake!'

I laugh and make a joke. I touch the young man's arm in gratitude (he doesn't like this; we are both practically naked but I hardly care).

I wait for a long time. What seems like a long time. Fifteen, twenty minutes, before the rescue boat comes to the shore. Ruan scrambles out, pale and cold-looking, and swims in the last bit of the way over the fringe of brown seaweed to the beach, which is stony down here and now looks sharp and sordid to me, with its rows of plastic machines, its pleasurecraft.

There is another story on my mind as I drive home. 'Miles City, Montana'. Alice Munro. A story about a near-drowning. The narrator's daughter Meg has a close shave in a swimming pool. She is rescued because her mother has an intuition as she walks towards a concession stand (what is a concession stand? some sort of kiosk, I suppose) to get cool drinks. *'Where are the children?'* flashes through her mind. Back she runs, just in time. Is it intuition or just a mother's natural, normal anxiety?

I think the point of the story is that a child who is looked after in the normal way, by parents who are protective, and normally anxious, tends to be safe and survive, while a child who is neglected . . . There is another, remembered boy in the tale, a boy who drowns. I could remember the description of his retrieved body, grotesque, with green weed in his nostrils. Usually in Kerry bodies are not retrieved, but perhaps that is not the case right here, Tralee Bay. It's more sheltered than the broad rough heartless ocean that stretches in front of our house, that beats eternally against the rocky shores of our parish. It's about that, as well as about the power of a mother's intuition.

I had no intuition. Just anxiety. I saw him. I saw him moving faster. I saw him being swept out. I admired him too, for getting off the bike and on to the banana boat, which was moored and big. The banana boat was exactly the right thing to head for. Of course I knew it was him, I recognised the way he carried his body. I recognised the way he cycled on a water cycle, as you know someone's way of walking. That's not intuition. It's familiarity. A mother's familiarity—Niall and John apparently did not recognise this at all. I knew it was Ruan, on the banana boat, in the rescue boat. Even as I was terrified to death, even when the friendly young woman's voice revealed alarm and said Ruan was not in the boat, but some other boy, I had a suspicion, in a deeply rational part of my mind, that the distant speck had the familiar shape of Ruan. The bits of the jigsaw that I had seen told me it was so.

He would have been saved anyway. The boat was on the way out before I reported the thing to the water sports centre. He was never in real danger.

That's what he said himself. In fact he insisted he was in no danger at all, that he had deliberately cycled out to the banana boat because he wanted to sit on it, that he could easily have cycled back. So why did he come back in the rescue boat? He had two answers to this. One was that the man in the boat offered him a lift. The other was that his 'go was up' (the bike was rented for an hour) and that the man wanted it back.

So maybe the man in the boat was a good psychologist? He was casual about the whole trauma, making little of it, to protect the macho feelings of the teenage boy. To protect his own feelings, as a businessman and owner of a water sports centre, competing with a strong offshore wind.

Ruan refused to talk at all about his experience, and was unusually cross and angry as we drove home.

Along the flat sunny roads of the plain, up to the alpine drama of the Connor Pass, down again to Dingle, and home. Home.

As we went along by Ventry Bay, I remembered the day we had found the kitchen full of smoke. Accidents. We could go back now and the house could be burnt to the ground, if I had in fact left the oven on—and I could have. I am increasingly absent-minded. I thought it unlikely that this would be the case. Just as I had, when the girl said 'It's not Ruan in the boat?', known that it was Ruan, because I knew that speck on the banana boat was a speck I recognised. Ruan. I felt that we still belonged to the lucky section of humanity that does not fall over the edge, usually. We still belonged to the charmed circle that may get an occasional premonition of disaster but does not actually experience it head-on.

And sure enough as we turn into the long grass of our field it's clear that the oven was not left on. The house is still standing at the end of its field, waiting for us to open the door and sleep there.

We are still safe. Alive and safe. We still belong to real life, the life that is uneventful, the life that does not get described in newspapers or even, now that the days of literary realism are coming to an end, in books. The protected ordinary uneventful life, which is the basis of civilisation and happiness and everything that is good: the desirable life. We still belong to the part of life that is protected from danger, by its own caution, by its own love, by its own rules, by its own belief in its own invulnerability. Usually.

But how reliable is that 'usually'? In a minute it can be swept away, on a freak wave, on an offshore wind, by a fast car or a momentary lapse of concentration. It is precarious and delicate, our dull and ordinary happiness, seeming sturdy as a well-built house but as fluttering and light as a butterfly on a waving clump of clover. As ephemeral as that; as beautiful and priceless.

Ruan's close shave happened on 16 July 1999. I thought about the event and wrote these thoughts down late that night and then fell asleep beside my husband in the wood-panelled bedroom we have shared, on holidays, for twenty years. In Fairfield, New Jersey, John Kennedy Junior, his wife and her sister were just taking off into the sunset in their Piper Saratoga 11 HP, on their way to a family wedding in Martha's Vineyard—the famous holiday resort five thousand miles from Dingle on the opposite shore of the Atlantic. An aviation expert, Mr Serge Roche, some days later described the Saratoga Piper as 'reliable.' By then, the newspapers were full of speculation about what had happened, and why John Kennedy Junior, his wife and her sister were at the bottom of the ocean.

Illumination

I WAS SPENDING THE summer at an artist's retreat in the hills on the west coast of America. The house where I lived was a brown wooden building, sheltered by a grove of pine trees where bobcats had their den. My room was large and plain and comfortable, with a wooden ceiling, a desk, an easy chair, and a wide bed covered by a blue patchwork quilt. A small balcony faced east to the rising sun, and in the mornings I sat there and read. Hummingbirds, like large insects, stood in the air near my head, making their sound which is more like a whirr than a hum. Rabbits looking like pictures cut from a children's pop-up book nibbled at the grass in the garden below, where agapanthus, shasta daisies and orange nasturtiums bloomed. And climbing up the wooden wall to the balcony railing, was a rambling rose bearing small pink roses which had no smell. All around me were layer upon layer of undulating hills, smooth and rounded, their long grasses the colour of pottery left too long in the kiln. Here and there among the dry hills were dark green stains, cool and inviting as oases. That was the forest. Redwoods, exotic pines, oak and arbutus, which here is called the madrone.

At night the coyotes barked, and the bobcats screamed, and it was said that a mountain lion roamed in the hills and sometimes came down to the house where the artists lived and worked. But no one had seen it for a long time. During the day, one saw only rabbits, and hummingbirds, and flowers. In the forest, hiding among the trunks of the redwoods, furrowed deeply like sticks of chocolate flake, small deer who would run, startled by the walker, and bound along the woodland trails as if on springs.

In the mornings, I wrote, sitting by the window, and spent an hour sitting outside on the balcony, beside the pink and scentless roses, catching the sun before it moved around to the south and the west sides of the house. I wrote a novel, doggedly, without hope or despair, trusting that sometime the work would find itself, although my experience told me that with novels this does not always happen. In the afternoons I went for a walk in the hills or in the woods, and in the evenings I read.

There was a good library in the house, warmly coloured, with dark wooden shelves, and a few thousand books, many left there by previous residents. The collection of biographies was particularly good and after a while I understood that the original owner of the house had been married to a biographer— her own works formed part of the collection, but there were many other lives there, captured between two covers. The Lives of Isak Dinesen, of George Eliot, of Anne Sexton, Sylvia Plath, Franz Kafka. I read, some swiftly: Anne Sexton, whose life was not edifying; Sylvia Plath, whose story we all know too well already. The other great writers had led longer and more varied lives, though all in their different ways were very strange. In the end, Isak Dinesen, or Karen Blixen, the lion huntress of Copenhagen, with her hooked aristocratic nose and intolerable snobberies, her incurable syphilis, tragic love affairs, and ridiculous fantasies, seemed the most balanced and normal. Such biographies make me wonder if an ordinary, sane person, lacking any stunning eccentricity could be a writer at all?

I was not alone in this wooden house. There were, during my month, two others in it, one a Chinese man of a very sweet disposition, a painter of abstract pictures. He had a studio in another building at some remove from the house, and went there in the mornings to make his paintings, which consisted of beautiful kaleidoscopic images built of thousands of minute coloured segments. They suggested fairgrounds, roller coasters, childhood, golden memories broken down into a million fragments. When he spoke about them it was in a stream of associations—he might mention macaroni, Taormina, the sea, Paris, Plato, Frida Kahlo, Ingmar Bergman, rice pudding, Shakespeare, Woody Allen, Avedon, strawberry ice-cream, all in one long intricate sentence. At first I tried to keep up with his train of thought but soon I abandoned it, realising that I could not go into that mysterious labyrinth and follow the thread to its meaning. Also there was a woman from Germany, Friederike, a composer who spoke very little. She spent the whole day and most of the evening in her studio, playing the piano, creating music which, I think, represented alienation and disconnection, the absence of harmony characterizing our world. Its randomness. There were many long pauses in her music and Li, the Chinese artist, told me that one of her compositions consisted only of fifteen minutes of silence, fenced between two single notes.

When he was not talking about his work, Li talked about food, in which he was very interested. He was an excellent cook and made delectable meals for the three of us every evening—not just Chinese, but Indian, French, American. He would go into the kitchen at six o'clock and by seven thirty an array of dishes would be laid out on the counter, ready to be eaten. Salads of chicory and baby tomatoes and feta cheese, homemade breads, spicy curries, or grilled fish or meat. Sauces of indescribable deliciousness, tart and sweet. We shared a bottle of white wine every evening, but he drank just a small glass.

When our meal was over, Friederike would go back to her studio of silence and I would retire to the library and read the stories of Karen Blixen, Anton Chekhov, William Trevor: the old masters. I knew I should pay attention to more gritty contemporary writers but once I had started on the clear sentences and meandering thoughts of Chekhov, the flowing fantasies of Blixen, once I had been transported on one night

to the idyllic summer woodlands of a Russian dacha painted
in Chekhov's water-colour prose, and on the next to the cool
slopes of the Ngong hills, embroidered like regal tapestries,
to stories which captured the essence of life in fifteen pages,
I could not revert to the urban jangle of irony, menace and
gruesome crime which is the stock in trade of contemporary
fiction. It would have been like moving from Beethoven's Fifth
Symphony to one of Friederike's pieces, with its jabs of sound,
its long silences, its love of dissonance.

The truth was my life was not dissonant, but whole and fulfill-
ing, while I was here in the golden sun-washed hills, with the
Pacific Ocean beating on a distant shore, with the merry hummingbirds and the sombre redwood trees, the dark library and
the bright meals. But it lacked what I had hoped to find here.
Brilliant insights into life and literature. An answer to a question
I couldn't even articulate, I had no answers to offer myself but I
had hoped to sit at the feet of philosophers, listen to discussions
that Plato might have organized, symposia where the dialogue
itself led to the solution of the problem, or to some great discovery. All my life I had been waiting for some answer to come
to me, from the conversation of others, or from a book, or from
the clouds themselves, or the sunlight on the ocean. And as yet
this had not happened.

My housemates did not like to walk in the woods, or in
the hills, or anywhere, Friederike preferred to do gymnastics,
and Li was afraid of mountain lions. The chances of being
attacked by a lion are one thousand times less than of being
struck by lightning. Li knew this—it was written out in our
guidebook—but he still did not want to take the risk. It would
be such a painful and messy way to die—although possibly, I
said, possibly not as painful or messy as being killed in a car
crash. But so terrifying, he said. We could both easily imagine
the moment when the victim sees the face of the lion, those

ferocious tawny eyes, the huge teeth bared within inches of
one's flesh. We could hear the deep growl, the deadly scream,
and feel the bottomless fear they would arouse, which would be
much worse than the pain, than death itself. The long golden
grass which grew abundantly on the slopes surrounding us, the
scrubby green bushes and the dense redwood thickets, provided
miles of hiding places for the canny lion. Li could imagine
them, everywhere.

'To him I am a mouse. Have you seen a cat take a mouse? I
do not want to be treated in that way.'

I thought, it would be worse. Noisier, for one thing. But
maybe to the terror the mouse feels it would be the same. That
is one of the many things I should know, as a writer, but can't:
how it feels to be a mouse, at the gate of the cat's mouth.

But anyway I didn't believe so much in the lion, and I
walked on my own, in the afternoons, between three and five
o'clock. Then the sun was still warm, which I liked, but my
day's work was done. I had a few favourite walks—one up the
golden hills to the top, from which I could gaze down over the
hills that rippled out to the coastline—in its habitual shroud
of mist there was always, from the high vantage point, a strip
of white foam visible, like a trimming of white fur on a winter
hood, on the far-off beach. My other walk led into the depth of
the woods, through colonnades of the ridged redwood trunks,
ferny groves, a babbling creek. I would see snakes, occasionally
hearing the menacing jingle of the diamond-patterned terror.
Deer. Red-tailed hawks and the beautiful harsh-voiced bluejay.
But never the mountain lion.

About a week into my stay at the cottage I followed a new trail.

In a clearing in the wood—known as the picnic grounds,
although nobody ever picnicked there—I noticed a gate which
I had not before observed. This was not surprising, because the
gate was constructed of logs, old and clothed with that pale

green moss that hangs on the oak trees, a strange dry lacy green which looked like something that would grow on an ancient coffin, or like the cobweb veil of a skeleton. The gate opened easily and I found myself on another track through the woods. I decided I would walk on it for ten minutes to see if it led anywhere of interest, then turn back—I didn't want to get lost. Mobile phones did not work here, and my companions would never find me if I failed to return to the house. Perhaps in a day or two Li would phone for help, but the woods, I knew without experiencing them, would be another world once darkness fell, a world where the coyote and the bobcats ruled, and the mountain lion. As I lay in my bed I heard the noises of the night—barks and howls and hoots and screams. It was comforting to lie tucked up under the patchwork quilt, watching the moon gleam coldly over the branch of the fir tree outside my window, and listen to the nocturnal symphony. But I did not want to be a member of the orchestra that produced it, or to hear it at closer range.

The trail went, slightly downhill, through the forest for about half a kilometre, through an avenue of tall redwoods, sentries to the gravel drive. I glanced at my watch. Eleven minutes had passed; something rustled in the leaves, and there was a quick scurrying sound in the undergrowth. I considered turning back but I went on.

In front of me there was a wide clearing. Nestling in the back, stretched out like a sleeping dog, was a white house, low and long. Behind it and around it a sheltering half moon of tall dark trees. There was a colonnaded porch all along the front of the house, and a stretch of lawn where shasta daisies and agapanthus grew, just as around our house. But this lawn was much bigger and so green and soft it looked like emerald silk, not grass. At one side was a swimming pool, open to the sun. Somebody was swimming and on the side of the pool were two women, one reclining on a lounger and one sitting at a poolside table.

I went over to them, realising that I seemed like an intruder.

As I came closer they both stared at me. The woman at the table was a middle-aged woman, dressed in a white blouse and beige skirt, and the other was young, wearing a spotted bikini, brown and yellow. They did not look frightened.

'I strayed off the trail,' I said. 'I'm sorry.'

I introduced myself, and told them I was staying at the artists' cottage, that I was a writer of fiction, and walked every day in the woods, for exercise and inspiration. The latter was not true, because the woods never inspired me, although I liked them well enough.

'Sit down. Have some lemonade, you must be thirsty.'

The older woman's voice was kindness itself. Her face was heart-shaped, like the chocolates you get in boxes made for lovers on Valentine's Day, and the irises of her slightly slanted eyes were of an unusual hazel colour, bright and penetrating. She wore gold framed spectacles, and her tawny hair was swept off her face and caught in a big tail at the back of her neck. She had exceptionally neat ears, which I noticed because they were studded with minute black earrings. Her name was Ramalina.

The younger woman's name was Isabel, and I assumed she was Ramalina's daughter. The person swimming in the pool, who had not stopped swimming, *was* her son, she told me: Marcus.

Isabel wrapped herself in a yellow silk wrapper, and sat at the table while I drank my lemonade. She was beautiful, with long black hair, eyes of a similar shade to her mother's, but with rounder and with more penetrating pupils. Her skin was smooth, and her lips thick and rather pale.

They lived here, the three of them, all year round, although this was an area mostly inhabited only during the summer.

'We have an apartment in the city,' Ramalina said, 'but we only go there for the Christmas shopping. We just seem to like it better here.'

'What about you?' I asked Isabel.

'Oh, I stay here too,' she said.

'You don't go to college?'

'No,' she said, and did not offer a further explanation.

I felt clumsy, as if I had been rude to ask such questions, although they had asked me a few, and in most company such questions would have been no more than polite meaningless words.

The swimmer climbed out of the pool and, dripping, came up and shook my hand.

'Marcus,' he said. 'How are you?'

As if I were an invited guest.

He was older than Isabel—brown and very slim, he looked at least thirty to me, or even older. He had reddish hair, like his mother, but of a darker shade. It was cut very short, in a sporty style, and this made his ears look exceptionally large, by comparison with hers. His feet, I noticed, were small and small toed, for such a tall man.

'Got to go up to the house,' he said. 'But call by again. Come to dinner.'

'Oh yes, please do, my dear,' said Ramalina.

I muttered something about not wanting to intrude but she pressed me, and her invitation seemed so heartfelt, so warm, so motherly, that I accepted it. I would come to dinner the next night.

Li had not heard of them.

'Lots of rich people have houses in this neighbourhood,' he said. 'It's probably some family from the city, on holiday here.'

'They live year round. The girl doesn't even go to college.'

'I'll ask around,' he said. 'I'll ask Kim.' Kim was the director of the program, who called to see us twice a week, and brought provisions from the town.

The following evening I went down the trail at about six o'clock. The sun was still warm on my bare arms, but the countryside was changing gear. The hummingbirds had gone to wherever hummingbirds go—their nests, presumably. One or two sudden flashes of blue indicated that some jays were still about, and their sharp squawks occasionally darted from the branches. The rabbits were out, eating the grass as if they were starving, and in our garden two small deer chomped doggedly at a hydrangea shrub, systematically stripping it of all its flowers and leaves.

The forest was cold and shadowy. Every moment the undergrowth rustled and the branches whispered. White owls hooted, animals cried. The walk to the picnic ground took an eternity. I considered turning back, and I do not know why I did not. Because I had promised to come to dinner? It was not that—Isabel and Ramalina and Marcus would wait—perhaps. Soon they would realise something had happened, they would dine, shrugging. Perhaps they had already forgotten that they'd invited me? That was very likely. The invitation had been warm, but whimsical. No doubt Ramalina was always issuing such invitations, knowing that most of them would never be taken up.

It was not fear of disappointing them that kept my feet on that forest path; it was my own fear. I did not want to give in to cowardice. On and on I went, my heart in my mouth, the primeval screams of the forest in my ears. We have always feared the forest, for it holds in its heart the wild creations of our nightmares, the flipside of our daylight selves, the threat of unimaginable madness. Our instinct is to overcome that threat and that fear, to tame or kill it. Karen Blixen, walking around her manor house at the foot of the Ngong Hills, didn't worry about prowling leopards. Even when she did not have her gun she didn't fear them. So why would I run in terror from a harmless forest, where a lion had last attacked hundreds of years ago, an unfortunate child of the Ohlone or the Miwok, who had lived in their grass huts in these mountains long ago, hunting and dancing and painting pictures which have vanished now forever from the face of the earth, and creating stories and songs, which have also vanished.

Finally I reached the house. And although it was still light the shadows cast by the trees made the roof dark, and in its windows lights fluttered. Nobody was on the lawn or the verandah or by the pool, which had that lonely tearful look swimming pools get at night, when the revels of the day are over. I walked up the wooden steps to the front door. It was half open, so I knocked and then walked in.

The hall was dappled with puddles of coloured light, deep red, ochre, flowing through a stained glass window on the landing above. There was a table made of polished applewood against the panelled wall, and on it a glass vase filled with fat pink roses, whose fragrance filled the room. Through an open door the sound of piano music filtered. I followed it and there in the drawing-room Ramalina and Isabel sat in the French window, while Marcus played the piano. I did not recognise the piece and it was mesmerising, and his playing seemed as good as that of the most professional pianists.

As soon as I entered the room Ramalina stood up and came to greet me, with a warm embrace. Isabel did not get up from her rattan chair, but she smiled and said hello, and her smile seemed full of genuine welcome. Marcus stopped playing and turned to grin at me.

'It's so great that you could make it!' Ramalina said.

She was wearing a white blouse again, a high necked Victorian one, and a long skirt of old gold silk which almost swept the floor. Isabel's black hair was piled on her head, and she was dressed in a black cocktail dress, short and girlish, showing off her long tanned legs. It looked good on her. Since I'd been walking in the woods, where snakes and ticks abounded, I was in my jeans and hiking boots. I had put on one of my nicer tops, in honour of the occasion, but I felt clumsy and rough around the edges, like a workman who finds himself in the drawing-room, to collect his wages after repairing the plumbing. Even Marcus was wearing a white shirt, and pale chinos, looking every inch the lord of the manor at rest. Ramalina sensed my unease, with her natural tact and thoughtfulness, and offered me some house slippers, which I accepted. I thought they would be the big flat shapeless fit-all-sizes slippers that some people have in a basket at their front door, but they were not. Silently, with a downcast look, Isabel handed me a pair of red moccasins, beautifully embroidered.

I slipped them on.

'They fit!'

'Yes, I thought this would be your size.'

Ramalina, it was, who smiled.

Isabel and Marcus at that moment exchanged the most fleeting of glances, and for the only time that evening I felt a prick of unease, although my feet had never felt so comfortable.

We ate immediately, in a dining room at the other side of the hall, a room of perfect proportions, beautiful furniture. On the wall hung a painting of a woman reading a letter, her face, circled by a white linen hood, the pale porcelain of the pictures by Vermeer, the dusky folds of her skirt so skilfully painted that I could feel the thick pink velvet under my fingers. So quiet she was, so absorbed in her reading, a reading that had happened hundreds of years ago and was still happening, here. The back of the white page was all the artist let us see, and a hint of a red seal, but there was no other clue as to the content of the letter except the gentleness of her eyelids. Beside her stood another woman, holding a gray bucket exactly like a bucket I had at home, and dusting a picture. She also held a letter, or perhaps an envelope, in her free hand. A small dog looked on, as often in a Chekhov story.

'What is it called?' I asked.

'*The Letter*,' Ramalina answered. 'It's anonymous.'

'Dutch?' I ventured, although I am often wrong about these things.

'Yes. From the Golden Age of Dutch painting.'

I nodded, pretending to know when that was, not sure about the dates. Seventeenth century probably. That is a century that I always feel is out of reach. That rich stillness of the uncluttered interiors. The durability of the clothes—ermine, velvet, linen. The strange porcelain complexions, skin the colour of bone. The eighteenth century I can grasp—we have the houses, and the sense of humour is familiar. The nineteenth seems like yesterday, and the Middle Ages like my schooldays. But the seventeenth is another country and this reader of letters, this bearer of buckets, belonged there. The startling clarity of the image made it simultaneously familiar and discomfiting, like a picture of one's mother's kitchen translated to the iconography of dreams.

The table was laid with silver and white linen napkins, two silver vases of lily of the valley, my favourite flower, decanters of white wine and red wine and iced water. Other food waited on a large trolley, in crockery bowls—salads, rice, vegetables, spiced chicken and lamb rolls. Fresh homemade bread, herbal, was beside it. The food was warm and seemed to have been placed on the trolley just moments before we came into the dining room, but there was no evidence of other people in the house, no cook or servant. Nor were they referred to. The food seemed to have been prepared in advance, by Ramalina, but she did not claim credit for it. In a way it seemed to have appeared without agency, although this could not have been the case. Of course, it was delicious, and the wine was smooth and lovely, from a local vineyard.

We talked about the area and the artists' centre where I lived, about what I was working on—a novel, a novel that was going nowhere. They asked me about my life at home and I told them what I wanted to reveal. I told them I taught literature sometimes, and lived in a house in the country, and would publish my novel next year, if I finished it. I did not tell them I was married, or that I had two children, aged fifteen and seventeen, who wondered why I had left them for a month and come away, nor did I mention that my last two books had received terrible reviews, been universally hated, and that my life as a writer was probably over now. And they did not ask any prying questions, but accepted what I told them as if it were the only thing in the world they wanted to hear and accepted it as if it was the complete truth.

When dinner was over, Ramalina and Isabel cleared the table and told me to sit in the front room with Marcus, and relax with a liqueur or a cup of coffee. Although Ramalina delivered this instruction in her usual warm and soft purr, it was an order; I would have liked to help with the washing up—I would have liked to see what the kitchen was like—but I followed Marcus back to the drawing-room, where a small log fire was now burning in the grate. Darkness had fallen; the big windows were black pools; branches and shrubs shuddered against them. The owl was hooting, a siren of loneliness, and in the distance an animal growled. Marcus went around and pulled silk curtains across the windows, shutting out the wilderness. He poured coffee and drinks and we sat by the fire and talked.

He told me about his music. He played the piano and the saxophone and the organ, and composed for all three. Sometimes he left the house and performed at concert halls in the city and all across the country, and he had been to Germany and England and France and Sweden and other places far away.

'But I prefer to compose here; here I work best. I can't create music anywhere else. The walls of the house inspire me.'

He laughed at his own pomposity but it was clear that he was speaking the truth.

Now that we were alone together I could see that he was

forty, at least. Could he be Isabel's brother? Ramalina's son? She looked about fifty, too young to have mothered this man. But she had introduced him as her son.

In this room, sipping the cointreau, smelling the roses and the pine wood in the fire, it seemed vulgar and inquisitive to ask such questions, even in one's own head. The atmosphere was so harmonious, so perfect, why try to disturb it with requests for facts and information? Anyway Li was going to make those inquiries. Back at the lodge, inquisitiveness would not be out of place. It would be natural there, in that world of rougher edges, less fine sensibilities.

Ramalina and Isabel spent a long time clearing up after dinner, an hour at least, which passed easily in Marcus's company. He told me music was the most important thing in the world, and he was happy with his compositions so far, but he knew his best work was yet to come.

'I don't know exactly what it will be,' he said. 'But I'll know it when I make it. And it will be very new and very beautiful, which is saying a lot, in the context of contemporary classical music.'

We discussed then interesting questions which had been bothering me for many months—especially since the disastrous publication of my last novel. I wondered if it was possible to make new fiction, by which I meant find a new template, a new mould, and also a new subject, and still create something which was, to use his word, beautiful? Post-modernism had failed, I said to him. The idea of the fragmented universe, mirrored in the fractured novel or work of art, was interesting, valid at the level of thought, but it had failed artistically because a fractured narrative is not enjoyable—it just doesn't work. But what is the point of continuing to write using the pre-modern template? And what subject can the new novel deal with? Traditionally the stories were about the conflict between the desire of the individual and the rules of the society. But does that sort of society exist, in our world, the western world, the only one we can honestly or usefully write about? Divorce is not a social disaster, homosexuality is legal and accepted. Nobody is forced to marry for money or to please their parents. There are taboos, but not so many, and there must be a limit to the number of explorations of pedophilia or psychopathic crime that the world can endure. So one is forced to write only what has been written, in a slightly different way, a million times already.

Marcus's answer was that in the perfect setting, by which he meant this house, his mother's house, the answer to this problem could be revealed, but he did not explain how.

'You talk as if the place were magical,' I said.

'Yes,' he said. 'It is the right atmosphere for the creation of great art. But still I will have to work, and try to make that good art myself.'

This led, naturally, to the questions: What is music for? What is writing for? What is life for?

But before we could discuss these questions the washing up was finished, and Ramalina and Isabel returned, padding so silently into the room I wondered if they had been in a corner, listening to us, unobserved, for some time. The conversation moved off in a different direction.

When I looked at my watch it was midnight.

Seeing my glance, Ramalina said:

'Why don't you stay here and go back in the morning?'

'I would rather go home.'

I did not like the idea of the track through the woods, the hoot of the night owl, the distant rumble of hidden animals. But I felt the strongest resistance to staying in this house. I never like overnighting anywhere, abruptly, in this way, so my resistance was automatic.

'Can I call a taxi?'

'You can call, but it won't come,' Marcus said. 'They never come out here, they get lost, and if they do promise to come, it costs not a small fortune but a large fortune.'

In his drawl, this sounded funny, for half a second.

There was a pause, during which they all waited for me to do the reasonable, civilized thing, and change my mind. But I didn't speak. Eventually Ramalina said, in a voice that was more chirpy and sharp than usual:

'Marcus will drive you home.'

He'd drunk half a bottle of wine and two cointreaus, but I said:

'Thank you. Sorry to put you to this trouble.'

Li had found out something about the family. They were called the Klarstads. They had lived in the house in the forest, Moss Lodge, for fifty years. Ramalina's husband's family had built the place as a holiday home; he had died fifteen years ago and since then she had lived there all the year round. It was known that Marcus was some sort of musician but he had the reputation of being a recluse; he gave no interviews and disliked being televised while performing, and he had not performed locally. Kim had not heard of the daughter, Isabel, but that was probably just an oversight: she was not known, for anything, and didn't leave home, so who would know about her?

'They're OK. They probably just need a bit of company,' Li said.

I called in in the early afternoon a few days later. The scene was exactly as it had been on my first visit. I walked down the drive between the fir trees, and sighed with pleasure when the low white house came into view. By the pool, Isabel reclined and Ramalina sat and Marcus swam, but languidly, in the pool.

The fragrance from the roses was stronger than before, something I attributed to the heat of the day. Even here, in this paradise, where the climate is temperate and invariably perfect, it was slightly too hot, while the rest of the nation sweltered in a terrible heat wave.

'Hello! Great to see you!' Ramalina called, as I approached

the poolside. Isabel smiled and nodded but as usual said little.
I could hear Marcus's body plashing in the water, a sound as
natural as the whirring of the hummingbird or the shiver of the
breeze in the leaves.

Ramalina offered me tea, and cucumber sandwiches, in
some sort of deference to my native tastes. Isabel, who had put
on her yellow silk robe soon after I appeared, glided across the
lawn and brought this snack from the house on wicker tray. We
talked about 'my day'. How was your day? Ramalina's manner
was as poised as that of a television presenter, it now seemed to
me. She smiled and penetrated me with her slanted golden eyes;
she was as controlled as if she was reading her questions from
a monitor.

'Did you go to finishing school?' I asked, rudely. Isabel raised
her eyebrows—an exceptional show of emotion for her—and
there was a loud whoosh in the pool, as Marcus pulled himself
out of the water.

'Why yes, I did,' said Ramalina, with her wide smile. 'How
clever of you to guess. As a matter of fact, when I was nineteen
I spent a year in a finishing school in Lausanne.'

'I didn't know they still existed.'

'They existed then!' she laughed. 'It was a wonderful year. I
met so many interesting people from all over the world, and I
saw so much of Europe. We travelled extensively, on the train,
to Paris and Rome and Trieste and London and Copenhagen.
Yes, it was a truly magical year for me.'

'When was that?'

'Oh, long ago,' she said, and smiled her rejection of the
question.

'Did you visit Dublin?'

'No, alas,' she said, smiling. 'And I would so love to visit
your beautiful city. I feel as if I had been there, I have heard and
read so much about it.'

Marcus came then, and we talked about *Ulysses* and
Dubliners, while he dried off in the sunshine. Ramalina and

Isabel left the pool and went into the house. She asked me to stay for dinner but I refused, and then said I would come the next evening, if I could get a lift home.

And every day or two for weeks I visited their house in the woods, and had tea or lemonade or dinner, and a pleasant easy conversation with Ramalina about my day and my work and what I was reading, and a long intense conversation with Marcus about literature and life.

Every day, I believed I was on the brink of finding out something wonderful, something radically important about the meaning of life and the meaning of fiction. I felt, as I walked through the redwood forest, through the whispering glades, the shifting pools of sunlight dappling through the long trailing branches, the promising ferns, that today an amazing truth would be revealed. A moment of illumination would come and that it would provide me with the answer I was seeking, the breakthrough I longed for, and needed.

I was not thinking of the kind of epiphany we talked of all the time, as we sat by the log fire after the dinners Isabel had cooked (for it was she who did all the work in the house, that I had noticed, so gradually that I was not surprised or dismayed). Not the Joycean moment of epiphany, where some ordinary Joe Bloggs realises that life is often sad, that we are mortal and lose the people we love, that loss must be tolerated, that compromise is the name of the game. I did not want one of those epiphanies which really just confirmed the truths that most sensible people know anyway, instinctively, and don't make much of a fuss about.

Nor yet did I hope for some big revelation about the nature of the universe. God exists. God does not exist. We will end. We will live on in some other form, our spirit will migrate to some other being, there is an afterlife, there is not an afterlife. The world will survive, the world will end, love matters, the world is beautiful and that is why we go on, and at the same time everything we know is doomed to extinction.

Maybe that last line was close to it, but it was not what I was looking for, not only that.

Some answer about writing, is what I wanted. What is it for? Not just to entertain people, with stories about other people, very like themselves. It must have some more profound and important purpose, surely, even in the context of our knowledge of our imminent extinction, perhaps especially in that context.

Every day, I felt I was on the brink. That the next day my brain, my self, would fill with light, that something wonderful would happen.

My period of residence in the lodge was drawing to an end. I had not said this, specifically, to the Klarstads. But they suspected it, they knew, as they knew most things.

'Stay on with us,' said Ramalina, with her most persuasive smile.

'Yes, do,' said Marcus. 'You can live here for as long as you like. It's easy to write here. You know that already.'

'Yes, I know that,' I said.

We were by the swimming pool, where they always were in the afternoons. Isabel wasn't there. In fact I had not seen her for a few days, but since I seldom talked to her I hadn't liked to enquire where she was. I knew such an enquiry would not be welcome, and would be met with a blank stare.

Ramalina and Marcus showed me the room I would have, if I stayed—at the end of the house, with a long window opening to a balcony, facing the rising sun, and another window to the south, directly onto the garden, with its oleanders and wisteria, and the branches of the redwoods like the drooping arms of ballerinas right behind. I loved my plain room in the lodge but this room was just as tranquil and at the same time much more beautiful. I could not imagine, I could not design, I could not conceive of, a room which more perfectly matched my taste, my requirements. Indeed when I stepped inside I felt I had been

there, many many times before, and I knew it was a room I
had dreamt of, often, in the dreams I often have of houses and
castles, about which I wander, from room to room, in search of
the perfect one.

'You'll write well here,' said Marcus.

He pulled me aside, and whispered, as his warm arm caressed
my neck and an electric bolt of pleasure ran through my body.

'You'll make a breakthrough here. Here, you will be
enlightened.'

And, as if in response, outside the window the lawn sprinkler
went on, shooting a delicate fountain of rain drops into the
air, and the sunlight caught them and transformed them to a
rainbow, dancing there in a myriad jeweled droplets outside the
window of my dreamed-of room.

We went back to the drawing-room, where Marcus played
a new piece on the piano, and never had he played so well,
and nothing he had composed was as moving and harmonious,
and at the same time unlike any music that had ever been
composed before, on this earth. The sun dappled the polished
floor and the rugs shone like soft jewels from some bazaar of
the *Thousand Nights*, when the orient was the land of magic
and mystery beyond all imagining. The glass bowl of pink roses
scented the air with a promise as tantalizing, and true, as that of
the music, which was, here is the answer you have been waiting
for. Tomorrow you will learn what you have been waiting for,
you will find out what you were born to know.

And then we had dinner, the most delicious dinner yet. We
served ourselves from the bowls and dishes on the sideboard,
and I dared to ask where Isabel was.

Ramalina's yellowish eyes sparkled at my question, but her
voice was as soft as a cat's fur when she answered:

'She's indisposed.'

I knew, from the way she flicked her golden braid, that I
would learn nothing further.

Well.

There is only one ending, as you who read stories know.

The next day, I woke later than usual, and when I opened my eyes something had changed. The sun was not shining, and the hummingbird was not whirring, and a gray fog filled the valley and blotted out the hills and the trees and the skyline.

Li said:

'Kim is picking me up at ten to go to the airport. What time is your flight?'

And I said:

'My flight is at one o'clock.'

'It won't take more than forty minutes to get down there. You should be OK. What time is your connection?'

'It's at eleven p.m.'

'So you'll land at what time?'

Li always said 'what time?' Never 'when?'

'Six o'clock tomorrow morning.'

That is when the flights come in, to Ireland, after the Atlantic crossing.

And as I said it I could see the west coast of Ireland as you see it from the plane at dawn, the jig-saw of tiny fields moist and green as lime jelly, and I could see as well the gray rain on the runway at Dublin, and I could feel the cold gray air on my skin, even as we sat and ate granola at the sun-washed table. And I knew I would go back to the fogbound beloved island, and struggle on towards an answer, like a woman who has stepped on the stray sod, and will wander around in one field for the rest of her life.

Literary Lunch

THE BOARD WAS GATHERING in a bistro on the banks of the Liffey. 'We deserve a decent lunch!' Alan, the chairman, declared cheerfully. He was a cheerful man. His eyes were kind, and encouraged those around him to feel secure. People who liked him said he was charismatic.

The board was happy. Their tedious meeting was over and the bistro was much more expensive than the hotel to which Alan usually brought them, with its alarming starched table-cloths and fantails of melon. He was giving them a treat because it was a Saturday. They had sacrificed a whole three hours of the weekend for the good of the organisation they served. The reputation of the bistro, which was called Gabriel's, was excellent and anyone could tell from its understated style that the food would be good, and the wine too, even before they looked at the menu—John Dory, oysters, fried herrings, sausage and mash. Truffles. A menu listing truffles just under sausage and mash promises much. We can cook and we are ironic as well, it proclaims. Put your elbows on the table, have a good time.

Emphasising the unpretentiously luxurious tone of Gabriel's was a mural on the wall, depicting a modern version of *The Last Supper*, a photograph of typical Dubliners eating at a long refectory table.

Alan loved this photograph, a clever, post-modern, but delightfully accessible work of art. It raised the cultural tone of the bistro, if it needed raising, which it didn't really, since it was also located next door to the house on Ussher's Island where James Joyce's aunts had lived, and which he used as the setting for his most celebrated story, 'The Dead'. In short, of all innumerable restaurants boasting literary associations in town, Gabriel's had the most irrefutable credentials. You simply could not eat in a more artistic place.

The funny thing about *The Last Supper* was that everyone was sitting at one side of the table, very conveniently for painters and photographers. It was as if they had anticipated all the attention which would soon be coming their way. And Gabriel's had, in its clever ironic way, set up one table in exactly the same manner, so that everyone seated at it faced in the same direction, getting a good view of the mural and also of the rest of the restaurant. It was great. Nobody was stuck facing the wall. You could see if anyone of any importance was among the clientele—and usually there were one or two stars, at least. You could see what they were wearing and what they were eating and drinking, although you had to guess what they were talking about, which made it even more interesting, in a funny sort of way. More interactive. It was like watching a silent movie without subtitles.

A problem with the arrangement was that people at one end of the last supper table had no chance at all of talking to those at the other end. But this too could be a distinct advantage, if the seating arrangements were intelligently handled. Alan always made sure that they were.

At the right end of the table he had placed his good old friends, Simon and Paul (Joe had not come, as per usual. He was the real literary expert on the board, having won the Booker Prize, but he never attended meetings. Too full of himself. Still they could use his name on the stationery). Alan himself sat in the middle where he could keep an eye on everyone. On his left hand side were Mary, Jane and Pam. The women liked to stick together.

Alan, Simon and Paul ordered oysters and truffles and pâté-de-foie-gras for starters. Mary, Jane and Pam ordered one soup of the day or and two nothings. No starter please for me. This

was not owing to the gender division. Mary and Jane were long
past caring about their figures, at least when out on a free lunch,
and Pam was new and eager to try everything being a member of
a board offered, even John Dory, which she had ordered for her
main course. Their abstemiousness was due to the breakdown
in communications caused by the seating arrangements. The
ladies had believed that nobody was getting starters, because
Alan had muttered, I don't think I'll have a starter, and then
changed his mind and ordered the pâté-de-foie-gras when they
were chatting among themselves about a new production of *A
Doll's House*, which was just showing at the Abbey. Mary had
been to the opening, as she was careful to emphasise; she was
giving it the thumbs down. Nora had been manic and the sound
effects were appalling. The slam of the door which was supposed
to reverberate down through a hundred years of drama couldn't
even be heard in the second row of the stalls. That was the
Abbey for you, of course. Such dreadful acoustics, the place has
to be shut down. Pam and Mary nodded eagerly; Pam thought
the Abbey was quite nice but she knew if she admitted that
in public everyone would think she was a total loser who had
probably failed her Leaving. Neither Pam nor Mary had seen
A Doll's House but they had read a review by Fintan O'Toole
so they knew everything they needed to know. He hadn't liked
the production and had decided that the original play was not
much good anyway. *Farvel*, Ibsen!

In the middle of this conversation Pam's mobile phone
began to play 'Waltzing Matilda' at volume level five. Alan
gave her a reproving glance. If she had to leave on her mobile
phone she could at least have picked a tune by Shostakovich or
Stravinksy. He himself had a few bars by a young Irish composer
on his phone, ever mindful of his duty to the promotion of the
national culture. 'Terribly sorry!' Pam said, slipping the phone
into her bag, but not before she had glanced at the screen to
find out who was calling. 'I forgot to switch it off.' Which was

rather odd, Mary thought, since Pam had placed the phone on
the table, in front of her nose, the minute she had come into
the restaurant. It had sat there under the water jug looking like
a tiny pistol in its little leather holster.

In the heel of the hunt all this distraction meant that they
neglected to eavesdrop on the men while they were placing
their orders so that they would get a rough idea of how
extravagant they could be. How annoying it was now, to see
Simon slurping down his oysters, with lemon and black pepper,
and Paul digging into his truffles, while they had nothing
but *A Doll's House* and soup of the day to amuse themselves
with.

And a glass of white wine. Paul, who was a great expert,
had ordered that. A sauvignon blanc, the vineyard of Du Bois
Pere et Fils, 2002. 'As nice a sauvignon as I have tried in years',
he said, as he munched a truffle and sipped thoughtfully.
'2002 was a good year for everything in France but this is
exceptional.' The ladies strained to hear what he was saying,
much more interested in wine than drama. Mary, who had been
so exercised a moment ago about Ibsen at the Abbey, seemed to
have forgotten all about both. She was now taking notes, jotting
down Paul's views. He was better, much better, than the people
who do the columns in the paper, she commented excitedly
as she scribbled. No commercial agenda—well, that they knew
of. You never quite knew what anyone's agenda was, that was
the trouble. Paul was apparently on the board, because of his
knowledge of books, and Simon, because of his knowledge of
the legal world, and Joe, because he was famous. Mary, Jane and
Pam were there because they were women. Mary was already on
twenty boards and had had to call a halt, since her entire life was
absorbed by meetings and lunches, receptions and launches.
Luckily she had married sensibly and did not have to work. Jane
sat on ten boards and Pam had been nominated two months
ago. This was her first lunch with any board, ever. She was a

writer. Everyone wondered what somebody like her was doing here. It was generally agreed that she must know someone.

One person she knew was Francie Briody. He was also having lunch, in a coffee shop called The Breadbasket, a cold little kip of a place across the river on Aston Quay. They served filled baguettes and sandwiches as well as coffee, and he was lunching on a tuna submarine with corn and coleslaw. Francie was a writer, like Pam, although she wrote so-called literary women's fiction, chick lit for Ph.D.s, and was successful. Francie wrote literary fiction for anybody who cared to read it, which was nobody. For as long as he could remember he had been a writer whom nobody read. And he was already fifty years of age. He had written three novels and about a hundred short stories, as well as other bits and bobs. Success of a kind had been his lot in life, but not of a kind to enable him to earn a decent living, or to eat anything other than tuna baguettes, or to get him a seat on an arts organisation board. He had had one novel published, to mixed reviews; he had won a prize at Listowel Writers' Week for a short story fifteen years ago. Six of his stories had been nominated for prizes—the Devon Cream Story Competition, the Ballymagash Young Authors, the Leitrim Lakes Mayfly Festival, among others. But he still had to work part-time in a public house, and he had failed to publish his last three books.

Nobody was interested in a writer past the age of thirty.

It was all the young ones they wanted these days, and women, preferably young women with lots of shining hair and sweet photogenic faces. Pam. She wasn't that young any more, and not all that photogenic, but she'd got her foot in the door in time, when women and the Irish were all the rage, no matter what they looked like. Or wrote like.

He'd never been a woman—he had considered a pseudonym but he'd let that moment pass. And now he'd missed the boat. The love affair of the London houses and the German houses

and the Italian and the Japanese with Irish literature was over. So
everyone said. Once Seamus Heaney got the Nobel, the interest
abated. Enough's enough. On to the next country. Bosnia or
Latvia or god knows what. Slovenia.

Francie's latest novel, a heteroglossial polyphonic post-
modern examination of post-modern Ireland, with special
insights into political corruption and globalisation, beautifully
written in darkly masculinist ironic prose with shadows of
l'écriture féminine, which was precisely and exactly what Fintan
O'Toole swore that the Irish public and Irish literature was
crying out for, had been rejected by every London house, big
and small, that his agent could think of, and by the three Irish
publishers who would dream of touching a literary novel as
well, and also, Francie did not like to think of this, by the other
five Irish publishers who believed chick lit was the modern Irish
answer to James Joyce. Yes yes yes yes. The delicate chiffon scarf
was flung over her auburn curls. Yes.

Yeah, well.

I'll show the philistine fatso bastards.

He pushed a bit of slippery yellow corn back into his baguette.
Extremely messy form of nourishment, it was astonishing that
it had caught on, especially as the baguettes were slimy and
slippery themselves.

Not like the homemade loaves served in the Gabriel on the
south bank of the Liffey.

Alan was nibbling a round of freshly baked, soft as silk,
crispy as Paris on a fine winter's day roll, to mop up the oyster
juice, which was sitting slightly uneasily on his stomach.

'We did a good job,' he was saying to Pam, who liked to talk
shop, being new.

'I'd always be so worried that we picked the wrong people,'
she said in her charming girlish voice. She had nice blond hair
but this did not make up for her idealism and her general lack of

experience. Alan wished his main course would come quickly. Venison with lingonberry jus and basil mash.

'You'd be surprised but that very seldom happens' he said.

'Judgments are so subjective vis-a-vis literature,' she said, with a frown, remembering a bad review she'd received fifteen years ago.

Alan suppressed a sigh. She was a real pain.

'There is almost always complete consensus on decisions,' he said. 'It's surprising, but the cream always rises. I . . . we . . . are never wrong.' His magical eyes twinkled.

Consensus? Pam frowned into her sauvignon blanc. A short discussion of the applicants for the bursaries in which people nudged ambiguities around the table like footballers dribbling a ball when all they want is the blessed trumpeting of the final whistle. They waited for Alan's pronouncement. If that was consensus, she was Emily Dickinson. As soon as Alan said, 'I think this is brilliant writing' or 'Rubbish, absolute rubbish', there was a scuffle of voices vying with each other to be the first to agree with the great man.

Rubbish, absolute rubbish. That was what he had said about Francie. He's persistent, I'll give him that. Alan had allowed himself a smile, which he very occasionally permitted himself at the expense of minor writers. The board guffawed loudly. She hadn't told Francie that. He would kill himself. He was at the end of his tether. But she had broken the sad news over the phone in the loo, as she had promised. No bursary. Again.

'I don't know,' she persisted, ignoring Alan's brush-off. 'I feel so responsible somehow. All that effort and talent, and so little money to go around . . . '

Her voice tailed off. She could not find the words to finish the sentence, because she was drunk as an egg after two glasses. No breakfast, the meeting had started at nine.

Stupid bitch, thought Alan, although he smiled cheerily. Defiant. Questioning. Well, we know how to deal with them.

Woman or no woman, she would never sit on another board. This was her first and her last supper. I feel so responsible somehow. Who did she think she was?

'This is a 2001 Bordeaux from a vineyard run by an Australian ex-pat just outside Bruges, that's the Bruges near Bordeaux of course, not Bruges La Mort in little Catholic Belgium.' Paul's voice had raised several decibels and Simon was getting a bit rambunctious. They were well into the second bottle of the Sauvignon and had ordered two bottles of the Bordeaux, priced, he noticed, at eighty-five euro a pop. The lunch was going to cost about a thousand euro.

'Your venison sir?'

At last.

He turned away from Pam and speared the juicy game. The grub of kings.

Francie made his king-size tuna submarine last a long time. It would have anyway, since the filling kept spilling out onto the table and it took ages to gather it up and replace it in the roll. He glanced at the plain round clock over the fridge. They'd been in there for two hours. How long would it be?

Fifteen years.

Since his first application.

Fifty.

His twelfth.

His twelfth time trying to get a bursary to write full time.

It would be the makings of him. It would mean he could give up serving alcohol to fools for a whole year. He would write a new novel, the novel which would win the prizes and show the begrudgers. Impress Fintan O'Toole. Impress Emer O'Reilly. Impress, maybe, Eileen fucking Battersby. And the boost to his morale would be so fantastic . . . but once again that Alan Byrne, who had been running literary Ireland since he made his confirmation probably, had shafted him. He knew. Pamela had phoned him from the loo on her mobile. She had tried her best but there was no way. They had really loved his work, she said. There was just not enough money to go round. She was so sorry, so sorry . . .

Yeah, right.

Alan was the one who made the decisions. Pamela had told him so herself. They do exactly what he says, she said. It's amazing. I never knew how power worked. Nobody ever disagrees with him. Nobody who gets to sit on the same committees and eat the same lunches, anyway. As long as he was chair Francie would not get a bursary. He would not get a travel grant. He would not get a production grant. He would not get a trip to China or Paris or even the University of Eastern Connecticut. He would not get a free trip to Drumshambo in the County Leitrim for the Arsehole of Ireland Literature and Donkey Racing Weekend.

Alan Byrne ruled the world.

The pen is stronger than the sword, Francie had learned, in school. Was it Patrick Pearse who said that or some classical guy? Cicero or somebody. That's how old Francie was, they were still doing Patrick Pearse when he was in primary. He was pre-revisionism and he still hadn't got a bursary in literature, let alone got onto Aosdana, which gave some lousy writers like Pam a meal-ticket for life. The pen is stronger. Good old Paddy O Piarsaigh. But he changed his mind apparently. Francie looked at the Four Courts through the corner window of the Bread Basket. Who had been in that in 1916? He couldn't remember. Had anyone? Tomás Mac Donagh or Sean Mac Diarmada or one of the signatories nobody could remember. Burnt down the place in the end, all the history of Ireland in it. IRA of their day. That was later, the Civil War. He had written about that too. He had written about everything. Even about Alan. He had written a whole novel about him, and six short stories, all so savage that they made Jonathan Swift look like Mary Poppins (he couldn't recall the name of any sentimental children's writer, because he had never read children's literature. The first book he read was *Crime and Punishment*, when he was nine. Before that he spent his time playing.) Those brutally brilliant satires were hardly going to find their mark if they never got published, and they were not going to get published if he did not get a bursary and some recognition from the establishment, and he was not going to get any recognition while Alan was running every literary and cultural organisation on the island . . .

At last. The evening was falling in when the board members tripped and staggered out of the restaurant, into the light and shade, the sparkle and darkness, that was Ussher's Quay. Jane and Mary had of course left much earlier, anxious to get to the supermarkets before they closed.

But Pam, to the extreme annoyance of everyone, had lingered on, drinking the Bordeaux with the best of them. They had been irritated at first but had then passed into another stage. The sexual one. Inevitable as Australian chardonnay at a book launch. They had stopped blathering on about wine and had begun to reminisce about encounters with ladies of the night in exotic locations; Paul claimed, in a high voice which had Alan looking around the restaurant in alarm, to have been seduced by a whore in a hotel in Moscow who had bought him a vodka and insisted on accompanying him to his room, clad only in a coat of real wolf-skin. Fantasy land. That eejit Pam was so shot herself she didn't seem to care what they said. Her mascara was slipping down her face and her blond hair was manky, as if she had sweated too much. It was high time she got a taxi. He'd shove her into one as soon as he got them out. He couldn't leave them here, they'd drink the Board dry, and if they were unlucky some journalist would happen upon them. He stopped for a second. Publicity was something they were always seeking and hardly ever got. But no, this would do them no good at all. There is such a thing as bad press in spite of what he said at meetings.

He paid the bill. There were long faces of course. You'd think he was crucifying them instead of having treated them to a lunch which had cost, including the large gratuity he was expected to fork out, 1200 euro of Lottery money. Oh well better than race horses, he always said, looking at *The Last Supper*. Was it Leonardo or Michaelangelo had painted the original, he was so exhausted he couldn't remember. He took no nonsense for the boyos, though, and asked the waiter to put them into their coats no matter how they protested.

Pam excused herself at the last minute, taking him aback.

'Don't wait for me,' she said. She could still speak coherently. 'I'll be grand, I'll get a taxi. I'll put it on the account.'

She gave him a peck on the cheek—that's how drunk she was—and ran out the door, pulling her mobile out of her bag as she did so.

Not such a twit as all that. I'll put it on the account. He almost admired her, for a second.

With the help of the waiter he got the other pair of beauties bundled out to the pavement.

The taxi had not yet arrived.

He deposited Simon and Paul on a bench placed outside for the benefit of smokers and moved to the curb, the better to see.

Traffic moved freely along the quay. It was not as busy as usual. A quiet evening. The river was a blending delight of black and silver and mermaid green. Alan was not entirely without aesthetic sensibility. The sweet smell of hops floated along the water from the brewery. He'd always loved that, the heavy cloying smell of it, like something you'd give a two-year-old to drink. Like hot jam tarts. In the distance he could just see the black trees of the Phoenix Park. Sunset. Peaches and molten gold, Dublin stretched against it. The north side could be lovely at times like this. When it was getting dark. The Wellington monument rose, a black silhouette, into the heavens, a lasting tribute to the power and glory of great men.

It was the last thing Alan saw.

He did not even hear the shot explode like a backfiring lorry in the hum of the evening city.

Francie's aim was perfect. It was amazing that a writer who could not change a plug or bore a hole in a wall with a Black & Decker drill at point blank range could shoot so straight across the expanse of the river. Well, he had trained. Practice makes perfect, they said at the creative writing workshops. Be persistent, never lose your focus. He had not written a hundred short stories for nothing and a short story is an arrow in flight towards its target. They were always saying that. Aim write fire. And if there's a gun on the table in Act One, it has to go off in Act Three, that's another thing they said.

But, laughed Francie, as he wrapped his pistol in a Tesco bag-for-life, in real life, what eejit would put a gun on the table in Act One? In real life, a gun is kept well out of sight and it goes off in any act it likes. In real life, there is no foreshadowing.

That's the difference, he thought, as he let the bag slide over the river wall. That's the difference between life and art. He watched the bag sink into the black lovely depths of Anna Livia Plurabella. Patrick Pearse gave up on the *peann* in the end. When push came to shove he took to the *lámh láidir*.

He walked down towards O'Connell Bridge, taking out his mobile. Good old Pam. He owed her. For each man kills the thing he loves, he texted her, pleased to have remembered the line. By each let this be heard. Some do it with a bitter look, some with a flattering word. The coward does it with a kiss, the brave man with a gun. That wasn't right. Word didn't rhyme with gun. Some do it with a bitter look, some with a flattering pun. Didn't really make sense. What rhymes with gun? Lots of words. Fun, nun. Bun. Some do it with a bitter pint, some with a sticky bun, he texted in. Cheers! I'll buy you a bagel sometime. He sent the message and tucked his phone into his pocket. Anger sharpened the wit, he had noticed that before. His best stories had always been inspired by the lust for revenge. He could feel a good one coming on . . . maybe he shouldn't have bothered killing Alan.

He was getting into a bad mood again. He stared disconsolately at the dancing river. The water was far from transparent, but presumably the Murder Investigation Squad could find things in it. They knew it had layers and layers of meaning, just like the prose he wrote. Readers were too lazy to deconstruct properly, but policeman were probably pretty assiduous when it came to interpreting and analysing the murky layers of the Liffey. Would that bag-for-life protect his fingerprints, DNA evidence. He didn't know. The modern writer has to do plenty of research. God is in the details. He did his best but he had a tendency to leave some books unread, some websites unvisited. Writing a story, or murdering a man, was such a complex task. You were bound to slip up somewhere.

Perfectionism is fatal, they said. Give yourself permission to err. Don't listen to the inner censor.

He had reached O'Connell Bridge and hey, there was the 46A waiting for him. A good sign. They'd probably let him have a laptop in prison, he thought optimistically, as he hopped on the bus. They'd probably make him writer in residence. That's if they ever found the gun.

City of Literature

THE BOARD FOR ARTISTS' Money Etc. had gathered for its AGM in the Dublin Literary Club. 'We'll pay above the going rate.' Two hundred euro. 'It's a friendly gesture'. Simon hoped the friendly gesture would compensate for the reduction of the Literary Club's grant from half a million euro per annum to zero. This cut had been Simon's first decision as chair of The Board. The action had won wide admiration. Internet commentators and callers to Liveline, who seemed to believe that a fascist dictator would solve all Ireland's problems, regretted that Simon was not in politics, noting that he possessed in abundance the leadership qualities that our government lacked. The secretary of one political party had rung him up and asked him to consider running for president, an offer which he declined, believing he had more power at the centre of Ireland's cultural life. As everyone knew, the one asset Ireland still possessed, untrammelled by debt or mortgage, was its creativity. Financially Ireland was bankrupt, but in its spiritual coffers a million cultural goldbars confirmed the real sovereignty of the nation. Simon liked to think of himself as Governor of the Bank of the Irish Imagination.

The room they were in, like all those in the Dublin Literary Club, was very beautiful. But it was also very cold. Wintry rain battered the lovely windowpanes.

'Victoria is looking for an electric heater,' said Simon cheerfully. Victoria was the secretary. 'We'll soon be as warm as toast. Just keep your coats on.'

Simon had replaced Alan as chair following Alan's tragic demise just after the AGM of 2007, the last meeting before the Bank Guarantee. Alan had been murdered by a disaffected novelist, Francie Briody, whose application for an award had been rejected in a year when dozens and dozens of writers— all of them useless, in Francie's view—had got pots of money. Understandably disappointed, he'd blamed Alan, and shot him. But in a way, Francie had given Alan a lucky break, Pam, a Board member and old friend of Francie, thought. He would never have survived in the era of austerity, given his aristocratic fondness for dispensing absurd largesse to those members of the artistic community who met with his approval, and of vintage wines and gourmet food to practically everybody.

'I won't detain you for long,' smiled Simon. He never detained anyone for long. Complementing that brilliant decisiveness which could guillotine a local drama society or condemn an emerging poet to a life of chick lit or bartending in Australia, was a talent for speed. Simon could get through an ordinary meeting in thirty minutes and an AGM in under an hour. He was much in demand as a chairperson.

'Where's Victoria? Never mind. I assume you've all read and agreed with the Minutes?'

He assumed right. They all *had* read the Minutes, since they were less than half a page long. Correspondence too was swiftly dispatched, whereupon Victoria returned. She sidled in next to Simon. 'They can't find the heater,' she whispered. 'They're going to borrow one from the Chinese take-away.'

'Question, through the chair,' Pam raised her hand.

Simon glared at her.

'I believe you have a letter from Francis Briody?'

'Yes, Pamela,' Simon smiled. 'And we'll discuss that as Item Five on the agenda. Is that OK with you?'

Pamela nodded humbly. She had learnt from Alan, before he died, that the key to survival was to always agree with the person in the seat of power.

It is one of life's many ironies that night is always darkest before the dawn. His murder of the Chairman of the Board for Artists' Money Etc. had brought Francie Briody the celebrity he had craved, as he wrote long experimental novels at his kitchen table and collected rejection slips by the hundred. He spent the first six years of the recession locked up in prison. This was not a bad place to be in the era of austerity. According to his cellmate, Marty, a drug baron implicated in the murder of more men than he could count, 'Boom or bust, it's all the same behind bars.' The diet hadn't changed, or the condition of the cells—neither of them had ever been good. The only difference, Marty asserted, was that there were fewer classes, due to cutbacks in funding. 'It used to be brutal. You'd be up half the night writing plays and memoirs and god knows what. We had one young one who was mad for sonnets. Sonnets, fucking sonnets, she couldn't get enough of them. That,' Marty asserted, 'was the worst.' He thought for a minute, as he rummaged in his mattress for one of his mobile phones. 'Apart from the sestinas. Are you into sestinas yourself?'

Francie assured him that he was not. 'I am a writer of prose,' he said quietly.

'Oh good,' said Marty.

Thanks to the lack of undue pressure from teachers of creative writing and art, Francie had plenty of time to do his own thing, namely write long experimental novels. Within a week of his arrival behind bars, Marty, whose ingenuity was indefatigable and contacts in and outside the walls innumerable, procured him a nice little laptop. All he asked in return was that his new pal should augment his supplies of his favourite substance by getting all his visitors to bring some in whenever they dropped by. (Francie's mother, sister, his friend Pam, and five of his former girlfriends, visited with some regularity. He was rather handsome.)

'What's that?' Francie wondered which of them would be

most likely to get her hands on heroin. Even his mother would be able to get some hash, he imagined, from the people who sold it at their local railway station, but he doubted if that would be enough for Marty.

Fry's Chocolate Cream. Marty could not get enough of it. He never touched drugs himself, and drank beer only on his birthday and at Christmas. He was a regular Holy Communicant and during the Abortion thing had founded a Pro-Life group in the men's prison (called 'Jail For Life', the venture had not been a success. As soon as the group was denied day release to participate in a Rosary for Life demonstration outside Leinster House, most of the members stopped attending meetings).

Now, however, Marty had a new interest. Literature. In addition to supplying his cellmate with a computer, he offered his services as reader and editor to Francie. Every novelist should have a special friend whose literary judgment they trust totally, Marty explained. Since he had attended dozens of creative writing classes in the course of his penitential career he knew things like that. Francie had never been to a writing workshop—too full of himself—and didn't know the most elementary tricks of the trade. In the forced conviviality of his shared cell, the concept of the friendly first reader made sense. Marty is not the friendly first reader he would have selected, perhaps, but there wasn't much choice. Nolan the warder did not seem literary. Lugs Beag next door couldn't read or write because after his first day at school he had spent his entire life on the mitch, and apprenticed himself to a drug dealer when he was four years old. 'He can text,' Marty explained. Texting was an essential skill in the drug business, Francie gathered. 'But he can't do ordinary writing. Pity. The lad's bright as a bullet.'

Marty himself had never been a great reader. As he was the first to admit, he was a workaholic, and in the limited spare time he permitted himself liked to watch football matches or television dramas. But he had been in prison on and off now

over a period of ten years, usually incarcerated in a cell which
lacked not only a toilet, but a television set. During this time
he had developed a fondness for Scandinavian crime fiction.
Henning Mankell was his favourite.

'Mankell always uses short sentences,' Marty said
thoughtfully, when he had read the first chapter of Francie's
novel. 'And you can understand what it is he's trying to say.'

He broke off a chunk of Chocolate Cream and offered it to
Francie. 'I love the bit about the fly on the cornflake.' Francie
smiled shyly. It was one of his own favourite passages: he had
devoted two pages to an in-depth account of the flight of the
bluebottle from the rim of the milk jug to the middle of his
bowl of breakfast cereal, where—after six further pages—said
insect eventually met his death by drowning. 'But it's too long.'
Marty's voice rose. He warmed to his theme and stood up the
better to emphasise his point. 'Twenty pages about a chap eating
a bowl of cornflakes is too much.' A tear rolled down Francie's
cheek. Marty sat down again. 'That's what I think anyhow, but
sure what do I know about . . . um . . . literary fiction?'

'Joyce devotes a lot of time to Bloom's breakfast,' Francie
defended himself. 'And then to Stephen's.'

A polite shrug was all the acknowledgment this insight
received.

With the repugnance of the genuine connoisseur forced to
consume literary swill, Francie agreed to have a go at Marty's
favourite novel. To his surprise he was up all night reading it by
the light of the torch his cell mate provided to all prisoners (in
exchange for two bars of Fry's Chocolate Cream.)

Simon arrived at the main item on the agenda: MONEY. The
electric heater had not yet been produced. Pamela snuggled
more deeply into her coat and wondered if it would be bad
manners to put on her gloves.

'We'll soon be out of here,' Simon glanced at her disapprovingly. Victoria, a pale girl who lurked behind large round spectacles like a rabbit peering over the edge of a burrow, pushed a mountain of papers in his direction.

'We're in a very healthy position, I'm glad to say,' Simon laughed. 'This year, we've received a record number of applications for Awards and Prizes. Ten thousand one hundred and fifty-seven, to be exact.'

The Board applauded. They went on and on clapping, once they noticed it got their circulation going again.

'Is there any pattern to their writing?' asked Pamela,

Simon looked at Victoria. Under the terms of the Haddington Road Agreement, she had had to read all ten thousand applications on top of her normal day's work as a clerical officer.

'I did a breakdown.' She seemed delighted to share her breakdown with the Board. It was nice to see her excited about something, Pam thought. Victoria always looked sad and exhausted, which she was, since she commuted every day from Portarlington to Kildare Street. She was one of those youngsters who had nabbed a job in the Civil Service in the nick of time, days before all recruitment stopped. Pam's own daughter, Saoirse Aine, had not been so lucky. Just a few years younger than Victoria, she considered herself fortunate to be employed as an indentured labourer in a uranium mine outside Calgary. (And she with a First Class degree in Civil Engineering.)

Victoria was reading her report with gusto: 'Twenty percent are memoirs of childhood, fifteen percent are about cancer, twenty percent are historical novels dealing with the Famine or the First World War, and thirty percent are first-person narratives told by half-witted people with funny accents.'

The Board clapped loudly again, and some stamped their feet. Laura frowned. Pam knew she was adding up the percentages to see if they came to a hundred.

'Anything on the Recession?'

'One or two.'

'Odd.'

'We're too close to it.' Laura had an opinion about everything. Her sort of nunnish Anglo-Irish accent made her seem even more of a know-all than she was. 'Writers need distance from an event in order to imagine the truth of it.'

'Indeed,' mused Paul. 'Still, you'd think it'd be easier for them to imagine how it feels to live through the Recession than how it felt to live during, say, the Famine. Or the First World War.'

'This is very interesting, folks, but let's not go off on tangents.' The one thing the Board never discussed was literature.

'We have ten thousand applicants. The bad news is that we have only two grants to award.'

The Board sighed dutifully.

'Naturally we'll blame the Troika,' Simon paused. 'I am proposing that we give the first award to Francis E. Briody.'

There was a silence for which stunned is the only reasonable description.

'But Francie Briody *murdered* our previous chairman.'

'That is not a consideration. Francie Briody has served his sentence. He has written a novel which has been highly acclaimed. He has already won three prizes.' Simon glanced at the application form. 'And a chapter was published last month in the *New Yorker*.'

'So why does he need a grant from us?' Laura again.

It was time for Pamela to atone for previous pusillanimity in defending Francie's cause.

'Francis Briody longs for our endorsement. This is his twelfth application for an award. We know how disappointed he was, last time we rejected him.' She gave them time to consider this. 'Speculation about his economic circumstances should not affect our decision. We should judge him on his literary merit.'

Merit was always a good word to use, at meetings.

'So you second my proposal? '

Pamela nodded.

'Excellent. And I propose we award our second grant to the poet Michael D. Higgins.'

'The *President?*' Laura, of course. '*Of Ireland?*'

'Victoria?'

She scanned the form. 'It doesn't say.'

'Is there an address?'

'1 Chesterfield Avenue, Dublin 7.'

'It's him all right.'

'Is he even allowed to apply for an award?'

'Victoria? Is there any regulation stipulating that Presidents of the country may not apply?'

Victoria shook her head firmly.

'In that case I propose we give it to him. He is a great poet.' The Board stared at him. 'Do I have a seconder?'

Laura found her voice, which was never lost for long.

'What if some pest of a journalist decides to make a big deal of it? The Sindo? Or Vincent Brown or Fintan O'Toole?'

Simon had a solution. He always had. They would ask the president to use a pseudonym. Michael D. Yeats or Seamus Biggins. Whatever. Victoria would think of something.

'Don't minute any of this, by the way.' said Simon.

Victoria laid down her biro.

'OK, meeting adjourned,' said Simon. 'Thank you once again for all your hard work.' They grinned uneasily. 'And now may I invite you to a little light refreshment? Victoria? Can you fetch the gourmet sandwiches?'

Victoria pattered downstairs. She had been up all night making sandwiches, as required under the terms of the Haddington Road agreement.

'Remember when we used to go to L'Ecrivain!'

'And Chapter One!'

'And The Playwright!'

'But these sandwiches will be special,' Simon licked his lips loudly, even though he knew perfectly well what was in the sandwiches. Some were ham, some tomato, and some ham and tomato. 'And I've got a nice little wine here, to wash them down. My own treat, of course—Victoria, record that in the minutes. Where is she?'

'Remember Alan and his vintage wines!'

'This is a Barolo,' said Simon. 'As good a little Barolo as I've ever tasted. Pamela?'

The wine flowed gently, chestnut and amber, into her glass. She walked to the window. It had stopped raining. The bare trees spread their branches wide, like the arms of sad ballerinas, or beggars in paintings. Beyond, acres of roofs and steeples were stacked against the Dublin mountains, a sort of sombre purple colour in the fading light. How tranquil everything looked! For centuries—so it must be—people had stood at this window as evening closed in and gazed at the city, stretched out before them like a child who has fallen into a sweet sleep.

The city was dreaming. Its people dreamt, and its poets and novelists and playwrights. Hundreds of them. It had always been so, and now there were more writers than ever. In studios by the river and town-houses in the suburbs, in artisan cottages rotten with negative equity and shiny canal bank apartments with mortgages which could never be paid, they sat at their laptops, wondering and analysing, pondering and pounding. Documenting the present, imagining the past and the future. Some were out to make a quick buck, others busy forging in the smithies of their souls the uncreated conscience of their race, or tracing the beauty of the individual in the nightmare of history. All trying, like poor Francie, like Pamela herself, to scratch one inky mark on the patient, wrinkled face of the city.

The shadows thickened in the Garden of Remembrance. One of the stone swans, the banished children of Lir, started to flap its wings. She heard them, the great wings, beating softly,

softly, a whisper in the dusk. And then a sliver of moon, thin as a cobweb, slid from the clouds, and swan was stone again.

I am a child of the earth, and of the starry heavens.

She went back to the table to grab a sandwich before they were all gone. She sipped her wine. Velvety as the distant mountains. *Plus ça change.* (She often thought in French when she drank red wine. Even when the wine was Italian.) It was, she knew, the Barolo you get in Lidl. That's not *la même chose* as the Barolo from the cellars of the fine restaurants they frequented in the good years, when a perk was a five-course lunch in a five-star restaurant, not a ham sandwich made by an overworked civil servant. It's still a Barolo, though. Much had changed, since the night of the Bank Guarantee. But some things had not changed all that much.

They wouldn't feel it now till Christmas. And she'd be flying out to Canada to visit Saoirse Aine.

The Coast of Wales

OPPOSITE THE FLOWERBED, WHICH dazzles the eye with crimson primroses and tulips the precise pink of dentures, a woman in a yellow anorak is bent over a tap. As she fills her blue watering can, her small dog waits—he's a Yorkie or a Scottie, one of those shaggy little 'ie' dogs. He is silent, which is good because dogs aren't allowed in here. Patiently he stares at the tap.

It's attached to a slim silver post and is almost invisible against the background of stone and milky misty sky. That's why I never noticed it before. Now this woman with the black dog illuminates it for me with that yellow anorak of hers. There's something new to learn every time I come here. For instance, I've found out that the potted plants I place carefully on the clay dry up very quickly, even when it rains. You need to come and water them every few days. Some people know this and they've rigged up clever permanent contraptions: containers like stone windowboxes, which they place on the concrete plinth, and fill with plants in season. It would be easier if you could sow something directly into the soil, but that's against the regulations.

The reason is that this is a lawn cemetery. That's another thing I've learnt: the term 'lawn cemetery', and what it means, which is that grass grows on the graves. And that men from the County Council cut this grass. They've been mowing regularly ever since spring got going, six weeks ago. These grass cutters also remove any unpermitted decorations—for example, teddy bears and plastic angels, Santa Clauses—from the graves, and throw them into the big skip by the gate. They also throw away withered flowers. You have to keep a close watch on your plants to make sure they don't decide to consign them to the skip before they're dead. All this cutting and throwing away, however, means the place is well kept. On sunny days it can look almost nice, at least after you get used to it.

I brought water in a bottle in my rucksack. And now I find out there's no need to carry water all the way from home. Water is heavier than it looks when it comes dancing out of the tap, light as stars.

This is what the graveyard looks like: an enormous housing estate, bisected by a thoroughfare. You can drive on this, and some people do, but I think that's inappropriate, like driving on a beach. Off this central artery are the cul-de-sacs, about twenty on each side. Hundreds of straight lines of graves, arranged symmetrically like boxy houses, with pocket-handkerchief lawns in front of each one. True, there is a certain amount of variation in the headstones, as there is in houses on estates, but, as with them, diversity is limited by planning restrictions. The headstones must not be higher than four feet and so they all measure exactly four feet—naturally everyone goes for as much height as they can get. Apart from this, some choice is permitted, although all headstone designs and inscriptions have to be vetted by the authorities. They're obviously tolerant; there are some pretty unusual headstones around. You hesitate to use the words 'bad taste' in connection with death—another thing I've learnt. Don't be judgmental about trivial things (and everything is trivial, by comparison with what's going on in this place.) But I can't warm to the shiny slabs with gold inscriptions and smug angels on top. The white marble is nicer, even when it comes with expressions of profound sentiments in lines apparently plagiarized from country and western songs, or the 'Funny Stories' page of some ancient schoolboy magazine.

His Life a Beautiful Memory, His Absence a Silent Grief.
Or:

Take care of Tom, Lord, as he Did Us, With Lots of Love and Little Fuss.

My favourites are the simple stones, plain gray, which have become more common, I'm pleased to report, over the past four or five years. (It's easy to date fashions in a graveyard.)

That's what I ordered for you. The style called 'boulder', the natural look that suits a man who wore tweed and spoke correct Irish, Welsh and Scots Gaelic. I thought it was a personal choice but I've discovered that most of the poets and writers, teachers and academics, in the graveyard are buried under similar stones. There's only one unique monument in the entire place: a wide slab of pinkish granite, thin as butterfly's wing. Only a name and a date inscribed on it in tiny Times New Roman.

The architect who designed Belfield.

Of course.

To tell the truth, I wouldn't mind one of those. A high modernist headstone that looks as if it were imported, at great expense, from Finland or some other crucible of understated good taste. But you could copy it and the next thing IKEA would be supplying the same thing in a flatpack at a fraction of the cost. They'd be all over the place.

I guess I'll stick with the country life look.

Unlike you, I know precisely how and where I will be buried (unless I am destroyed in a plane crash or murdered and chopped up into little bits and my body never found). I'll be under a homespun boulder on Row C, in the section called St Mark's, down near the wall and the old Church of Ireland. I thought when I was shown the spot that it was pretty, because it was in the shelter of the old church, with its bell tower and stone walls. The newer section of the graveyard, St Elizabeth's, didn't appeal to me one bit. It's a huge flat field that stretches despondently to the Irish Sea. The undertaker, who encouraged me to think very carefully before I made a decision, pointed out that as time went on St Elizabeth's would look 'less bleak.' The trees will grow, he said, in his mild, and mildly ironic tone. He takes death in his stride, and thinks in the longer term.

But how much time have I got?

From St Mark's there is a fine view of the Dublin mountains, today a rich eggy yellow. The gorse. Easter egg time, almost everything in nature is yellow. Not only has it a fine view, always desirable in houses or graves, St Mark's also has the virtue of age, being in the oldest part of the graveyard, where un-burnt corpses can no longer be buried—there's not enough room. For them, poor skeletons, no choice. It's St Elizabeth's; they'll have to grin and bear it, and wait for the trees to grow. But there's still space for little urns of ashes in the old section, just because not that many Dubliners choose cremation, and of those that do many don't get a grave—their ashes are scattered in some scenic spot where they used to go on their holidays, or kept at home on the mantelpiece. Some of yours are at home too. I'm planning to scatter them on a nice headland near the place where *we* went on holiday on Anglesey, where almost everyone speaks Welsh. But I rather like having them in the house so I'll probably hold on to some. That means your ashes will be in three different places. There's no rule against it; that's the beauty of ashes. You could never dismember a body and bury bits in various places—except in vey exceptional circumstances, such as Daniel O'Connell's.

I'd have thought such ideas unhealthy, even disgusting. And terrifying. Before. Life is for the living was my motto, not that I expressed it one way or the other. But now the dead are always on my mind and I'm quite an expert on graves and graveyards. I could set up an online advice centre and may do that when I get over your death. I have quite a lot of plans for that time, for the time when I get over it, when my energy returns and I start out on a new life as a person who has lost her husband but has survived. A widow, to use that word all widows I have met—they're all over the place—can't stand. People tell me that you'd want me to start a new life, to be happy. I suppose it is a safe bet that you wouldn't want me to be actively miserable. You didn't get a chance to express any preferences one way or the other but others step into the breach. You should get a dog. Aren't you lucky it all happened so quickly? A massage would make you feel so much better. The sort of things we'd have a good laugh at, between ourselves, over dinner. I reckon we ate about 14,000 dinners together and so had at least 14,000 good laughs. 28,000? More. It would be so great to have just one more dinner so I could tell you about all that's been happening, relay all the comments: the sublime, the absurd, the in between.

Quite a long dinner, we'd need, to tell the whole story.

They mean well.

St Mark's is not really as nice as I first thought. The church and the ivy-covered wall block the sun in the afternoon, so our grave is often in cold shade. Today for once I came in the morning, and through the muslin haze the sun is shining on you. I take my plastic water bottle out of my rucksack and pour water on raggedy white chrysanthemum and the purple flower, a senettia. It's not the kind of flower you liked, or I like, but it was the only thing in the flower shop that looked healthy enough to survive in this graveyard for any length of time. And it has lasted and looks quite good here on the grave, which needs all the flowers it can get. The boulder hasn't come yet—they're waiting for a good block of granite. As if blocks of granite come rolling down the hill when they feel like it. You'd think they'd have a regular supplier. In the meantime all you have is a little wooden marker with your name on it, and dates. It has been a great help to me, especially at the beginning when I couldn't remember where the grave was. It took me a while to remember to turn left at Mary Byrne's grave, which is next to that of Enrico Cafolla, Professor of Music—easier to remember than Mary Byrne, beloved wife, Mom and Nana. (The word 'granny' seldom appears on head-stones.) I never go astray now.

There isn't enough water in the bottle. The flowers are alive, but thirsty. The white petals of the chrysanthemum are turning to straw. The senettia is such a strong regal purple, a deep dyed purple, that its thin blade-like petals could never turn brown, but they're getting limp. I decide to walk back to the tap and get more water. It'll take about ten minutes, to go there and back, but I have plenty of time now. That is another thing. Before I had no time for anything. Now time seems to stretch endlessly in front of me, like the sea out there in front of the railway. But the sense of a wide expanse of ocean is an illusion. There is a coast that you can't see over the horizon. Wales. The land I love because it brought us such luck. After four years waiting we conceived a child there, on the first night of a holiday at Beaumaris. It's a mere sixty-six miles (nautical) away. Just because you can't see it doesn't mean it doesn't exist. And it's closer than, say, Ballinasloe.

As I go back towards the tap, I notice the woman I saw earlier. The woman in the yellow anorak. She's busy at a grave. No doubt she's a widow, like me, like most of the graveyard visitors, who spent their lives taking care of husbands and have no intention of stopping now, just because they're dead. So they keep coming to the graves to pull up the weeds, to water the flowers, to plant new things. The woman in the yellow anorak is touching her headstone with both hands, and talking to it. As I pass I hear what she's saying. 'Sandra came to dinner yesterday and we watched *Fair City*. I miss you so much, my dearest darling.'

The dog is nowhere to be seen.

The tap.

That's where the dog is, tied to the silver post by his leash. He's a Scottie, I can see it now, I remember the difference. Black, with that long, sceptical, Scottish head.

'Hi, little dog,' I say. 'Excuse me while I fill this empty ginger ale bottle with water.'

I turn on the tap and squeeze the mouth of the bottle so it fits over the lip of the tap. This is not a good idea.

Just then a hearse comes through the gate, followed by two

black limousines; after them the straggle of ordinary cars. A few people stand at the corner, paying their respects as the hearse passes and swings quietly around the corner, making for St Elizabeth's.

I used to hate the sight of a hearse. My heart would sink if I met one on the road. But I no longer fear them now that I've met death face to face, tried to shoo it away, and lost the battle. Now I can cast an indifferent eye on every hearse that passes by, because I've driven behind yours.

Just as the hearse turns around the corner this thing happens. The plastic bottle dislodges from the tap and a strong gush of water splashes onto the dog. Startled by the sudden cold shower, he breaks free. He can't have been tied very tightly. Off he dashes, in the direction of the woman in the yellow anorak.

And he runs right under the second big limousine, the one which probably contains the more distant relatives who are nevertheless too important to come in their own cars. I see him, all the funeral followers on the side-lines see him. The only person who does not see him is the driver of the limousine. He is such a tiny dog, the size of a well-fed rat. Dogs aren't allowed in the graveyard. The driver isn't expecting one to run out in front of him.

How ghastly. First your husband, then your dog.

This had occurred to me, in connection with dogs. And cats. Their mortality. If I get a dog, as so many people advise, it will die sometime. And by the time it dies I will have grown to love it, even though a dog is no substitute for a husband. I'd be bereaved all over again in a different way. An easier way. But bereavement is never easy.

The hearse glides slowly along the road to St Elizabeth's. The first limousine turns the corner and follows it, and the second limousine turns too.

The driver still doesn't realise he has just run over a widow's dog.

But no.

No. It's OK. The dog is OK.

The car passed over him and just left him behind like a jellyfish on the beach when the tide goes out. Alive, with no more than an expression of mild surprise on his narrow little face. He scampers off over the graves towards the spot where the woman he loves, who has seen none of this, is busily engaged in a conversation with someone she loves but who doesn't exist.

Animals don't know what we humans know.

All the people standing by the side of the road, including me, laugh, some more heartily than others.

His lucky day, someone says.

Yes. There's quite a bit of luck involved, when it comes to the crunch, in matters of life and death.

A short pause. We consider this observation, and savour the taste of profound relief. An exquisite taste.

I turn off the tap.

Then I kick the bottle and let the water spill over into the bed of crimson primroses, tulips the exact colour of dentures. I decide not to return to our grave. It's pointless. Unless the brash senettia, the weary chrysanthemum, get some rain and manage to soak it up, nothing I can do will keep them alive.

The mourners shake themselves, remember why they're here, and start to process sedately along the track that leads to St Elizabeth's, the railway line, and the Irish Sea. The haze has burnt off now and the water sparkles, blue as silk close to land, and a deep dark indigo, like a firm line of ink, on the horizon.

You still can't see Wales.

But it is there, all right.

Éilís Ní Dhuibhne was born in Dublin. She was educated at University College Dublin and has a BA in English and a PhD in Irish Folklore. She worked for many years as a librarian and archivist in the National Library of Ireland, and now teaches on the MA for Creative Writing at University College Dublin and for the Faber Writing Academy. The author of more than twenty books, including five collections of short stories, several novels, children's books, plays, and many scholarly articles and literary reviews, her work includes *The Dancers Dancing* (1999), *Fox Swallow Scarecrow* (2007), and *The Shelter of Neighbours* (2012).

MICHAL AJVAZ, *The Golden Age.*
The Other City.
PIERRE ALBERT-BIROT, *Grabinoulor.*
YUZ ALESHKOVSKY, *Kangaroo.*
FELIPE ALFAU, *Chromos.*
Locos.
JOE AMATO, *Samuel Taylor's Last Night.*
IVAN ÂNGELO, *The Celebration.*
The Tower of Glass.
ANTÓNIO LOBO ANTUNES, *Knowledge of Hell.*
The Splendor of Portugal.
ALAIN ARIAS-MISSON, *Theatre of Incest.*
JOHN ASHBERY & JAMES SCHUYLER, *A Nest of Ninnies.*
ROBERT ASHLEY, *Perfect Lives.*
GABRIELA AVIGUR-ROTEM, *Heatwave and Crazy Birds.*
DJUNA BARNES, *Ladies Almanack.*
Ryder.
JOHN BARTH, *Letters.*
Sabbatical.
DONALD BARTHELME, *The King.*
Paradise.
SVETISLAV BASARA, *Chinese Letter.*
MIQUEL BAUÇÀ, *The Siege in the Room.*
RENÉ BELLETTO, *Dying.*
MAREK BIENCZYK, *Transparency.*
ANDREI BITOV, *Pushkin House.*
ANDREJ BLATNIK, *You Do Understand.*
Law of Desire.
LOUIS PAUL BOON, *Chapel Road.*
My Little War.
Summer in Termuren.
ROGER BOYLAN, *Killoyle.*
IGNÁCIO DE LOYOLA BRANDÃO, *Anonymous Celebrity.*
Zero.
BONNIE BREMSER, *Troia: Mexican Memoirs.*
CHRISTINE BROOKE-ROSE, *Amalgamemnon.*
BRIGID BROPHY, *In Transit.*
The Prancing Novelist.

GERALD L. BRUNS, *Modern Poetry and the Idea of Language.*
GABRIELLE BURTON, *Heartbreak Hotel.*
MICHEL BUTOR, *Degrees.*
Mobile.
G. CABRERA INFANTE, *Infante's Inferno.*
Three Trapped Tigers.
JULIETA CAMPOS, *The Fear of Losing Eurydice.*
ANNE CARSON, *Eros the Bittersweet.*
ORLY CASTEL-BLOOM, *Dolly City.*
LOUIS-FERDINAND CÉLINE, *North.*
Conversations with Professor Y.
London Bridge.
MARIE CHAIX, *The Laurels of Lake Constance.*
HUGO CHARTERIS, *The Tide Is Right.*
ERIC CHEVILLARD, *Demolishing Nisard.*
The Author and Me.
MARC CHOLODENKO, *Mordechai Schamz.*
JOSHUA COHEN, *Witz.*
EMILY HOLMES COLEMAN, *The Shutter of Snow.*
ERIC CHEVILLARD, *The Author and Me.*
ROBERT COOVER, *A Night at the Movies.*
STANLEY CRAWFORD, *Log of the S.S. The Mrs Unguentine.*
Some Instructions to My Wife.
RENÉ CREVEL, *Putting My Foot in It.*
RALPH CUSACK, *Cadenza.*
NICHOLAS DELBANCO, *Sherbrookes.*
The Count of Concord.
NIGEL DENNIS, *Cards of Identity.*
PETER DIMOCK, *A Short Rhetoric for Leaving the Family.*
ARIEL DORFMAN, *Konfidenz.*
COLEMAN DOWELL, *Island People.*
Too Much Flesh and Jabez.
ARKADII DRAGOMOSHCHENKO, *Dust.*
RIKKI DUCORNET, *Phosphor in Dreamland.*
The Complete Butcher's Tales.

RIKKI DUCORNET (cont.), *The Jade Cabinet.*
The Fountains of Neptune.
WILLIAM EASTLAKE, *The Bamboo Bed.*
Castle Keep.
Lyric of the Circle Heart.
JEAN ECHENOZ, *Chopin's Move.*
STANLEY ELKIN, *A Bad Man.*
Criers and Kibitzers, Kibitzers and Criers.
The Dick Gibson Show.
The Franchiser.
The Living End.
Mrs. Ted Bliss.
FRANÇOIS EMMANUEL, *Invitation to a Voyage.*
PAUL EMOND, *The Dance of a Sham.*
SALVADOR ESPRIU, *Ariadne in the Grotesque Labyrinth.*
LESLIE A. FIEDLER, *Love and Death in the American Novel.*
JUAN FILLOY, *Op Oloop.*
ANDY FITCH, *Pop Poetics.*
GUSTAVE FLAUBERT, *Bouvard and Pécuchet.*
KASS FLEISHER, *Talking out of School.*
JON FOSSE, *Aliss at the Fire.*
Melancholy.
FORD MADOX FORD, *The March of Literature.*
MAX FRISCH, *I'm Not Stiller.*
Man in the Holocene.
CARLOS FUENTES, *Christopher Unborn.*
Distant Relations.
Terra Nostra.
Where the Air Is Clear.
TAKEHIKO FUKUNAGA, *Flowers of Grass.*
WILLIAM GADDIS, JR., *The Recognitions.*
JANICE GALLOWAY, *Foreign Parts.*
The Trick Is to Keep Breathing.
WILLIAM H. GASS, *Life Sentences.*
The Tunnel.
The World Within the Word.
Willie Masters' Lonesome Wife.
GÉRARD GAVARRY, *Hoppla! 1 2 3.*

ETIENNE GILSON, *The Arts of the Beautiful.*
Forms and Substances in the Arts.
C. S. GISCOMBE, *Giscome Road.*
Here.
DOUGLAS GLOVER, *Bad News of the Heart.*
WITOLD GOMBROWICZ, *A Kind of Testament.*
PAULO EMÍLIO SALES GOMES, *P's Three Women.*
GEORGI GOSPODINOV, *Natural Novel.*
JUAN GOYTISOLO, *Count Julian.*
Juan the Landless.
Makbara.
Marks of Identity.
HENRY GREEN, *Blindness.*
Concluding.
Doting.
Nothing.
JACK GREEN, *Fire the Bastards!*
JIŘÍ GRUŠA, *The Questionnaire.*
MELA HARTWIG, *Am I a Redundant Human Being?*
JOHN HAWKES, *The Passion Artist.*
Whistlejacket.
ELIZABETH HEIGHWAY, ED., *Contemporary Georgian Fiction.*
AIDAN HIGGINS, *Balcony of Europe.*
Blind Man's Bluff.
Bornholm Night-Ferry.
Langrishe, Go Down.
Scenes from a Receding Past.
KEIZO HINO, *Isle of Dreams.*
KAZUSHI HOSAKA, *Plainsong.*
ALDOUS HUXLEY, *Antic Hay.*
Point Counter Point.
Those Barren Leaves.
Time Must Have a Stop.
NAOYUKI II, *The Shadow of a Blue Cat.*
DRAGO JANČAR, *The Tree with No Name.*
MIKHEIL JAVAKHISHVILI, *Kvachi.*
GERT JONKE, *The Distant Sound.*
Homage to Czerny.
The System of Vienna.

JACQUES JOUET, *Mountain R.*
Savage.
Upstaged.
MIEKO KANAI, *The Word Book.*
YORAM KANIUK, *Life on Sandpaper.*
ZURAB KARUMIDZE, *Dagny.*
JOHN KELLY, *From Out of the City.*
HUGH KENNER, *Flaubert, Joyce and Beckett: The Stoic Comedians.*
Joyce's Voices.
DANILO KIŠ, *The Attic.*
The Lute and the Scars.
Psalm 44.
A Tomb for Boris Davidovich.
ANITA KONKKA, *A Fool's Paradise.*
GEORGE KONRÁD, *The City Builder.*
TADEUSZ KONWICKI, *A Minor Apocalypse.*
The Polish Complex.
ANNA KORDZAIA-SAMADASHVILI, *Me, Margarita.*
MENIS KOUMANDAREAS, *Koula.*
ELAINE KRAF, *The Princess of 72nd Street.*
JIM KRUSOE, *Iceland.*
AYSE KULIN, *Farewell: A Mansion in Occupied Istanbul.*
EMILIO LASCANO TEGUI, *On Elegance While Sleeping.*
ERIC LAURRENT, *Do Not Touch.*
VIOLETTE LEDUC, *La Bâtarde.*
EDOUARD LEVÉ, *Autoportrait.*
Newspaper.
Suicide.
Works.
MARIO LEVI, *Istanbul Was a Fairy Tale.*
DEBORAH LEVY, *Billy and Girl.*
JOSÉ LEZAMA LIMA, *Paradiso.*
ROSA LIKSOM, *Dark Paradise.*
OSMAN LINS, *Avalovara.*
The Queen of the Prisons of Greece.
FLORIAN LIPUŠ, *The Errors of Young Tjaž.*
GORDON LISH, *Peru.*
ALF MACLOCHLAINN, *Out of Focus.*
Past Habitual.

The Corpus in the Library.
RON LOEWINSOHN, *Magnetic Field(s).*
YURI LOTMAN, *Non-Memoirs.*
D. KEITH MANO, *Take Five.*
MINA LOY, *Stories and Essays of Mina Loy.*
MICHELINE AHARONIAN MARCOM, *A Brief History of Yes.*
The Mirror in the Well.
BEN MARCUS, *The Age of Wire and String.*
WALLACE MARKFIELD, *Teitlebaum's Window.*
DAVID MARKSON, *Reader's Block.*
Wittgenstein's Mistress.
CAROLE MASO, *AVA.*
HISAKI MATSUURA, *Triangle.*
LADISLAV MATEJKA & KRYSTYNA POMORSKA, EDS., *Readings in Russian Poetics: Formalist & Structuralist Views.*
HARRY MATHEWS, *Cigarettes.*
The Conversions.
The Human Country.
The Journalist.
My Life in CIA.
Singular Pleasures.
The Sinking of the Odradek.
Stadium.
Tlooth.
HISAKI MATSUURA, *Triangle.*
DONAL MCLAUGHLIN, *beheading the virgin mary, and other stories.*
JOSEPH MCELROY, *Night Soul and Other Stories.*
ABDELWAHAB MEDDEB, *Talismano.*
GERHARD MEIER, *Isle of the Dead.*
HERMAN MELVILLE, *The Confidence-Man.*
AMANDA MICHALOPOULOU, *I'd Like.*
STEVEN MILLHAUSER, *The Barnum Museum.*
In the Penny Arcade.
RALPH J. MILLS, JR., *Essays on Poetry.*
MOMUS, *The Book of Jokes.*
CHRISTINE MONTALBETTI, *The Origin of Man.*
Western.

NICHOLAS MOSLEY, *Accident.*
Assassins.
Catastrophe Practice.
A Garden of Trees.
Hopeful Monsters.
Imago Bird.
Inventing God.
Look at the Dark.
Metamorphosis.
Natalie Natalia.
Serpent.
WARREN MOTTE, *Fables of the Novel:
French Fiction since 1990.*
*Fiction Now: The French Novel in the
21st Century.*
Mirror Gazing.
Oulipo: A Primer of Potential Literature.
GERALD MURNANE, *Barley Patch.*
Inland.
YVES NAVARRE, *Our Share of Time.*
Sweet Tooth.
DOROTHY NELSON, *In Night's City.*
Tar and Feathers.
ESHKOL NEVO, *Homesick.*
WILFRIDO D. NOLLEDO, *But for
the Lovers.*
BORIS A. NOVAK, *The Master of
Insomnia.*
FLANN O'BRIEN, *At Swim-Two-Birds.*
The Best of Myles.
The Dalkey Archive.
The Hard Life.
The Poor Mouth.
The Third Policeman.
CLAUDE OLLIER, *The Mise-en-Scène.*
Wert and the Life Without End.
PATRIK OUŘEDNÍK, *Europeana.*
The Opportune Moment, 1855.
BORIS PAHOR, *Necropolis.*
FERNANDO DEL PASO, *News from
the Empire.*
Palinuro of Mexico.
ROBERT PINGET, *The Inquisitory.*
Mahu or The Material.
Trio.
MANUEL PUIG, *Betrayed by Rita
Hayworth.*

The Buenos Aires Affair.
Heartbreak Tango.
RAYMOND QUENEAU, *The Last Days.*
Odile.
Pierrot Mon Ami.
Saint Glinglin.
ANN QUIN, *Berg.*
Passages.
Three.
Tripticks.
ISHMAEL REED, *The Free-Lance
Pallbearers.*
The Last Days of Louisiana Red.
Ishmael Reed: The Plays.
Juice!
The Terrible Threes.
The Terrible Twos.
Yellow Back Radio Broke-Down.
JASIA REICHARDT, *15 Journeys Warsaw
to London.*
JOÃO UBALDO RIBEIRO, *House of the
Fortunate Buddhas.*
JEAN RICARDOU, *Place Names.*
RAINER MARIA RILKE,
The Notebooks of Malte Laurids Brigge.
JULIÁN RÍOS, *The House of Ulysses.*
Larva: A Midsummer Night's Babel.
Poundemonium.
ALAIN ROBBE-GRILLET, *Project for a
Revolution in New York.*
A Sentimental Novel.
AUGUSTO ROA BASTOS, *I the Supreme.*
DANIËL ROBBERECHTS, *Arriving in
Avignon.*
JEAN ROLIN, *The Explosion of the
Radiator Hose.*
OLIVIER ROLIN, *Hotel Crystal.*
ALIX CLEO ROUBAUD, *Alix's Journal.*
JACQUES ROUBAUD, *The Form of
a City Changes Faster, Alas, Than the
Human Heart.*
The Great Fire of London.
Hortense in Exile.
Hortense Is Abducted.
*Mathematics: The Plurality of Worlds of
Lewis.*
Some Thing Black.

FOR A FULL LIST OF PUBLICATIONS, VISIT: www.dalkeyarchive.com

RAYMOND ROUSSEL, *Impressions of Africa.*

VEDRANA RUDAN, *Night.*

PABLO M. RUIZ, *Four Cold Chapters on the Possibility of Literature.*

GERMAN SADULAEV, *The Maya Pill.*

TOMAŽ ŠALAMUN, *Soy Realidad.*

LYDIE SALVAYRE, *The Company of Ghosts.*
The Lecture.
The Power of Flies.

LUIS RAFAEL SÁNCHEZ, *Macho Camacho's Beat.*

SEVERO SARDUY, *Cobra & Maitreya.*

NATHALIE SARRAUTE, *Do You Hear Them?*
Martereau.
The Planetarium.

STIG SÆTERBAKKEN, *Siamese.*
Self-Control.
Through the Night.

ARNO SCHMIDT, *Collected Novellas.*
Collected Stories.
Nobodaddy's Children.
Two Novels.

ASAF SCHURR, *Motti.*

GAIL SCOTT, *My Paris.*

DAMION SEARLS, *What We Were Doing and Where We Were Going.*

JUNE AKERS SEESE,
Is This What Other Women Feel Too?

BERNARD SHARE, *Inish.*
Transit.

VIKTOR SHKLOVSKY, *Bowstring.*
Literature and Cinematography.
Theory of Prose.
Third Factory.
Zoo, or Letters Not about Love.

PIERRE SINIAC, *The Collaborators.*

KJERSTI A. SKOMSVOLD,
The Faster I Walk, the Smaller I Am.

JOSEF ŠKVORECKÝ, *The Engineer of Human Souls.*

GILBERT SORRENTINO, *Aberration of Starlight.*
Blue Pastoral.
Crystal Vision.

Imaginative Qualities of Actual Things.
Mulligan Stew. Red the Fiend.
Steelwork.
Under the Shadow.

MARKO SOSIČ, *Ballerina, Ballerina.*

ANDRZEJ STASIUK, *Dukla.*
Fado.

GERTRUDE STEIN, *The Making of Americans.*
A Novel of Thank You.

LARS SVENDSEN, *A Philosophy of Evil.*

PIOTR SZEWC, *Annihilation.*

GONÇALO M. TAVARES, *A Man: Klaus Klump.*
Jerusalem.
Learning to Pray in the Age of Technique.

LUCIAN DAN TEODOROVICI,
Our Circus Presents . . .

NIKANOR TERATOLOGEN, *Assisted Living.*

STEFAN THEMERSON, *Hobson's Island.*
The Mystery of the Sardine.
Tom Harris.

TAEKO TOMIOKA, *Building Waves.*

JOHN TOOMEY, *Sleepwalker.*

DUMITRU TSEPENEAG, *Hotel Europa.*
The Necessary Marriage.
Pigeon Post.
Vain Art of the Fugue.

ESTHER TUSQUETS, *Stranded.*

DUBRAVKA UGRESIC, *Lend Me Your Character.*
Thank You for Not Reading.

TOR ULVEN, *Replacement.*

MATI UNT, *Brecht at Night.*
Diary of a Blood Donor.
Things in the Night.

ÁLVARO URIBE & OLIVIA SEARS, EDS.,
Best of Contemporary Mexican Fiction.

ELOY URROZ, *Friction.*
The Obstacles.

LUISA VALENZUELA, *Dark Desires and the Others.*
He Who Searches.

PAUL VERHAEGHEN, *Omega Minor.*

BORIS VIAN, *Heartsnatcher.*

LLORENÇ VILLALONGA, *The Dolls'
Room.*

TOOMAS VINT, *An Unending Landscape.*

ORNELA VORPSI, *The Country Where No
One Ever Dies.*

AUSTRYN WAINHOUSE, *Hedyphagetica.*

CURTIS WHITE, *America's Magic
Mountain.*
The Idea of Home.
Memories of My Father Watching TV.
Requiem.

DIANE WILLIAMS,
Excitability: Selected Stories.
Romancer Erector.

DOUGLAS WOOLF, *Wall to Wall.*
Ya! & John-Juan.

JAY WRIGHT, *Polynomials and Pollen.*
The Presentable Art of Reading Absence.

PHILIP WYLIE, *Generation of Vipers.*

MARGUERITE YOUNG, *Angel in the
Forest.*
Miss MacIntosh, My Darling.

REYOUNG, *Unbabbling.*

VLADO ŽABOT, *The Succubus.*

ZORAN ŽIVKOVIĆ , *Hidden Camera.*

LOUIS ZUKOFSKY, *Collected Fiction.*

VITOMIL ZUPAN, *Minuet for Guitar.*

SCOTT ZWIREN, *God Head.*

AND MORE . . .